"You amaze me, Alexandria," Frederick said.

"Sometimes I amaze myself," Alexandria replied.

"Do you realize what you've done?"

"I've taken a hotel room with you. When I left Paris, I told my friend that I wanted to have an adventure—and I am."

"And why have you singled me out?" he asked with an intense expression in his eyes.

"Do you think I purposely singled you out, Frederick?"

"When a young lady is as forward as you, Alexandria, one wonders if there is an ulterior motive behind her actions."

Alexandria turned away from his piercing gaze.

"Never mind," he said as he let his hand curl about hers. "Let us enjoy each other."

"Yes, indeed, Frederick."

Fawcett Popular Library Books
by Katheryn Kimbrough:

#36

Katheryn Kimbrough's

Saga of the Phenwick Women

ALEXANDRIA,

THE
AMBIVALENT

FAWCETT POPULAR LIBRARY • NEW YORK

SAGA OF THE PHENWICK WOMEN #36—ALEXANDRIA,
THE AMBIVALENT

Published by Fawcett Popular Library, a unit of CBS
Publications, the Consumer Publishing Division of CBS Inc.

ISBN: 0-445-04655-4

Printed in the United States of America

First Fawcett Popular Library printing: May 1981

10   9   8   7   6   5   4   3   2   1

Dedicated To
MARSHA STONE

BOOK 36—ALEXANDRIA, THE AMBIVALENT

CAST OF CHARACTERS

ALEXANDRIA MUZAKOVA	A pretty young ballerina.
Monique Dupree	Her mother, a woman of vast experience.
Count Philippe de Marco	Monique's fiancé, a man of tremendous wealth and influence.
LETITIA PHENWICK	Alexandria's best friend, also a ballerina.
Luke Phenwick	Letitia's distant cousin.
OLIVER PHENWICK	Luke's son.
Joyce Phenwick	Luke's wife.
HAYDEN PHENWICK	Luke's younger brother.
Daniel Charles Phenwick	Another cousin, head of Medallion, London.
Louise Phenwick	His wife.
CHARLES PHENWICK	
Augustus "	
Timothy "	Their sons.
Baron Conrad von Klootz	A Prussian nobleman.
Major Kramer	A Prussian officer.
VLADIMIR POPKIN	A pianist with the LeVeque Ballet Company.
Madame Roselle Ivanovich	A choreographer and Letty's mentor.
JEREMIAH JAMES	Letty's long-time Negro friend, a dancer.
WORTH BASSETT	A wealthy businessman, Jeremiah's patron.
Tiziano Spolini	An Italian impresario.
Georges LeVeque	Producer of the LeVeque Ballet Company.
MANUEL CATALON	A waiter at La Petite Fleur Café, Paris.
GUY CROISANT	A fanatical student.
Joachim Holtzer	A German baker
Anna Holtzer	His wife.

| ROMULA HOLTZER | His daughter. |
| Gertrude Hauser | His sister-in-law. |

Reader's Note: For complete genealogy of the Phenwick family, see volume 35 of the Phenwick Saga: LETITIA, THE DREAMER

PROLOGUE

The mind of the artist has always provoked
fascination because of the inherent ambivalence that
seems to compel it in two different directions: that
of the extreme creative personality which is often
in opposition to the sensual, lustful personality. In
essence these are the same, since they are both
motivated by the creative urge. Yet these two
extremes in the personality spectrum frequently
are in conflict and intrude upon each other: devotion
to artistic pursuit in contrast to the fulfilling of
carnal instincts. On the surface it appears that the
artist is primarily dedicated to his or her art, but
beneath the exterior appearances, there often exists
an inner turmoil of emotions and sensual desire.
Are these not, in the final analysis, essential
ingredients necessary for being a creative individual?
In any case, such was the basic conflict within
Alexandria Muzakova in that era which was still
strongly influenced by the Victorian standards of
morality inherited from the nineteenth century.

Over the period of time that Letitia Phenwick and Alexandria Muzakova shared a room together at the Dance Academy in Somerset, England, the two young ladies grew to be the best of friends. A bond of unity welded them. Similar in size and both extraordinary beauties, it was paradoxical that they did not have a greater sense of competition between them. A deep love had evolved, and each was the sister the other had never had.

Letty bore the Phenwick name; therefore she was shown preference over Alexandria, although the latter was perhaps technically better as a dancer. To court a Phenwick was to flirt unabashedly with the Phenwick wealth. But Letty refused to permit herself to be used or to be given position above Alexandria. It was often wondered if, had the shoe been on the other foot, Alexandria would have been as generous as her friend. Still, to those who had come to know the young ballerinas to any degree of understanding, it was obvious that each was equally concerned for the other's highest good.

The young ladies had emerged from two widely different backgrounds. In a sense, each was largely self-educated through her own determination to succeed. Practically from infancy, Alexandria knew that she was destined to become a great ballerina. Conversely, it was she who reenforced the drive in Letty to aspire to accomplishment and success.

Alexandria and Letty had attracted the attention and admiration of Charles and Timothy Phenwick, Letty's distant cousins. Tim was definitely in love with Letty, but her feelings for him were not as strong. Charles, the eldest, was more passive in his emotional responses, and while he greatly admired Alexandria's beauty and talent, his amorous enthusiasm was somewhat lacking. At times it seemed that Charles and Alexandria were paired off more out of convenience than for any other reason.

Still, the drums of destiny were beating in the

distance to the cadence of war. Most people were unaware of the political and economic implications, of what was at stake, nor was theirs a vast interest or knowledge about international affairs. Kaiser Wilhelm was only a name that was occasionally heard as he conspired to unite the German lands. The houses of royalty throughout Europe were collapsing and frenzy and desperation had begun to prevail. And as monarchies crumbled, the tattoo of the war drums was heard with deeper urgency than ever before.

ONE

1914

"**Will spring never appear?**" Monique Dupree exclaimed. "I loathe this nasty cold and damp. We should have wintered on the Côte d'Azur. The climate is so much nicer in the south of France than it is here in Paris."

"You know it was impossible for me to get away," Count Philippe de Marco replied indulgently to his fiancée. "I have business to which I must attend."

"Business, business!" the woman replied, pouty and sullen, "I didn't think nobility concerned itself with business."

"There, you see how mistaken you can be, my precious Monique," Philippe returned. "There was a time when we of so-called noble birth could sit about in country salons and act foppish and, I might add, just a bit ridiculous, but that was when there was far more inherited wealth than there is today. Were it not for business, I would be on the brink of beggary."

"Don't be silly, Philippe; you are rich," Monique

said as she examined her likeness in the ornately decorated mirror. Raven-black hair glistened in a stylish arrangement. Her exquisite features in a long oval face were artistically well proportioned; her body was beautifully contoured, and on any number of occasions she had posed for artists. Nearing her early forties, she had the appearance of a woman ten years younger, with only a hint here and there of maturity lining its way into her features.

"If I am rich, my dear, it is because I have made myself so through persistent industry and tenacity," Philippe returned. Tall, with elegant posture and bearing, he was considered to be one of the most handsome men on the Paris social scene. Twice married, he was in his late forties, but he, too, had the façade of a man much younger than his actual years. "Come along, Monique; we will be late for our appointment."

"One should be fashionably late, I always say." Monique brushed a speck of powder from her cheek and eyed the man in the mirror. His look of impatience could not be disguised by a congenial smile. She turned to him, reaching her hands for his. "My darling, you have not kissed me in at least ten minutes. And you know how my lips ache in anticipation of yours."

"The impetuous Monique," Philippe commented as he took her in his powerful embrace. As he disengaged his lips from hers, he stared deeply into her eyes. "But, my dear, your kisses hold such a persuasive invitation that if we allow this to progress, we will miss our appointment altogether."

"We can telephone that we will be late."

"No, dearest Monique, it is your daughter, and we cannot disappoint her," Philippe said gently. "I am so anxious to meet her at last."

"My daughter?" Monique repeated.

"Do you fear my meeting her, that I might find

her far more attractive than you, my dearest?" Philippe teased. "You have always told me she was a beauty. But how could she be other than that with a mother as lovely as you, my precious?"

"I have never feared competition with any woman," Monique replied, "certainly not from my daughter. And to prove my point, I will stop embracing you this very minute and we will go and meet her. But let me stress, I was extremely young when she was born to me. My first husband, Josef Muzakova, was much older than I."

"Why do you keep telling me that? Are you afraid that seeing you with your daughter will make you appear older or less attractive to me? How absurd! Come along, then."

Monique Dupree had had little contact with her daughter over the years. A child got in the way of her profession, which was the oldest, and one that was constantly in demand. Her beauty had attracted an opulent clientele, and she managed to live in luxury and to keep her daughter in private schools, after a meager beginning and the drudgery of having _____ Muz____ ds or Alexandria. _____ se to Alexandria's age as _____ re."

_____ known ___ ttracted Philippe's was convenient for her, and she very quickly learned how to use her natural assets.

The Café du Clair was on a small side street just off the Champs Elysées, where students and artists gathered. It was hardly Monique's choice of a meeting place; yet, upon seeing the quaintly decorated café, she decided that it would be appropriate for a first meeting between her husband-to-be and her only daughter.

"It is most colorful," Philippe commented as he glanced about. "There was a time when I used to sneak off to places like this to absorb local atmosphere. I suspect, however, that our dress is a bit conspicuous for the establishment."

"Does it make you feel uncomfortable?" Monique asked as she scanned the bearded faces and the purposely peasant-type costumes.

"I can adapt if you can, my darling."

"My life has been one of adapting, one way or another." ·

"So I have gathered," Philippe said kindly. "Were the weather warmer, it would be pleasant to sit outside."

"Perhaps we can simply meet Alexandria here, have a glass of wine with her and persuade her to go elsewhere with us to dine. I wonder where she is. We are at least ten minutes late." She looked around before turning back to Philippe to observe his curious interest in an attractive young lady across the room. She knew only too well that expression of interest in his eyes. "That, I assure you, is *not* Alexandria."

"I beg your pardon?"

"That attractive young lady who has captured your interest is *not* my daughter," Monique said. "Still, in some ways she remin̶̶̶̶̶̶̶̶̶̶̶̶̶̶ I would judge she is clo̶̶̶̶̶̶̶̶̶̶̶̶̶ well as practically her siz̶̶̶̶̶̶̶̶

The young lady who had a̶̶̶̶̶̶̶̶̶̶̶̶̶̶̶̶̶̶̶̶ interest rose and crossed to where the handsome, well-dressed couple was standing. After eying them curiously, she smiled. "Are you Madame Dupree?"

"I am Monique Dupree. How do you know me?"

"I am Letitia Phenwick, Alexandria's very good friend. She has told me very much about you, and a psychic sense told me that you must be Alexandria's mother."

Monique smiled appropriately and introduced Philippe as her fiancé.

"Alexandria was briefly detained," Letty continued. "She asked if I would come and intercept you for

16

her. I have a table for four over there, where it isn't quite as busy as it is here. Won't you join me?"

"Did you say your name was Phenwick?" Philippe asked after they had seated themselves at the table.

"Yes."

"Is that an English name?" Philippe inquired. His eyes seemed to be decoding Letty's expression.

"I suppose it may be of English origin," Letty replied, "but I am an American."

Philippe frowned. "Ah, I know so little about Americans. Are you from New York?"

Letty laughed. "No. I've been in New York, but my home is Savannah, Georgia."

"Alexandria has mentioned your name in several letters," Monique commented as she watched what appeared to be an exchange of fascination between Philippe and Letty. She knew the man only too well. "Alexandria seems to be quite fond of you, Letitia."

"And I love Alexandria as if she were my own sister. We confide everything to each other."

"Everything?" Monique arched an eyebrow. *"Everything?"*

"She has told me so much about you—I mean—well, that is, I feel as if I know you, Madame Dupree." Letty felt as if she had suddenly begun to blush.

Monique smiled knowingly. "I, too, have known very few Americans. There was a diplomat once—ah, but I do not recall much about him."

"You are a ballerina, too, are you not, Letitia?" Philippe asked.

"We leave next week for Amsterdam for the opening performance of the LeVeque Ballet Company," Letty answered. "It will be my debut as a professional dancer, as it will be Alexandria's. I aspire to dancing, but it is yet to be proved if I can honestly be called a ballerina. In my opinion, Alexandria is a far superior artist to me."

17

"You are modest, Letitia," Monique remarked. "Alexandria has written nothing but praise about your dancing."

"Is Savannah, Georgia near Boston?" Philippe asked after he had considered the statement.

"No, goodness no! I declare, Boston is way up in the north and Savannah is way down in the south."

"Oh, I see." Philippe ordered a bottle of wine. "Have you ever been to Boston?"

"No, I haven't been. But I do have relatives in Boston."

"Hmm." Philippe tried to appear disinterested. "I should one day like to see Boston."

"So would I." Letty tried not to appear to be too eager. "The Phenwicks of Boston own Medallion Enterprises, a very large company with many subsidiary units. There's a Medallion in London, too, but it's not near as far-reaching as the parent company in Boston. My cousin Tim told me all about it."

Fortunately Alexandria Muzakova entered the café as Letty was doing her best to maintain a conversation with those who were strangers to her. Attractive in a black dress, Alexandria's beauty was understated, yet she was so lovely that no amount of conservative attire could keep her beauty from showing through. Lithe and stately, she moved like a dancer. Attention turned to her, and she appeared to be oblivious of it. Gracefully she pushed her way through the room and smiled with recognition as both Philippe and Monique rose to greet her.

"Mama!" Alexandria warmly embraced her mother and kissed her cheek. "I see Letitia has found you."

"Dearest Alexandria," Monique said, trying not to gush, but beneath her façade she was a sentimental woman. "I am so pleased you sent Letitia ahead. We might have not waited for you." Another kiss. "Now, since I have written so much about him, I want you to meet Count Philippe de Marco."

"My pleasure, Count de Marco," Alexandria said formally.

"No, dear Alexandria, it is *my* great honor." Philippe bowed and kissed her hand. "With your mother being the beauty that she is, I was certain that you would be attractive, but I confess, I am overwhelmed by your loveliness. As your father-to-be, I must say that I could not be more pleased if you had been actually sired by me."

Alexandria eased her hand from Philippe's hold and took a seat beside Letitia. "Did you have difficulty recognizing Mama?"

"They were conspicuous," Letty replied. "Besides, you have a strong resemblance to your mother."

"Only in appearance," Alexandria returned, softly nudging Letty's leg. "I have my profession; Mama has hers."

"Is that really necessary, Alexandria?" Monique asked.

"I merely meant it as a way of explaining that you were not in the arts, Mama. I hope you didn't take it wrongly."

The wine arrived. Philippe sampled it and gave his approval.

"I had suggested to Count de Marco that we would simply have wine here and go elsewhere to dine," Monique commented after the wine was poured. "Letitia will join us, of course."

"I will," Letty replied, "if you don't think I will be intruding."

"I wanted Mama to meet you as much as she wanted me to meet Count de Marco," Alexandria said, clasping Letty's hand beneath the table to indicate that she wanted her friend to remain with her. "Is that an Italian name?"

"De Marco?" Philippe questioned. "Yes, the name is very much Italian, but I am very much French. The Italian influence is distantly in my family. You know how royalty is, with all of the arranged

19

marriages." He laughed. "I am constantly asked that question, and I've even considered changing it to Dumarc—but why? I'm used to de Marco."

"I prefer de Marco," Monique commented. "I think it gives you an air of distinction and mystery."

"Distinction, perhaps, but not mystery. What is mysterious about an Italian name?" Philippe again laughed and raised his glass. "To a new alliance, Alexandria, to my new daughter."

"And to my new *step*father," Alexandria returned.

"And shall we drink to your new careers?" Monique asked. "Both Alexandria's and Letitia's, that they may be extremely successful."

"Thank you, Mama."

"We plan to marry in April," Monique said awhile later. "I would like you to be my maid of honor, Alexandria."

"We will be dancing on tour in April."

"But can't you get away for a few days?"

"That may be difficult to arrange," Alexandria replied, "but I will see what can be done when you know the exact date."

"Maybe we will have to check your schedule and plan to have the ceremony performed wherever you may be," Philippe stated. "After all, a civil ceremony can be performed anywhere."

"We will discuss that later," Monique said. "I think we should go to André's for supper. It is nice, but one does not have to be extremely well-dressed to go there."

"Letitia and I dressed for the Café du Clair," Alexandria related. "Had we known you had other plans, we would have dressed accordingly. Very well, André's it shall be."

"I must say, you sounded almost hostile when you spoke with your mother," Letitia observed later that night, after they had spent several hours with Philippe and Monique.

20

"I cannot help it," Alexandria replied. "Mama always brings a rebelliousness out in me."

"I declare, she seems to be very sweet, to me."

"She is sweet—when she wants to be," Alexandria returned. "Shall we walk back to the hotel?"

"It's a bit chilly."

"The chill will make us walk faster, after all that food we consumed," Alexandria remarked. "And I'm lightheaded from the wine. I need the exercise."

"So do I, for that matter." Letitia locked her arm about Alexandria's as they accelerated their gait. "I found Count de Marco quite interesting and—well, regal."

"Mama has always had a way of attracting interesting men," Alexandria confided. "That's the sort she has made up her mind she wants. Monsieur Dupree, her last husband, was extremely interesting. He was much older than the Count, and quite wealthy. I'm certain Mama married him less for his charm, wit and attractiveness and more for his money."

"What about for love?"

Alexandria laughed cynically. "I doubt if Mama even married my father for love. He was a means of escape for her from a family situation she found unbearable. She was just a child when she married. Mama's love is for wealth and the fine things in life. She can endure almost anything if she is surrounded with finery. Even during the times she has not been married, Mama always managed to live well and to keep me in school. I'm pleased about that. I'm certain I would have found it difficult to cope with the string of men who sought Mama's favors. I could not do that, but then, I've never been in the position where I have had to even consider doing it. For that reason alone, I am truly grateful to Mama."

"I never really knew my parents," Letty confessed, "since I was raised by my grandfather. I can't

21

imagine what my reactions would be to my mother if she did—I mean, if she lived as yours does. But from what little I've seen of Madame Dupree, I thought she was very nice, and I cannot help but admire her."

"Mama can be many things. She's like a chameleon, adapting to every situation. That is why she has been so successful," Alexandria explained. "I wish I could learn greater adaptability. It must be a distinct advantage to be able to do."

"I received a letter from Tim today. He and Charlie are hoping to be in Amsterdam for our opening," Letty said as they hurried through the streets and avoided or ignored the attention they attracted.

"Both Charles and Tim are sweet," Alexandria commented, "but I suspect we will both be abundantly exhausted after the opening night performance—and probably still a bundle of nerves."

As they turned a corner, the girls practically ran head-on into a tall, handsome man in his forties. He caught himself before he collided with them.

"Excusez-moi," he said awkwardly. *"Je regrette—* ah, blast! Do either of you speak English?"

"Un peu," Alexandria replied.

"Un per? Whatever that means. Anyway, I'm sorry for nearly bumping into you," he said. "Damned if I'm not lost. Excuse the French—I mean, the English."

"You cannot find your way?" Alexandria asked, affecting an accent.

"Then you do speak English! Good. I'm looking for the Montmartre. Do you know where that is?"

"We are going near there, if you would care to walk along," Alexandria said. Letty nudged her.

"Don't get me wrong," the man returned. "I'm just lost, I'm not looking to pick up—er—to meet anyone. I'm a married man, you see, from Denver, Colorado. That's in the United States."

"I have heard of Denver, Colorado," Alexandria

said as they walked along the wet street. "Are you in Paris on holiday?"

"I'm—yes, you might say that."

"Have you been in Paris for only a short while?" Letty asked.

"Hey, isn't that an American accent? Southern?" the man questioned.

"I'm from Savannah, Georgia."

"Well, if that isn't something!" As they reached an intersection, he introduced himself. "My name's Luke Phenwick."

"Phenwick?" Letty questioned as goose bumps came over her.

"Spelled with an *f*?" Alexandria asked.

"No, with a *p h*." Luke laughed awkwardly. "Guess it's a kinda unusual spelling."

"I'm Alexandria Muzakova, and this is—"

"I'm Letitia—" Letty swallowed hard. "I'm Letitia Phenwick."

"Huh?"

"With a *p h*."

"You're a Phenwick?"

"I'm a Phenwick woman," Letty corrected.

"A *Phenwick woman?* Holy cow! My wife, one of my sisters and my two sisters-in-law are all known as Phenwick women. Don't tell me there are other ladies known as Phenwick women outside my own family."

"Perhaps we are related, Mr. Phenwick," Letty said politely.

"My wife's named Joyce, and my sisters-in-law are Carol and Olga. Sound familiar?" Luke asked.

"Vaguely."

"Oh, yeah, and my sister—not Lola, she's not a Phenwick woman, so to speak—my other sister is named Peggy."

"Peggy? Cousin Peggy Phenwick bought me a hat," Letty returned, now becoming even more

23

excited. "Cousin Peggy from San Francisco and Boston."

"That's my sister. Small world, isn't it? Letitia?" Luke snapped his fingers. "Not Letty?"

"Letty."

"The ballet dancer?"

"The same."

"Well, I'll be—Peg told me to look you up while I was in Paris, but I've never been much for keeping up with distant kin—not like Peg is. Besides, I don't know nothing about ballet dancing. Well, I'll be—!"

"Have you ever heard of Adam Truff?" Letty asked, as if seeking further verification of Luke's identity.

"Joyce and I were at Adam's bedside when he died," Luke replied. "I loved that man. He was part of the family. Good ol' Adam! Can we go somewhere to get better acquainted?"

"We've just come from supper," Letty replied. "And our hotel room is quite small and cramped."

"A cup of tea?" Luke offered.

"You go with your cousin, Letitia; I'll go on back to the hotel and get to my exercises," Alexandria said.

"Are you certain you won't join us?"

"Positive." Alexandria smiled. "It was a pleasure meeting you, Mr. Phenwick."

"The pleasure was mine, Miss—uh—"

"Muzakova."

"Is that a Russian name?"

"Moravian. Perhaps we will meet again. Good night."

"Shouldn't we walk you to the hotel, Alexandria?"

"I can manage on my own; it's only in the next block."

"You two look enough alike to be sisters," Luke commented as Alexandria darted down the street without looking back.

24

"We are practically like sisters in many ways. Neither of us has sisters of our own," Letty related.

Luke escorted Letty into a hotel dining room, where they ordered tea. Although the place was dimly lit, he sat for several minutes studying her appearance.

"Yes, I can see you have the Phenwick features. Do you have any idea how we are related?"

Letty laughed. "Cousin Peggy explained that my great-grandfather and your father were half-brothers. My great-grandfather was Prentise Phenwick."

"Uncle Prentise, for crying out loud! Well, I'll be. It makes me feel old to think that my first uncle was your great-grandfather. But I guess there's no changing that, is there?"

"Is your wife with you in Paris?"

"No, Joyce is back in Denver. She wanted to come, but—well, her health hasn't been the best lately, not since—well, she's been emotionally upset," Luke said.

"I'm sorry to hear that. Then you must be here on business."

"In a sense." Luke glanced around to see that they were not being overheard. "You see, I'm with the military. Actually, I'm Major Luke Phenwick. I received my rank during the Spanish-American War. I didn't see active military service, merely did desk work, and, quite frankly, my commission was purchased. But since that war, I've been involved off and on in military intelligence work. My cousin Xan got me into it, and I guess he was responsible for getting me reactivated."

"Is there a war somewhere?"

"Not yet."

"I beg your pardon?"

"There are always threats of war," Luke explained. "And it's the hope of my superiors that through intelligence interaction, wars can be averted."

"There must be serious concern that some kind of

25

conflict is going to erupt, if you've been called back into active service," Letty speculated.

"You sound quite knowledgeable about such things."

"Only from what my cousin Tim has told me. I really know nothing about it."

"The fact is, and I trust you will keep this confidential, I'm in Paris as an aide to meet with several German military persons. I can tell you no more about that, and I probably shouldn't have even mentioned it."

Letty stared straight forward as a dark feeling of apprehension came over her. "What is—what is the nature of Mrs. Phenwick's illness?"

"It's psychological in nature," Luke replied. "She has become very fearful since our only son left home. We have just the one child. Frankly, leaving home was the best thing Oliver could have done for himself, but it has badly affected Joyce."

"Oliver? Is Oliver Phenwick your son?"

"Have you met him?"

"I was introduced to him at a party given in London," Letty replied. "He was only there briefly, then he just seemed to disappear. Is Oliver in some kind of danger?"

"Why do you ask that?"

"The day after I met him, I happened to be in the garden of the Daniel Charles Phenwick home when I found a piece of partly burned paper that appeared to be identification of some sort which bore Oliver's name."

Luke stared strangely into space. "My son has temporarily given up his identity. I pray it *is* only temporary. Please do not ask me any more about the matter. I regret that I brought up my son's name."

"Cousin Luke—?" She put her hand atop his in an attempt to draw him back into conversation.

"I'm sorry."

26

"Perhaps if you're still in the area next week, you can come to Amsterdam to see me dance. I should like to get to know you better."

"I can make no promises, Letty. My time is not my own." Luke forced a smile. "Would you care for more tea?"

"Thank you, no. Another drop of anything and, I declare, I'm apt to explode right here on the spot."

"Then permit me to walk you to your hotel. Perhaps we can manage to dine together in the next day or two and become better acquainted, Letty."

Letty did her best to carry on a light conversation as Luke walked her back to the hotel; however, it was difficult because he appeared to be deep in contemplation. After he left her, a picture of Oliver Phenwick came to her mind and remained there—and with it came a sensation of fear.

TWO

Alexandria Maria Muzakova stood tall before the looking glass, observing the reflection of her unadorned beauty. She had the tendency to be overly critical about certain aspects of her appearance; still she had to agree with those who praised her regal pulchritude. High cheekbones accented her dark, almond-shaped eyes with almost an oriental quality that glistened with a touch of mystery. The long, slender neck held her head high. Sullen lips were drawn in practically a straight line, so as not to betray what inner thoughts or attitudes she had, yet there was always just a hint of a smile. While she spent many hours a day dancing and her body was strong, the muscles of her calves and thighs were curved and soft-appearing, while her torso was a picture of artistic perfection. In many ways Letitia was similarly structured, except that there was more a quality of roundness to her.

In the time the girls had known each other, they had become extremely close and sharing. What sense of competition they might have had, was well covered over. Their intimacy could not have been more sincere if they had been born fraternal twins. Alexandria often expressed that she thought they were soul-mates who, having been born on different sides of the world, were destined to be together.

As Alexandria studied the depth of her eyes, the wisp of melancholy sadness which was more an illusion than fact, she thought of her mother and part of the structural beauty she had inherited from her. She did her best not to be critical of Monique Dupree and her way of life, but she held a resentment toward her. Still she reasoned that Monique had done the only thing she could have to earn money to raise her daughter and educate her as well as possible. Alexandria tried to rationalize that it wasn't so much a moral issue, since she rarely reflected about such things, as much as it was a matter of social acceptance, as if Monique's occupation as a courtesan affected the attitudes of others toward herself. She was determined that under no circumstance, would she ever permit her body or her passions to be denigrated as Monique's had been. She found her mother's outlook shallow compared to the depth of her own, thus reasoning that that set her apart as an artist in contrast to the banal existence of those who prostituted themselves.

As Alexandria slipped into a pink sheer peignoir, a sense of extreme femininity came over her, and she appraised the qualities that defined her gender. It was not so much self-adulation as it was physical appreciation. She loved her body for the outward loveliness that it was, but she never lost sight of the fact that, in the ultimate reality, it was the temple in which her spirit—her soul, if you will—the essence of her immortality dwelled. She often ruminated on matters of the spirit, of the truth of her being, not in a prescribed religious sense, but as a philosophical actuality. The body was the

29

structure through which the soul of the artist was expressed.

The telephone rang. Alexandria eyed it curiously before she went to answer after three rings. Apprehensively she lifted the receiver as a fleeting fear concerning Letitia rushed into her mind. Why? Was the man who claimed to be Luke Phenwick really Letty's distant cousin?

"Hello?"

"Alexandria Muzakova?" the man's well-modulated voice asked.

"This is Alexandria Muzakova. Who is this?" she asked in French, which was more of a second language to her than English was.

"This is Count Philippe de Marco."

"Count de Marco?" A vision of the man flickered into her mind.

"First, let me tell you how delighted I was to have finally met you this evening," Philippe said in that cultured voice of his. "I have heard so very much about you from your mother, of course. I must say, however, that I was far more impressed than I had intended to be . . . impressed with both you and your friend Letitia."

"That is interesting of you to say, Count de Marco."

"Not merely idle flattery, mam'selle." The tone of his voice changed. "I wish to see you at your earliest convenience, Alexandria, if I may."

"To see me?"

"You—alone. It is most urgent that I do so." A pause. "Tonight?"

"That is impossible. I am already prepared to retire and I have an enormously busy schedule tomorrow."

"Not too busy, I trust, that you cannot spare a few minutes for me, Alexandria. What I have to discuss with you is of vital importance, both to myself and your mother and indirectly to you. I beg of you to find time for me."

"I will be in rehearsal until mid- to late afternoon."

"Will you take tea with me?" Philippe questioned, a plea in his voice.

"I will be exhausted, and I usually rest after rehearsal."

"The early evening, then?"

Alexandria considered the situation. "Can you be more explicit about what you wish to discuss?"

"Not over the telephone. It is a matter far too confidential for that."

Again Alexandria contemplated the situation. "You obviously know my hotel, or you wouldn't have been able to reach me here. There is a small café two doors to the north of the hotel entrance. I will meet you there at four-thirty for tea."

"If it is not an atmosphere where we can speak in absolutely privacy," Philippe replied, "I know another place close by. I regret having disturbed you this hour of the night. I will explain tomorrow."

Letty quietly entered the room and, seeing Alexandria at the telephone, she tiptoed into the dressing room.

"Very well, Count de Marco."

"I thought it was agreed that you would address me as Philippe, Alexandria."

"I feel awkward doing that."

"But you mustn't feel awkward. I am soon to be your stepfather."

"Yes, I know. Very well; Philippe, if it will please you."

Letty had begun to disrobe when Alexandria finished the telephone conversation. Alexandria was standing staring at the instrument when Letty emerged from the dressing room.

"What is it, Alexandria? You seem to be in a strange state," Letty asked as she turned her back to her friend. "Unbutton me, if you please."

"I am merely fatigued," Alexandria said as her fingers worked at the buttons.

31

"If you're ever away, remind me not to wear this dress. I'll never be able to get out of it by myself." She laughed. She turned to her friend as she began to remove the garment. "Who was that on the telephone?"

Alexandria appeared perplexed. "That? It was Count de Marco. He wishes to speak to me in private."

"Not tonight, surely."

"No, tomorrow."

"Why such a concerned expression, Alexandria?" Letty asked a few moments later after she had donned her nightdress. "Is something wrong?"

"I don't know. It strikes me as odd that Count de Marco wishes to speak to me in private."

"He seemed a very likeable sort to me," Letty commented as she sat on the side of the bed.

"I do not dislike him, but he does present a mystery," Alexandria returned as she began to brush her hair. "Exercises, Letitia."

"What?"

"You've not done your exercises."

"I'm far too tired."

"You'll be far too stiff to dance properly tomorrow if you neglect them."

"You're such a mother hen at times." Letty reluctantly got to her feet and made a meager attempt at doing her exercises. "Back home in Savannah, at Moss Grove, when I used to gather eggs, I'd try to take eggs from under a hen who wanted to sit, and she pecked at me. That's what you remind me of: peck, peck, peck."

"I am concerned for you, Letitia, that is all."

Letty went up behind her friend and hugged her. "I know you are, Alexandria, I know you are. I'm sorry if I seem to be so irritable." She went back to her exercises.

"Did you have an interesting chat with your cousin?" Alexandria asked as she set the hairbrush

32

on the bureau. "He's a most attractive man. I couldn't help but notice that."

"Luke is one of Cousin Peggy's older twin brothers. He's Oliver's father."

"Oliver?" Alexandria's interest picked up. "No wonder his son is such a dashing creature."

"Creature?"

"Person," Alexandria corrected herself.

"Oliver certainly made an impression on you, didn't he?"

Alexandria went toward the bed. "I found him provocatively interesting. Yet I doubt that he even noticed that I was at the party in London. Does Luke have an identical twin?"

"Very much identical, from what I gather. Cousin Peggy had mentioned them on occasion, and even to this day she can be confused by their identities," Letty said as she did the last of her routine movements. "I think that it would be exciting to have an identical likeness of yourself. John Adam, his twin, lives in San Francisco, while Luke lives in Denver, Colorado, so they are rarely at the same place at the same time."

"Does Oliver have siblings?" Alexandria asked as she stretched out in the bed.

"He apparently was the only child of Luke's and Joyce's who lived. I don't recall details and I'm far too tired to attempt to recall them." Letty fell onto the bed. "I immediately took a liking to Luke. I don't always like my relatives at first meeting, but I found a deep sincerity in him. I hope I have the opportunity to get to know him better."

Alexandria reached to turn out the light on her side of the bed. "I have no doubt that you will, Letitia. We'll discuss it at another time."

"Good night, Alexandria."

"Good night."

In no time, Letitia was breathing heavily in sleep, but Alexandria remained wide awake. She could not put events of the day from her mind, particularly the telephone conversation she had had with Philippe de Marco. Why had that so disturbed her? What was behind the urgency he expressed? It took conscious effort to force such thoughts from her mind and ultimately fall asleep.

Rehearsal the following day was grueling. Both Letitia and Alexandria wondered where they would get the energy to last out the session. Still, they, like all the members of the LeVeque company, had tremendous endurance, which was part of the prerequisite for being a ballet dancer in the first place.

When they were finally dismissed, Alexandria was on the verge of collapse. She wanted only to soak in a hot tub for at least two hours. Instead, she spent only fifteen minutes in the hot water, and another fifteen in a horizontal position on the bed while Letitia bathed.

"It's only a suggestion, Alexandria," Letty said as she toweled herself, "but, if you like, I'll go meet Count de Marco and explain that you simply can't make it."

"But I can make it," Alexandria protested. "I am already regaining my strength."

"Your strength, perhaps, but not your enthusiasm," Letty returned.

"I am most anxious to learn what Count de Marco has on his mind. That curiosity alone will spur me on." She pushed herself from the bed.

Letty watched as Alexandria slipped into a conservative black woolen dress, the plain lines of which gave her an almost austere appearance.

"Alexandria, I've been thinking," Letty said as she stood, towel-draped. "You don't suppose the count has some sort of impropriety in mind, do you?"

"What a question to ask!" Alexandria shot from across the room. "Philippe is to be my stepfather."

34

"That is no reason for him not to have strange notions."

"How silly you are, Letitia. I am certain the count is every inch a gentleman."

"Are you?" There was cynicism in Letty's voice.

"But of course."

"I confess I was beginning to feel quite uncomfortable last evening at supper when he stared at me as he did," Letty commented. "I felt as if he were attempting to disrobe me with his eyes."

"You have a notorious imagination, Letitia." Alexandria laughed. "I suspect the disrobing was all in your imagination."

"I think not."

Alexandria went to her and cocked her head. "Why do you say that?"

"The word that comes to mind to describe his look is 'salacious,'" Letty returned. "It's a word I never use; still, that is what I perceived. Promise me you'll be careful, Alexandria."

"Salacious?" Alexandria laughed again, but her expression changed when she saw the deep concern in Letty's expression. "You are well aware that I can handle myself in situations with men."

"With young men—and perhaps inexperienced ones, but the count reeks of confidence and persuasion. Just be wary."

Alexandria kissed Letty on the cheek as they embraced. "I will take extra precautions for you, Letitia."

"No, do it for yourself. Please."

"Very well. Now I must go." Alexandria started for the door, stopped and went to the dresser, where she found a small bottle of perfume and put some behind each earlobe. She only briefly glanced back, smiled and left the room.

Letty sat on the bed and worried.

THREE

Alexandria had always maintained a self-confidence regarding her ability to withstand aggressive advances of men. She didn't like Letty's use of the words *impropriety* and *salacious*. Certainly not naïve, she was aware that both implied threats to women, but she somehow felt herself impervious to such things. Still, she, too, had detected the unmistakable underscoring in Philippe de Marco's attitude.

Fortunately, as Alexandria left the hotel, she was distracted by a short parade of patriotic advocates who were in the process of rallying support for French nationalism. Such rallies were not uncommon, and, to her way of thinking, they were all just so much noise. The shouting was so intense and her knowledge of idiomatic French so limited that she really could not grasp the actual theme behind the rabble-rousing. Torchlights flickered in the wind, and the staccato distant drumbeat seemed to thrill the crowd into a kind of unity of purpose.

Just as she was about to enter the prearranged

meeting place at the café, a group of opposition supporters began to converge on the otherwise peaceful demonstration. Before a melee began, Alexandria entered La Petite Fleur Café. The small establishment was practically vacant after the majority of the patrons had disgorged from the place to investigate the excitement.

A short, dark-complected waiter showed her to a table in the back. Although he appeared sleepy and uninterested, he mumbled, "There is a war coming. I can feel it. But then, there is always a war coming. Do you wish to order?"

"War?"

"No, food."

Alexandria was momentarily flustered by his bleak philosophy. "I am expecting a gentleman."

"Ladies are forever expecting gentlemen: they are often disillusioned. Will you have wine?"

"No, only tea, thank you."

The waiter shrugged, and shuffled off in the direction of the kitchen.

As a crescendo of rowdy voices swelled outside, Alexandria repeated the waiter's morose prediction about the coming of war. Increasingly she had overheard similar statements, even in England, when she would stroll in Green Park of a Sunday afternoon. Of course, there was always that sort of commentary there. She wondered if people simply couldn't tolerate the idea of peace, and life without a war was boring and unexciting. Still she tried to maintain a sanguine attitude, clearly optimistic in spite of the pessimism around her.

The proprietor and two of the waiters ran dashing through the café and outside, where they quickly closed the shutters to protect the window glass.

When her waiter arrived with the teapot and cups, Alexandria questioned the closing of the shutters.

"A preventive measure, mam'selle," he replied in

dry tones, as if such demonstrations were everyday occurrences. "It costs nothing to close shutters, but it is expensive to replace window glass. Madness and complete irresponsibility prevail when mobs are incited. Well, there is certain excitement about wars. And when it comes, all of those people out there will be rallied to a common cause. It's paradoxical."

"You speak like an educated person."

"Educated through observation and experience, mam'selle, little more." He shuffled away, swiping his towel across the surface of tables en route, to sweep away crumbs as he moved.

A crashing sound against the shutter preceded Count Philippe de Marco's entrance into the café. He looked slightly ruffled by the experience, but quickly gathered his wits and went directly to where Alexandria was seated. With his old-world gallantry, he bowed and kissed the back of her hand before he took a seat opposite her.

"At first I thought the mob was expressing some personal vendetta against me," Philippe said humorously, "but I have never been so popular—or unpopular, as the case may be. How lovely you appear this evening. Who would dream that you had had such a rigorous day of rehearsal?"

"I don't feel particularly lovely, Philippe," Alexandria replied. "And as a matter of fact, any display of good humor you see is merely a preconditioned façade I've managed to erect. I really should not be here."

"But it is most imperative that you are, mam'selle."

Another loud noise came from outside the café.

"It sounds as if the war has already begun," Alexandria observed.

"The war?" Philippe questioned. "But of course, you have heard the constant rumors of war—they're everywhere. I am not unconvinced that such demonstrations as those going on outside are not purpose-

38

fully perpetuated by the government to incite the plebians into exaggerated states of patrotism. That is a simplified yet truthful observation."

Alexandria poured the tea. "Since I am in such a state of fatigue, Philippe, can we get on with what you wanted to discuss?"

Philippe glanced around him to ascertain that they were not being overheard. "Ah, for that I could have not asked for a more appropriate overture than all that hysteria going on outside, Alexandria. Or perhaps 'prelude' would be a better expression. Whatever. The fact is that war is imminent. Where and when it will break out is anyone's guess at this time."

"You say that with surety."

"There is no doubt of the fact in my mind, and in every other knowledgeable mind in Europe. England, France, Germany, Russia—who knows where the first cannons will explode?" Philippe repositioned himself. "Ah, but the art of war and the fine arts, such as you find yourself in, are never truly in conflict."

"The art of war?" Alexandria questioned.

"But of course; war is an art in the true sense of the word, particularly now, when the forces of imperialism and the struggle for power have reached sword's point," Philippe said. "Do not scowl away the pretty expression on your face, Alexandria. It doesn't become you. But I mustn't stray from the major theme of my discourse. I told you last night that I was predominantly French, despite my misleading Italian name. The fact is I am nearly half Prussian, and I will tell you at the outset that my sympathies lie with Kaiser Wilhelm."

"Am I to be shocked by such a statement, Philippe?"

"Not necessarily, although I had expected more of a reaction from you," Philippe replied. "Let me detour a moment and explain that I own a considerable

39

amount of land along the Rhine; perhaps a good half of my estate is there. I do, of course, own considerable property here in France. I believe France, even with Russian assistance, is incapable of withstanding Germany's superior might; therefore, it is propitious of me to side with strength. Do you follow what I am saying?"

"You think that France and Germany will be at war and that the latter will triumph, meaning that you wish to insure the safety of your property," Alexandria repeated without any sort of reaction. "But what has all this to do with me?"

"You know of my plans to marry your mother."

"I do, but I've not been able to sort out why precisely you wish to do such a thing," Alexandria bluntly stated. "Surely you and Mama are consorting together without the benefit of legal sanction."

"You are quite outspoken, aren't you, Alexandria?"

"I've been known to be."

"Well, then, let me put it this way. It is a matter of propriety."

"Propriety?" Alexandria repeated as she recalled Letty's use of the same word.

"I am not an old man but I am vulnerable, as all men are," Philippe continued. "I have no heirs, at least no immediately direct heirs. Were I to meet mishap at any time, your mother would have no legal leg to stand on as far as my estate is concerned."

"Do you love Mama?"

"But of course! I would not consider marrying her if I did not."

Alexandria toyed with the spoon. "I wonder."

"You are dubious?"

"I am pragmatic, Philippe—not coldly calculating, but practical," Alexandria explained. "Go on with what you were saying."

Philippe readjusted himself in the chair and stared deeply into Alexandria's eyes before he continued. "In the event of my demise and the subsequent

40

transition of your mother, dear Alexandria, you would find yourself in the position of heiress to my fortune, with the title of Countess de Marco."

"I am unimpressed with titles." Alexandria emptied her cup, observing Philippe over the rim of it before she put it back on the saucer. He was waiting for her to go on. She finessed by reaching for the teapot and refilling her cup. "What is it you *really* want from me, Philippe?"

"What do I want from you?" He smiled and sat back, with his fingertips pushing against each other. "You *are* clever. Far more clever than I had imagined. I admire your pragmatic nature."

The short waiter, with his compulsive gesture of sweeping crumbs, imaginary or not, from the tables, unobtrusively wandered toward where the couple was seated.

"I am practical enough to know that one does not bestow a title and fortune upon another without sufficient provocation," Alexandria stated.

"Do you have political alliances?" Philippe asked.

"None whatsoever."

"You are technically a French citizen because of your mother, but you do not even list French as your nationality."

"True."

"Then it wouldn't matter to you if France won or lost the war that is on the brink of starting?"

"Not particularly. As I said, I have no political alliance. What is it you wish from me?" Alexandria had become insistent. She looked up to see the waiter standing at the next table. "What is your name?"

"Mine?" the waiter questioned. "Manuel Catalon. Why do you ask?"

"I merely wished to know how to address you," Alexandria said. "You have a Spanish name."

"I am from Seville," Manuel replied, his mustache

twitching slightly as he spoke. "Why do you ask my name?"

"Merely to give you directions to bring us a fresh pot of tea. Leave this; bring another."

Manuel nodded and departed for the kitchen.

"You are clever, Alexandria. I hadn't noticed the waiter so near at hand," Philippe said. He sat forward. "Well, then, I'll get more precisely to the point. You are correct. One gets nothing for nothing —including a title and a fortune. I wish to propose you assist in the art of war in behalf of Germany."

"Assist? How?"

"Simply by passing strategic information."

"To become a spy?"

"Oh, no! Nothing so dramatic—merely to be a liaison, a courier, as it were, a go-between," Philippe explained. "You will be in a position to do so, touring about as you do with the ballet company. And, as I've observed, you are clever."

"You wish me to be a liaison, nothing more?"

"That's all." Philippe smiled. "As you must have presumed, I have investigated your background."

Alexandria sat rigid. "Did you do that prior to meeting Mama?"

"No, shortly after."

"And is that why you eventually proposed marriage to her?" Alexandria perceptively asked.

Philippe looked blank for a moment. "I love your mother."

"Because she is *my* mother?"

"No, because she is the fabulous Monique Dupree."

"But you're a man of nobility and Mama is—well, of peasant stock."

Manuel appeared with the second pot of tea. He eyed them both before he sauntered away.

"I have looked into the background of your friend, Letitia Phenwick, and she indeed is a member of the extraordinarily wealthy Phenwick family of Boston," Philippe said as he took another approach.

42

"I, also, have learned through an old acquaintance, Vladimir Popkin, that, because of her family's wealth, she has been given eminence in the LeVeque Ballet Company over you, who are perhaps a better dancer."

"Letitia is my best friend in all the world, and I love her dearly."

"But isn't some jealousy there, envy on your part?"

"Not in the least."

"Still, with wealth, you, too, could purchase a position of eminence with the LeVeque Ballet Company, or any other such organization, after the war. Think about it, Alexandria."

"This is all preposterous!"

"Is it?" Philippe leaned back again. "Think about it, Alexandria. Don't make a hasty decision. There is ample time."

Alexandria drank from the teacup. Her immediate reaction was to denounce Philippe as a fraud. But was he? Oughtn't she consider the entire situation before she reacted on impulse? "Were I to accept your offer, Philippe, what guarantee would I have that I would become your heiress?"

"It would all be spelled out legally in writing in a will that could not be broken under any circumstance," Philippe replied. "I give you my word on that."

Alexandria stifled a yawn. "You will forgive me. I am on the verge of collapse. That being the case, I suggest that I give you no answer at this time, and take the entire situation under consideration—as you suggested, Philippe."

"How soon may I have your answer?" he asked.

"The day after tomorrow. Press me for a reply before then, and I will have to answer in the negative," Alexandria stated. "Now I must beg that you excuse me, or I will have to be carried to my room."

"By all means; I will see you to your hotel."

43

After Philippe paid for the tea and the couple left the café, Manuel Catalon sauntered over to the table to sweep up his gratuity and to clear the dishes. He swore in Spanish. "Ordered a fresh pot of tea and they didn't even touch it." He shrugged and carried the things to the kitchen.

FOUR

Throughout her life, Alexandria had never been one to form close attachments to others. She cherished solitude and privacy to the point that she often felt as if she purposely isolated herself in her own little world. Much of it was a carry-over from her lonely childhood. She did not remember her father. Her earliest recollection was of traveling to Paris and sharing a tiny room with her mother, who by then had changed her name from Maritza to Monique. But little Alexandria was in the way of her mother's new-found profession, and when she was old enough, the child was hustled off to a private school run by Franciscan nuns.

Feeling rejected and unwanted, Alexandria kept to herself, dwelling in a world of fantasy and wishful dreaming. Only one nun, Sister Magdela, who was old enough to be her grandmother, took special interest in the starkly staring child. It was through the kindly sister that Alexandria first learned about ballet. Sister Magdela had seen two different performances by a second-rate company, but she was so impressed that she wished in a fleeting moment that the direction of her life had been different. Since it was too late to alter that situation, she imbued Alexandria with her dreams.

By the time Alexandria was eight years old, Sister Magdela suddenly died. The child was broken-hearted and begged her mother to put her in another school, where she could learn to dance. Monique was not easily persuaded, but when Alexandria refused to eat for nearly two weeks and appeared to be in a state of extreme depression, the Mother Superior called the mother in for a conference. Alexandria was transferred, began eating again and managed to shake the severe depression.

These thoughts replayed in her mind as Alexandria sat in the large, fairly comfortable chair in the small hotel room where Letty was stretched out asleep on the bed. In all honesty, Alexandria had to admit that Letitia Phenwick was the first real friend she had ever had, or had ever allowed herself to have, other than Sister Magdela, of course. But her friendship with Letty was different. She had been more open with her about her thoughts and ambitions, her feelings and her philosophy than she had ever been with anyone. Something about Letty seemed to magnetically draw her out. And over the time they had known each other, a tremendous closeness had developed between the two.

Alexandria stared at her sleeping friend. Did she, in all honesty, feel envy or jealousy toward her? No. The fact is, and that was unusual under the circumstances, she never had a sense of competitiveness with Letty. Each helped the other and wished for the other's success. Was that what true friendship actually was? A deeper emotional attachment had developed between the two young ladies, the kind of love Plato had described, a love grown out of sharing and caring, a love more real and universal

46

than that expressed by lovers whose emotions were predicated on a carnal relationship.

When Letty expressed her feelings for Tim Phenwick, Alexandria was pleased. Her only regret was that she could not feel toward Tim's brother Charles as Letty felt about Tim. Still Alexandria never encouraged her to consummate such feelings, and contrarily urged Letty to devote herself to the art of dancing, to establish herself before she considered marriage or deep emotional ties with any man, be it Tim or any other. That attitude was not born out of jealousy, but from honest concern for Letty's eventual triumph and success.

Now, as she observed her sleeping friend, Alexandria thought of the proposal made to her by Philippe de Marco and the suggestion that she would have to always take a second place to Letty because her family's wealth could buy her a place of importance. Alexandria knew from observation that such was often the case even in artistic circles. She had heard many tales from other dancers about how those who were most successful were sponsored by their family or patrons of great wealth. Heretofore Alexandria had rejected such notions, believing that she could make her own way to eventual fame and fortune. Still, she realized that, more often than not, reality was in direct opposition to ideology, and dreams were, at best, illusions. Would she in some way be betraying Letty by accepting Philippe's offer?

It was the ethics of the situation that most disturbed Alexandria. Since she really had no patriotic feelings or sense of belonging to any country per se, nor did she have political leanings one way or the other, she could rationalize that she would do well to ally herself with the winning side. Imperialist Germany was strong, and she had met several Germans who had compelled her interst. Yet uncertainty clouded her thoughts and she wanted more information.

Letty stirred and, as if awakening from a bad dream, her eyes blinked open and she suddenly sat up, leaning on her elbows. The room was dark except for the street light that came in through the window. In that dim light, Alexandria could see her friend's look of alarm. Letty reached to the bed beside her as if wanting to touch Alexandria, but found the place vacant.

"Alexandria?" Letty called in a whisper.

Alexandria hesitated a moment before she replied. "I'm here, Letitia, in the chair."

"What are you doing there?"

"Simply going through my thoughts. Did you have an unpleasant dream?"

"I was reliving the horrible fire at Moss Grove," Letty explained. "Why must I be haunted by that? And I saw Aunt Mattie being consumed by flames while she called for me to help her. Oh, Alexandria, I might have been able to save her!"

Alexandria moved to the bed and caught her friend in her arms. "It's all right, Letitia. It was only a dream. You couldn't have possibly saved your Aunt Mattie. You must stop condemning yourself for that."

Letty cried, sobbing deeply and leaning heavily against Alexandria for support. "I know it was only a dream and I did all that I possibly could do to save Aunt Mattie, but the horror of it keeps replaying over and over again. Sometimes I fear I may end up as mad as she was."

"You will not end up mad, Letitia. Put that idea from your head once and for all," Alexandria said soothingly. "Now dry your eyes and wash your face. Shall I get the salts for you to inhale?"

"No. Not that." Letty hugged her again. "I'll be all right now. I think I'm fully awake. I don't know what I'd do if I ever awakened from one of those nightmares and you weren't here to comfort me."

Alexandria rose from the bed to allow Letty to get up.

"We must think about supper," Alexandria said as she went to switch on the light.

"Did you nap?" Letty asked as she washed her face at the basin.

"I daydreamed in the chair, but I feel refreshed."

"I forgot to tell you, we have an invitation for supper," Letty announced, the thought just occurring to her.

"From whom?"

"Jeremiah James."

"Your Negro friend?"

"You know Jeremiah. He asked for you and made a special point of inviting you to join them."

"Them?"

"He's with his patron, Worth Bassett. It will be fun, Alexandria. Don't look that way. Besides, Mr. Bassett is most influential. It can't hurt to get to know him better."

Alexandria did her best to keep the frown from remaining, but she found it difficult. "Very well, if we are to be their guests. My money is short until we get to Amsterdam."

"Of course we're to be their guests," Letty returned as she went to the bureau closet. "You can wear that black woolen dress you have on, if you like, but for goodness' sake, put my pearl necklace on. I think you dress too plainly at times."

"Are you criticizing me?"

"Not at all. Just showing my concern for your appearance. It might do well if you were to impress Mr. Bassett."

"I've heard he doesn't care much for ballerinas."

"You listen to too many rumors, Alexandria. Even so, we're Jeremiah's friends."

"*You're* Jeremiah's friend," Alexandria corrected.

"I'm the one from Savannah. If anyone should be prejudiced, it should be me," Letty lightly commented as she chose a soft blue dress that had been given to her by her cousin Laura, altered to fit her after her cousin had tired of it.

"I'm not prejudiced," Alexandria objected. "I simply do not know Jeremiah well enough to call him my friend."

"Whatever. The pearls are in the top drawer, and I insist that you wear them."

Alexandria began to catch part of Letty's enthusiasm and her mood brightened. It amused her to see her friend in such eager anticipation over seeing Jeremiah again. Yet, as she reflected while putting the pearls about her neck, if she felt any sense of jealousy, it was for Letty's friendship with Jeremiah —and she couldn't explain why that was.

Always precise and proper, debonair Worth Bassett was the epitome of manners and affluence. The man, who never admitted his age, was in the latter part of his thirties, but he looked considerably younger. He was clean shaven, and his hair had grown longer than it had been when Letty had last seen him. He smoked expensive Turkish cigarettes and wore cologne with an exotic spicy fragrance.

Thinner than when they had last met, Jeremiah appeared far more handsome and mature, the boyishness fading from his manly physique. His face was a light bronze with darker highlights, and he had developed what seemed to be an aristocratic air that mirrored Worth's influence over him. Dressed in fashionable gray, the youth could not help but attract attention wherever he went. His smile broadened and looked to be all teeth when he beheld Letty and Alexandria coming toward him.

"No, Jeremiah," Worth reprimanded. "Let them come to you."

"But Miss Letty is my oldest and dearest friend."

"When will you ever get over that foolishness of calling her *Miss* Letty? Savannah is a century away from here," Worth stated. "I've done marvels in

50

polishing you in every way I possibly can, but you still persist in harking back to the past, to referring to Letitia Phenwick as you have always done. Sometimes I think it a mistake for you to continue your relationship with her."

"And sometimes, Worth, I think you try to have too much dominion over me," Jeremiah snapped back.

"Really? Do you?" He took a cigarette from a gold case. "We'll discuss that at another time, Jeremiah. But lest you forget, you are where you are today because of me." Abruptly Worth changed. "Ah, Miss Phenwick and Miss Muzakova! How delightful to see you again."

"Thank you, Mr. Bassett," Letty said. She started to embrace Jeremiah, but Worth loudly cleared his throat and she stopped in mid-action. "How wonderful you look, Jeremiah."

"Jeremiah always looks wonderful," Worth inserted. "He's a commodity, and commodities must perpetually be well packaged. I've arranged for us to have a private dining room. If you two insist upon showing a display of your childhood emotions, wait until we are ensconced there."

Jeremiah smiled broadly and rolled his eyes toward Worth. "It is good to see you again, Miss Alexandria."

"Likewise, Jeremiah."

The four were escorted to the floor above and into the aforementioned private chamber. If Worth was uneasy about the situation, he did not show it.

"I'll take the liberty to order for us, if that is satisfactory," Worth said.

Jeremiah exchanged a quick look with the two young ladies. "It will be satisfactory, Worth." He held chairs, first for Alexandria, then for Letty.

Worth ordered in impeccable French.

"I've learned some Russian," Jeremiah explained, "and a little German, but I've not even begun with French."

51

"You will, dear boy, you will." Worth turned toward Alexandria. "Before these two begin reminiscing, Miss Muzakova, let me inquire about the progress of your career."

"As you probably know, the LeVeque company opens in Amsterdam next week," Alexandria said, and watched as the waiter poured the wine. "Both Letitia and I seem to be progressing nicely."

"Jeremiah will be dancing with your company when you are in Berlin next month. I only trust Georges LeVeque has not made his choreography too French for the German tastes."

"With Madame Ivanovich keeping a tight rein over us," Alexandria replied, "I believe we have more Russian influence than French."

"I should hope so," Worth commented. "German culture is so very different from French. I would call German decidedly masculine, compared to the feminine French. Wagner's music, for instance, while romantic in its own idiom, certainly has strong masculine overtones, not like, shall we say, the music of Massenet or Debussy and that crowd. And of course, music of the Latins is far too saccharine for my tastes."

"Yet you don't appear to me to be extraordinarily masculine yourself, Mr. Bassett," Alexandria observed. Immediately following, she was nudged by Letty's leg. "It's true. Artistic men, I have found, are not especially masculine."

Worth remained unruffled. "I respect your candid observation, Miss Muzakova, and admittedly concur with it. But, you see, it is for that very reason that the masculine appeals to me."

The conversation through supper was a bit touch-and-go. Worth made no attempts to disguise or soften his brittle remarks and he seemed to delight in Alexandria's equally brittle retorts.

Before the evening ended, it was arranged that Letty and Jeremiah would have luncheon the following day, since Worth would be dining with his old friend, Count Philippe de Marco. The latter announcement was made for Alexandria's benefit and she knew it, but she refused to react outwardly to it.

FIVE

Alexandria slept restlessly that night and awakened fully conscious before dawn. With Letty sound asleep beside her, Alexandria got up as she observed light beginning to brighten the sky. She stood at the window and watched the sparse early-morning activity in the street below. Convincing herself that the motive behind supper the previous evening was to let her know that Worth Bassett was a friend of Count de Marco, she felt as if she were being coerced into making a decision to comply with Philippe's proposal. Yet in the back of her mind, she couldn't conceive how Philippe and Worth could possibly be friends. She could only conclude that they must be in some way involved with business matters.

As the thought of Philippe's proposal became more intriguing to her, Alexandria decided to do a little investigating on her own, as it were. Despite the hour of the morning, she made a resolution to call on her mother.

Letty was not disturbed by Alexandria's quiet

moving about to prepare to leave, nor did she respond when the door was opened and closed as Alexandria left the room.

Having had observed a misty rain falling, Alexandria carried a sturdy British umbrella as she left the hotel lobby. Coat pulled tightly about her, she hurried through the rain-wet streets as unobtrusively as possible. Only early-morning workmen stopped briefly to view her movements and entertain speculative thoughts. She stopped long enough to pick up a bouquet of fresh flowers from a street vendor. She only prayed that her mother was alone and that she would not be too upset by her visit at such an unexpected hour.

Only twice before had Alexandria been to Monique's flat in rue de Chance, in an unpretentious middle-class section. She lived in a second-floor walk-up. Alexandria braced herself as she reached the door. She rapped as quietly as she could, yet sufficiently loud to awaken the occupant. There was no response at first. She rapped again. Padded footsteps.

"Who is it?" Monique asked in French.

"Alexandria."

"Alexandria *who?*"

"Your daughter."

Sound came from down the corridor as the door was unlocked from the inside. Monique had struggled into a robe, her hair was wrapped and she yawned unceremoniously as she curiously eyed her daughter. "Have you any idea of the time?"

"It's almost six-thirty. I have a rehearsal at nine and I had to see you," Alexandria said before her mother could eject her.

"Six-thirty in the morning? I haven't been up at this hour since God knows when," Monique blurted. "Well, you're here and I'm up. Come in, come in. The neighbors will be squawking if they hear us chatting in the hallway."

55

Alexandria followed Monique's scuffing footsteps into the flat, where she was led directly to the kitchen.

"Are you alone?" Alexandria cautiously asked.

Monique raised an eyebrow and made a contemptuous expression, the meaning of which escaped her daughter. "I will fix coffee. Facing the day at this hour is one thing, but to face one's child at the same time is quite another matter. Fortunately I retired quite early last night—and alone, for your edification. I've had sufficient sleep. I simply am not fully awake. Bear with me, Alexandria."

Alexandria sat rigidly at the round kitchen table and avoided critically scrutinizing the unkempt condition of the room. To occupy her time, she scraped crumbs from the tablecloth before her. Fully aware of her mother's early-morning disposition, she thought it judicious to wait until Monique was less groggy before she stated her business.

Monique stood at the stove as if staring at the coffeepot would make it brew faster.

"I brought flowers."

"So I see."

"Shall I put them in water?"

"They'll wilt if you don't."

Alexandria went to the cupboard for a container, put water in it and delicately arranged the flowers. "They're lilies from Holland."

"Force-grown in a hothouse, no doubt. Horticulturists are always tampering with nature," Monique commented. "Get cups and saucers while you're at the cupboard. There's milk on the window ledge."

A tabby gray cat sauntered in from the next room and stretched as if the word "milk" had been her entrance cue. She went to Alexandria and brushed through her legs.

"Hermione is up to her old tricks, I see. Better give her a saucer of milk or she'll pester you to death," Monique ordered. She yawned and scratched. "Do you always rise this hour of the day?"

"Not always quite this early, Mama," Alexandria said as she put milk in a saucer. "Here you are, Hermione." She stroked the cat's back as she lapped the milk.

"Then what is the occasion, and why have I been blessed with your presence hardly after the crack of dawn?" Monique went to the bread cupboard, removed half a loaf and cut off two slices. "There's marmalade and cheese, if you like."

"Thank you, no, Mama."

"You don't want my marmalade and cheese, Alexandria—what do you want?"

"Just coffee will be fine." Alexandria again positioned herself beside the table. "Are you excited about your marriage to Count de Marco?"

Monique shrugged, with a blasé expression. "Do I look excited?"

"Not especially. But it is early in the morning." Alexandria arranged the cups and saucers. "If I had more free time, I would come and clean your kitchen for you."

"Phoebe will be in tomorrow or the next day. I do not worry about it." Monique belched. "When you have known as many men as I have, you will understand why the prospect of marriage holds little excitement."

"But you will have the title of countess and greater wealth than you have ever known," Alexandria said enthusiastically.

"Even the title of queen wouldn't make it any different."

"But you should be flattered that the count proposed marriage to you," Alexandria remarked.

"I was overwhelmed, if you want to know the honest truth," Monique replied. "Monsieur Dupree left me well enough taken care of financially that I can live comfortably the rest of my days. Alas,

57

Philippe became infatuated with me practically the moment we met; and after he had visited me a time or two, he impetuously fell in love with me. Some men have the tendency to be overly romantic, while others—well, never mind that."

"It must give you great comfort to know that the count is in love with you."

"Do you mean 'at my age'?"

"Not at all, Mama. You're sensitive."

Monique poured the coffee. "I am practical."

"Are you in love with Count de Marco, Mama?"

"I make him think that I am."

"But are you?"

"I have learned to play men for all I can get out of them," Monique replied candidly as she fingered the lilies. "I can be quite an actress when it comes to the roles I play. It will be a lark, I think, to become a countess."

"Does he have any children?"

"None—at least—well, I believe we can assume there are none."

"And others of his family?"

"There are a few distant relatives, but they are unimportant to him."

Alexandria drank from the coffee cup. "If you are not in love with him and you don't need money, why are you marrying Philippe de Marco?"

Monique looked down and picked up Hermione before she replied. "Do you think I've not asked myself that question a million times? Oddly, I never come up with a satisfactory answer."

"Mama, are you doing it for me?" Alexandria asked.

"What a foolish notion!" Monique scolded. "Did you hear that silly question, Hermione?"

The cat purred.

"Alexandria, you are my only child—fortunately—" Monique said after a measured silence. "I suppose I love you, but not always as a mother should. And

I've supported you as best as I could. You've had no complaints. Once you've become a prima ballerina—isn't that what they call them?—you'll be fully on your own. I look forward to that day."

"Enough so that you would purchase a place of importance for me with a ballet company?" Alexandria questioned.

"Is that a proposal? I am not that well off."

"I meant by marrying Count de Marco."

"Who told—that is, where did you get such an outrageous notion?" Monique stared into the coffee cup before she added more sugar to it.

"Mama—?"

"Hermione, this daughter of mine has most ridiculous notions."

"Do I, Mama?" Alexandria looked deeply into her mother's eyes. "I have always loved you, Mama, more than you will ever know."

"Who else did you have to love?"

"And you've loved me more than you've ever shown, I know that now. I used to hate what you did to earn a living. I even felt guilty being educated by money acquired that way. And maybe I stood away from you because of your profession. I simply didn't understand."

"The lilies have no odor. I know they're hothouse."

"Listen to me, Mama."

"I'm not deaf."

"I know you're not. But I suspect I've been blind to many things."

"Perhaps you need eyeglasses."

"Don't make light of what I have to say. You know what I mean. Oh, there are hundreds and thousands of things I've wanted to say to you through my life. Most of them weren't kind, or merely tolerant at best."

"It is nice to know a mama is tolerated. I suppose I should be thankful for that." Monique put the cat aside and went to get the coffeepot. "It's too early in

59

the day for this sort of scene, Alexandria. It's liable to give me gas."

"Do you have an agreement in writing with Count de Marco?"

"We have an agreement."

"In writing?"

"Should it be in blood? What are you getting at, Alexandria? You confuse me." She poured the coffee. "Yes, I have a written agreement with Philippe; it is all perfectly legal. I wouldn't have married him otherwise. I am to be his sole heiress, except—"

"Except?"

Monique took the coffeepot back to the stove. She spoke without turning around. "I didn't love your father. I didn't love Monsieur Dupree. I don't believe I have much feeling of love for Philippe—perhaps a little. But I have had an obligation—not for my own survival, Alexandria, but for yours. There were times when I detested you because of that obligation to you, but I loved you too much to abandon you. Every time I stared up at a stained and cracked ceiling, I knew I was doing what I was doing for you." She turned slowly around, tears in her eyes. "You see, Alexandria, I once had dreams, not pretentious ambitions, perhaps not even grand ideals, but I did have dreams. I swore when Josef Muzakova was killed that I would see my dreams fulfilled in you. I could have never been a ballerina or an actress or anything as sophisticated as that, but I wanted luxury and the fine things of life, not the drudgery. I vowed that somehow some way, you would have a different life than I had ever known. Can you understand what I'm saying?"

"Perfectly well, Mama. I want to be angry. I want to scream that I don't want you to sacrifice yourself for me." She rose and went to where Monique was standing. "I can't. It's too late for that, isn't it? You will be Count de Marco's only heiress—except for me. But then, I'll actually be your heiress, won't I?"

"Let me do this for you, Alexandria; please let me do this for you."

Alexandria wrapped her arms about her mother and held her tightly. "Mama, I love you—I do love you so very much."

"And I love you, Alexandria, more than I've ever shown you."

"But you have shown me often in many different ways." She kissed Monique. "Love cannot be bought or sold, but it's good to know that it exists. If only I could find a way to make you happy, Mama, if only—"

"You can by becoming a great ballerina. I will triumph through you." She kissed her again and wiped her eyes. "Now my coffee is getting cold."

Alexandria watched as her mother padded back to the table and sat with effort. Then she went up behind the older woman and put her hands to her shoulders. "How long have you known Count de Marco?"

"Four, maybe five months—it seems forever. Why do you ask?"

"Just curious, Mama, that's all. It is getting late and I have rehearsal at nine o'clock sharp," Alexandria said.

"What was so urgent that you awakened me this hour of the morning?"

"It isn't important now. I wanted to see you, to touch and to kiss you."

"You're far too sentimental for your own good, Alexandria," Monique uttered. "You'll have to get over that if you really wish to succeed in this world."

"I'll try to remember that." Alexandria kissed her mother again. "Thank you for the coffee—and the conversation."

"Coffee's cheap—conversation's cheaper."

"Goodbye, Mama." She went toward the door. "I'll let myself out."

"Alexandria—"

"Yes?"

"I don't really mind being awakened this hour. Come again, if you like." Monique sipped from the coffee cup. "Oh, and Alexandria . . . I forgot to thank you for the lilies. They're very nice. Come here, Hermione; Mama will give you a bit of bread and cheese. You'll like that, won't you?"

Alexandria hurried from the flat.

SIX

Rain was still drizzling as Alexandria walked tall from Monique Dupree's home. What her mother had revealed to her had realistically altered Alexandria's attitude about several matters; but it also raised questions that had no easy answers. Umbrella aloft, she hurried back to the hotel room and preparation for the day's rehearsal.

The morning rehearsal went so well that the majority of the company was given a two-hour break at noon. Letty, who always seemed to have accelerated energy after a lengthy period of physical exercise, eagerly prepared to meet Jeremiah James for luncheon. Since Alexandria had taken Letty into her confidence concerning certain aspects of her conversation with her mother, she asked Letty to attempt to get specific information from her young friend.

Even back at Moss Grove in Savannah, wearing overalls, and barefoot, Jeremiah had always had a radiant appearance about him, as if some kind of magical aura of happiness surrounded him. His leaner face accentuated his fine features, but he still had that boyish quality that most people found appealing. He seemed taller to Letty, but that may have been because he held himself proudly erect and walked with ever-increasing confidence and pride of accomplishment. Not the slightest trace of a southern Negro accent remained in his speech, and there was such polish in his manners and attitude that no one could possibly have guessed at his plantation background. Always a quick student with the ability to learn and retain, the thing he needed most was encouragement, and that presently he received in large doses.

Jeremiah embraced Letty as they met. His large lips kissed her soft cheek as she squeezed him with the joy of reunion.

"Miss Letty, I declare you are prettier every time I see you," Jeremiah exclaimed.

"And you are more and more handsome, Jeremiah," Letty returned as she studied his face.

"I met a woman in Moscow, a psychic," Jeremiah said as they went to their table, "who told me a lot of very interesting things about myself. I don't know that I believe all that she told me, if I believe any of it. Still I found it fascinating."

After they had ordered, Letty reached across the table and held his large bronze hand in hers. "Tell me about your psychic friend."

Jeremiah laughed as if to conceal embarrassment. "I don't know how much stock to put into what she said. She told me that I was an old soul, that I had lived many, many lifetimes, and, that I had been reincarnated over and over again."

"Reincarnated?" Letty questioned. She had heard the word, but knew nothing about the subject.

She says that everyone has lived many lives," Jeremiah explained; "that is the way that the soul learns and matures. According to her, every soul lives as both a male and a female in alternating lives; furthermore, the soul goes into every race. This is not my first life in the Negro race, but it is the first one after an extremely long time in both the Oriental and Caucasian races. It's strange, but when she told me this, something within me confirmed that it was true. It was logical to me."

"I'm afraid I just don't know about such things," Letty confessed, "but I do find it most interesting. Go on."

"She explained that I had chosen this body, this life, my parents, the entire situation because I had a need to learn certain lessons. She said I had been a dancer in several previous lives—not a ballet dancer, but other kinds. That is why it was easy for me to learn to dance in this lifetime and why I will excel as a dancer. But she also advised me that there would be many complications for me to face and resolve. She even told me about you, and that we had lived together in many different experiences in the past and that you, too, had previously been a dancer."

"That makes goose flesh come to me."

"That's the way I was affected when I first heard her," Jeremiah added. "In one life, you and I were husband and wife—only you were the man and I the woman. In another life we were brothers; and in still another we were mother and daughter. She further told me that although I was in a man's body in this life, my masculine and feminine were equal and the same, which is why I have both the physical prowess and the emotions to be an artist. The magic is in the believing, she said, believing that I can accomplish."

"Your masculine and feminine are equal? I don't understand."

"We are all both masculine and feminine in basic nature," Jeremiah related. "That's what she told me, and I can believe her. That's why the soul goes

65

from one gender to the other, back and forth in a series of lifetimes, to gain balance between the magnetic feminine and the dynamic masculine. Worth is of the opinion that all artists, especially dancers, have neither a stronger masculine nor feminine side, but that these two aspects are closely in balance or in the process of being balanced." He laughed. "You see how I've changed, Miss Letty?"

"You absolutely amaze me, Jeremiah. Do go on."

"I don't believe there's much more I can tell you, other than that she told me that we were both destined for notable success."

Their conversation digressed to small talk about their families and recollections about the past until after their meal arrived, and the matter of Jeremiah's psychic reading was dropped.

"So you will be dancing with the LeVeque company in Berlin," Letty stated as a means of turning the conversation from what it had been.

"I will be dancing with you in Leipzig, Salzburg, Prague and Zürich," Jeremiah recited. "And there is a possibility of Vienna. Perhaps even other arrangements will be made. I leave that to Worth."

Letty hesitated before she said, "Tell me about Mr. Bassett."

"What do you want to know about him?"

"I really don't know him at all. And after last night, I'm more confused than ever about the man," Letty admitted.

Jeremiah found her statement amusing. "Worth likes to remain a mystery. Even to me, he is still somewhat of a puzzle. I can tell you this: that he is the most unusual person I have ever known."

"Do you get along well with him?"

"Extremely well. He is the first person who ever treated me as a whole individual," Jeremiah explained. "I don't mean to say that you weren't always my friend. Worth has uncovered much in me, brought out aspects of myself that I never dreamed were

66

there. He's a hard taskmaster, don't mistake me on that point, but he is also compassionate and understanding."

"Do you constantly live with him?"

Jeremiah pondered before he spoke his next words. "Miss Letty, there are certain phases of my life I can't discuss with you—not at this time, perhaps never. Suffice it to say that Worth guides and directs me in all ways. I admire him and I am appreciative of what he has done for me."

"Have you become too dependent upon him?" Letty asked.

"Too dependent? I find that a strange question."

"Look how you've changed. You're not the same Jeremiah I knew six months ago," Letty said. "You've become very much like Worth Bassett. You talk like him, your mannerisms are his, even your attitudes and outlook. I'm certain your parents wouldn't recognize you, the way you've become."

"Do you find what I've become objectionable?"

"Why, I—I don't know, Jeremiah. Perhaps not. Still, I see Worth Bassett in everything you do."

"Worth is *not* a dancer."

"All right, your dancing is uniquely you, but everything else is him."

Jeremiah put his hand to hers. "Miss Letty, who is your mentor?"

"My—?"

"Who do you pattern yourself after?"

"Why, no one. I'm simply me."

"Are you? What if I told you that I, too, have seen a remarkable change in you?" Jeremiah questioned. "But, you see, I was aware of that change coming way back in Savannah. Your mentor is Madame Roselle Ivanovich. It is perfectly right. She was your teacher, and the one person who recognized your talent. Worth is to me what Madame Ivanovich is to you, only he is something even more to me."

"Are you happy with him?"

Again Jeremiah considered the question. "Yes, I would say I am happy with him. If people from the past do not recognize me, then it only proves that I have progressed and they have not. I believe that progress is the most important thing in life; without it there is stagnation and regression."

Letty closed her eyes. "I hear Worth Bassett's words."

"That is the nicest thing you could say to me, Miss Letty."

Letty scrutinized his face, the smile, the look of confidence and determination. "Yes, I can see that it is." She forked a morsel of food, giving her attention to it as she gathered her thoughts. "What is the source of Worth Bassett's wealth?"

"The source?" Jeremiah turned his head to the side. "He has inherited part of his wealth. He has many business interests other than the arts. He has never fully discussed his affairs with me."

"He mentioned lunching with Count de Marco. Are they connected in business in some way?" Letty asked, getting to the information Alexandria had asked her to learn.

"I believe they must be. I've only met the count on two occasions," Jeremiah related. "Once we went to his home. From what I gather, both he and Worth have international business interests. As to what these are, I cannot tell you. I know there was mention of France, Germany and England in a business sense, and that they did say something about wanting to establish in the United States. Worth has not taught me about business matters. Whenever I bring up the subject of business, he explains that I am an artist and should not concern myself with such things. And I believe he is correct, because I find the whole realm of business to be confusing. Worth says I must take care of first things first, and when it is time to enlarge my education, it will happen."

"So trusting, aren't you, Jeremiah?"

"I have every reason to be, Miss Letty, every reason."

Their conversation was interrupted by the appearance of the rakish Tiziano Spolini, who always made an entrance with a flourish of eccentricity and affectation. His eyes glistened as he spied the young dancers, and he made a direct path to where they were seated.

"Ah, Signorina Phenwick!" the Italian exclaimed as he kissed the back of her hand. He clicked his heels together before he reached to shake Jeremiah's hand. "And Signor James. What a coincidence that I should run into you both here!"

"Won't you join us, Maestro?" Jeremiah asked.

"But I am interrupting you."

"Your presence is always welcomed," Letty said.

"Then by all means." Tiziano snapped his fingers for the waiter to bring him a chair. The maneuver was accomplished in seconds. As he sat, he ordered a glass of wine. "One rarely finds good Italian wine in Paris, but the French wines are passable. I don't find them in the least offensive. I hope I am not interrupting anything important."

"We were discussing Mr. Worth Bassett," Letty said.

"Ah, Signor Bassett! He sometimes strikes me as being a dilettante in the ballet world. But then, aren't we all, at one time or another?" He laughed at his humor. "Do not mistake me, since I know he is an extremely close ally of Signor James, and I make an effort to not offend anyone. I don't always succeed, but I do make the effort."

"Do you know Count Philippe de Marco?" Letty asked, as she observed a frown of concern on Jeremiah's face.

"De Marco is *not* Italian! I know that for a fact," Tiziano stated. "And I know for a fact that he is as much German, on his mother's side, as he is French.

69

But he is clever. Imagine a French-German with an Italian name! He is practically international. And he, too, is a dilettante as far as ballet is concerned."

"Count de Marco is?" Letty questioned.

"He was speaking with Georges LeVeque and me just the other day about becoming a patron of a young dancer," Tiziano explained. "One wonders what the motives are behind such gestures. Oh, excuse me, Signorina, I did not mean to imply that your cousin Signora Donnally had devious motives in sponsoring your career."

"And you think Count de Marco may have devious motives?" Letty asked.

"I did not mean to imply that in the least." Tiziano quickly changed the subject. "Signor James, I have been just this morning arranging for you to dance in Roma and Milano. The Italians will love you. Diaghilev drives a hard bargain, but I believe things will be worked out to the satisfaction of all involved."

"Have you heard from my cousin Laura?" Letty asked.

"Ah, the magnificent Signora Donnally! I do not like people to hate me, but some persons are narrow-minded by nature. Signora Donnally will be at the opening in Amsterdam, then she will sail back to the United States, where her husband is most insistent that she return. She has become disillusioned by me, but fortunately you were able to make her see reason, Signorina. For that I am eternally grateful." A change of thought entered Tiziano's mind. "It is peculiar that we should mention Signora Donnally and Count de Marco in practically the same breath. The count expressed a desire to meet your cousin. I had completely forgotten about that."

"Count de Marco wishes to meet Laura?"

"Perhaps it has to do with his desire to become a patron." Tiziano shrugged and finished his wine.

"The life of an impresario is one of confusion and haste. You must excuse me."

Shortly after Tiziano left, Jeremiah took care of the check and walked Letty back to the rehearsal hall. They parted with the promise to lunch together again in the near future.

Before the rehearsal began, Letty pulled Alexandria aside and related all she had learned about Worth Bassett and his relationship with Philippe de Marco. The data were sketchy and fragmentary, but Alexandria had a clearer picture of the man with whom she was dealing.

SEVEN

Before returning to her room after rehearsal, Alexandria stopped at the café called La Petite Fleur, two doors north of the hotel. Had it not been raining, she would have walked along the Seine as she gathered her thoughts. The small establishment was almost fully occupied. She had to share a table with a young male student who introduced himself as if apologizing. The bearded, shaggy-haired, intellectual-looking youth, Guy Croisant, was preoccupied with reading; he merely peered at Alexandria over his eyeglasses with quiet interest and went back to his book.

Despite the din of chatter in the large room, Alexandria perceived the familiar shuffle of the waiter's footsteps when he came to take her order.

"Merde! Water everywhere! Why must people drip all over my floor?" the waiter muttered as he stood beside her. "May I take your order, mam'selle?"

"A cup of tea, if you please."

"Ah, it is you, mam'selle. Only tea?" Manuel Catalon eyed Guy.

"I am sharing this gentleman's table because this place is so crowded. Miguel, isn't it?"

"No, mam'selle, Manuel, but you were close." He dusted crumbs from the table in front of her. "I will bring your tea."

Alexandria glanced over to the table where she had been with Philippe de Marco the previous evening. Two young lovers were seated there, oblivious to everything and everyone but themselves. She turned back and stared at the checked tablecloth as she attempted to sort out her thoughts and the information she had received. As she felt herself being stared at, she raised her eyes to observe Guy Croisant again peering at her over his glasses.

"Do you wish something?" she questioned as she tried to decipher his intense expression.

"There's going to be a war, you know?"

"I beg your pardon?"

"War. It's coming," Guy said. "The revolution was fought to abolish the monarchy, only to have another brand of imperialism take its place. I suppose it is inevitable. The masses are incapable of governing themselves. So they are again dominated by a select few who claw their ways to positions of supremacy and authority."

"I know little about politics," Alexandria commented as a means of dismissing the young man's statement.

"That is all part of the strategy: keep the masses in ignorance," Guy persisted. "I believe the wealth of the world is controlled by only a small group of people, maybe not more than a dozen or so. And I believe they are the ones responsible for putting individuals in power and the ones who pull the strings behind wars. Wars are all a matter of economics, anyway." He held up the book he had been reading. "Have you ever read Nietzsche?" Finding an underlined paragraph, he read:

It is mere illusion and pretty sentiment to expect much from mankind if it forgets how to make war. As yet no means are known which call so much into action as a great war, that rough energy born of the camp, that deep impersonality born of hatred, that conscience born of murder and cold-bloodedness, that fervor born of effort in the annihilation of the enemy, that proud indifference to loss, to one's own existence, to that of one's fellows, that earthquake-like soul-shaking which a people needs when it is losing its vitality.

And I always believed Nietzsche to be a compassionate philosopher."

"I've never read Nietzsche," Alexandria replied. "Furthermore, I freely confess that I have no interest in such things. If you don't mind, Monsieur Croisant, I have other matters on my mind and I would be pleased if you would not disturb me."

"Ah, that is the very passivity of the masses, the loss of vitality Nietzsche speaks of," Guy went on. "How can you be so complacent in times as these?"

Manuel brought the tea.

"Is there another place available, Manuel?" Alexandria asked.

"There with the little old lady in the corner, mam'selle."

"Good. I'll move there."

"Is everyone so blind?" Guy shouted.

"Nor are they deaf, monsieur," Manuel replied. "Another outburst such as that and I will have to ask you to leave."

Alexandria was unable to concentrate on her thoughts as she sat opposite the quiet old lady. Her attention periodically went back to Guy Croisant. She quickly finished her tea and left the café. Manuel watched as she left, then shuffled toward the table and dusted away imaginary crumbs before he went to the kitchen.

"She was here again," Manuel said into the telephone, "and we know that she is staying at the hotel two doors down. She *almost* remembered my name. Perhaps she will come in again when we are not so busy and I can engage her in conversation."

"Be extremely cautious, Manuel," the voice at the other end said. "She must not be permitted to know that she is being watched."

The following day was devoted to packing and taking care of last-minute arrangements. Only a short rehearsal was called during the morning hours, after which the dancers were given time to prepare to travel to Amsterdam.

"It's the beginning," Letty said as she fastened her valise. "We're on our way!"

"Such excitement, Letitia," Alexandria commented. "You'll work yourself into quite a state of anxiety if you're not careful."

"How can you be so coldly indifferent, Alexandria?"

"I only *seem* to be coldly indifferent. I suppose that's part of the ambivalence of my nature. A protective façade is always a marvelous disguise."

"I lack your flair for mystery." Letty sat on the bed. "Do you have plans for the rest of the afternoon?"

"I do."

"Oh." Letty sounded dejected. "Are they—?"

"Confidential," Alexandria interrupted. "And I will tell you no more about it."

Letty watched as Alexandria quietly moved about, gathering and packing her belongings. Letty sighed and lay back to sort her own mind.

Alexandria was met by a chauffeur-driven motorcar at the hotel entrance. The driver informed her that he would take her to a meeting place with

Count de Marco and advised her to sit back and enjoy the ride.

The destination was about twenty kilometers out of Paris. Rain was still falling and gloom hovered everywhere. The country road was bumpy and Alexandria was bounced about before the vehicle turned into the driveway of a country house. A high stone wall surrounded the property, and the interior side of the wall was lined with tall poplar trees.

"Is this the château of Count de Marco?" Alexandria inquired as the chauffeur opened the door for her.

"No, mam'selle. It is just a meeting place the count has arranged. This way, please." The middle-aged chauffeur led her to the front door. "I will wait for you in the automobile."

The door was opened to Alexandria by a man who was a good ten years older than the driver. The butler, if that is indeed what he was, glanced at the car and the chauffeur. Without comment, he motioned for Alexandria to follow him.

The château was old, with antique furnishings. Built on two levels, Alexandria judged that it must contain at least twelve rooms, possibly more. She was shown into a dark, musty-feeling library. The walls of books were dust-covered and probably hadn't been read in fifty years.

Alexandria went to the window and watched a gaggle of geese splash around in the water, delighting in the continuing rain. An apprehensive sensation came over her and she wished she had arranged to meet Philippe de Marco in a place that was familiar to her.

"Ah, my dear Alexandria!" Philippe exclaimed as he rushed into the room. "Forgive my delay. I was in conference with my legal advisors and solicitor. There are so many odds and ends to clear up in such a short period of time. May I offer you wine?"

"Thank you, no. I do not imbibe much of alcoholic spirits," Alexandria stated.

"Do you mind if I indulge?" Philippe asked as he stepped toward a crystal decanter.

"Please do."

Philippe deliberately took his time in pouring the wine. "Well, have you reached a decision?" He toasted her health.

"I wish to further discuss the matter, Philippe."

"By all means. What more is there you wish to know?"

Alexandria preferred not to sit, rather to move about the room as she spoke. "Why have you selected me to be the liaison for the information you wish to have passed?"

"Because you are Monique's daughter."

"But in truth, didn't you know about me prior to the time you met my mother?"

"I beg your pardon? Where did you get such a foolish notion?"

"It seemed a possibility." Alexandria crossed away from him. "Very well, I will accept your offer on condition that you deposit fifty thousand francs in an account for me in a Swiss bank."

"Fifty thousand?" Philippe whistled. "Go on."

"Do you agree?"

"That depends on the rest of your stipulations."

"I also want it fully in writing that I am to be your heiress, after my mother, regardless of what happens to her or to you," Alexandria stated.

"What could possibly happen?"

"That is not the point. The situation is, I want to know beyond any question of doubt that I will be legally protected and will be your heiress no matter what your status with Mama becomes."

"Ah, I see. You think that my marriage to your mother may not be successful and, were I to disassociate myself from Monique, you would still be protected. Without a question I agree to that."

"Why do you agree so quickly?"

"Because in my mind there is no doubt that I will make a success of my marriage to your mother," Philippe replied with a broad smile. "Alexandria, I deeply love your mother."

"Do you know of her past?"

"Exactly."

"And you still love her?"

"With tremendous passion."

"I don't understand about love, I mean love between a man and a woman," Alexandria said. "How can you be certain that love actually exists between the two of you?"

"How can one be certain of anything? I just know the feelings I have within me." He went to her and placed his hands on her shoulders. "Alexandria, were I a younger man, the only other woman I might possibly choose would be you. Since I know of your career, your dreams and ambitions, I could never hope for such an arrangement. But by marrying your mother, in the end I will have from you what I most desire—and that is, lest you get the wrong idea, the very thing you are showing me now. You have an investigative sense. In time, when you've done your work for me well and we get to know each other far better, I will explain many other things to you in full detail."

"What sort of things?"

"You see! That is what I like about you. You are clever, Alexandria, I know that. It is the clever people who survive, and you are a survivor." Philippe sipped from the glass of wine. "Do you have any other demands?"

"What I've stated is primarily what I want, in addition to what you posed at our last meeting."

"Very well, it is done."

"Why are you so anxious to please me?"

"Because I want your assistance."

"Why mine?"

78

"Suffice it to say at this time that there is a definite reason," Philippe replied. "My solicitor is in the next room. I will call him in to add the amendments to the contract he has drawn up."

"You are prepared, aren't you, Philippe? How could you have been certain that I would agree to the deal?"

"Because you accepted to come out here today. Had you refused, I would have known that you were not in agreement." Philippe went to the door. "Shall I call in my solicitor? One further thing: I will not want you to sign this document until you have legal advice to ascertain that it is fully valid."

"Very well, call him in."

During the return drive to Paris, Alexandria reread the contract several times, searching the words for any hidden meanings that might be tucked away therein.

Because she had no official legal advisor of her own, Alexandria contacted Georges LeVeque to get the name of a representative. The document did not spell out what her actual duties were to be, so that she felt relatively safe in showing it to an impartial stranger.

Having received his approval, Alexandria had the attorney notarize her signature. She kept one copy, which Philippe had already signed, and sent the other copy back with the chauffeur.

The unwritten part of the agreement was that she was to begin her mission once she received verification that the fifty thousand francs had been deposited in the Swiss bank. Since there seemed to be expediency wanted in the entire situation, she presumed that the account would be opened within a day.

Had she properly protected herself? Alexandria had a feeling that something wasn't quite right, but she didn't know what made her sense that. Well, it was done. She had agreed and signed the contract. Whatever second thoughts she might have, she had to dismiss them without further consideration.

EIGHT

Less than two-thirds of the seats were occupied in the concert hall for the first performance of the LeVeque Ballet Company. The promotion had been sufficient, but the fledgling troupe of dancers was virtually unheard of; and without support or critical acclaim, it was considered fortunate that the attendance was what it was.

Georges LeVeque was relying on his limited reputation for having presented various concerts and sponsored other small dance groups; but having his own company struck most people as being a bit pretentious and overstepping his realm. Yet the critics were not only favorable to the premiere performance of the young company. Though they noted a few technical matters, which was to be expected, overall praise was given to the promise of the company and individual performances were singled out as outstanding. Both Alexandria and Letitia were among those who appeared to be outstanding, and the pas de deux they danced together received special acclaim for precision and technique. One reviewer actually had the audacity to suggest that a special ballet for Siamese twins should be written to show off the talents of the young ladies.

The second of the three performances in Amsterdam was much better attended as result of opening-night reviews, and the third performance was nearly sold out. The gradual increase in attendance was most encouraging. With all due consideration, the Amsterdam program had to be deemed a success in more ways than one.

Georges LeVeque and Tiziano Spolini met privately with Madame Roselle Ivanovich, and it was decided that a *pas de trois* would be created for Letty, Alexandria and Jeremiah for the Berlin debut.

"Don't you think you are rushing matters?" Roselle wisely asked. "Neither Letitia nor Alexandria lacks talent, but they are painfully without experience. I do not believe they should be expected to progress so rapidly. Maybe a *pas de trois* for Salzburg or Zürich, but not so soon as Berlin. The German critics are much harsher and far more demanding than the Dutch. True, Bassett has given Jeremiah James recital exposure in Berlin, but we do not know yet how he can perform with others. I do not know what all the rush is."

"We must capitalize upon our tremendous reviews," Georges stated.

"I don't believe, in all honesty," Roselle commented, "that they were all that tremendous. Favorable and highly praising in some aspects, true, but we must remain objective and not lose our heads."

"Madame Ivanovich speaks from experience," Tiziano acknowledged. "You must listen to her, Georges."

"I have always known Letitia Phenwick had talent," Roselle remarked. "And with the Phenwick support behind her, I can see why she was singled out by the critics—a guilder here, a guilder there. And I am aware that, because she danced with Letitia, Alexandria Muzakova would naturally be noticed. But why she should have received the notices that she did, somewhat baffles me, unless she too has suddenly received a patron."

"Most perceptive of you, Madame Ivanovich," LeVeque replied. "Most perceptive indeed."

"Ah!" Roselle widened her eyes before she frowned a question. "Who is her sponsor?"

"At the present he wishes to remain anonymous," LeVeque said. "Such wishes must be adhered to, isn't that so, Tiziano?"

"Most definitely," the Italian responded.

Roselle wore a practiced expression that was devoid of any emotion. Whatever her reaction was to the information, she kept it well to herself.

During the day of the third performance in Amsterdam, two significant events occurred. The first was the civil marriage ceremony between Monique Dupree and Count Philippe, at which Alexandria was maid of honor. Just before the rites were enacted, Philippe took Alexandria aside and presented her with the information and the number of the account he had had set up for her in the Swiss bank. Along with the financial data, he advised her that she would be sent flowers that evening, among which would be the information she was to pass on. Further instructions were to be given prior to departing from Amsterdam.

Alexandria viewed the ceremony with detachment. Later she was surprised to learn that her mother had asked for a duplicate copy of the marriage certificate, which she presented to her daughter for safekeeping. It all seemed a mere formality.

On that same day, Luke Phenwick arrived in Amsterdam, late for the opening performance, but with plans to see the final one. Locating the hotel where the company was staying, he sent word around to Letty that he would be present at the theater that night and suggested they have a light supper afterwards.

Staying at one of the finest hotels located near the royal palace, Luke spent the afternoon quietly reviewing thoughts that had been disturbing him and making preparations for a most important meeting to take place two days hence. During that period he did take time to scratch out a letter to his wife back in Denver. He deeply missed Joyce. Since his career with the military had begun, he unfortunately had to be away from her a great deal of the time. He regretted the situation. In the past, Oliver had been at home to comfort his mother. How greatly Joyce had been affected by the turn of events in Oliver's life! She had fought, as with her very life, to keep him at home, and begged that he reconsider once he had made the decision to leave on his foreign mission. Xan Phenwick had been the persuading factor in the matter.

Luke had not tried to influence his son's decision one way or the other. He could only remain supportive of whatever the boy chose to do. Joyce could not honestly give her support to the plan. She irrationally bemoaned that her only child was being torn from her breast and would be flung into the ever-present shadow of death and goodness knows what else.

Peggy Phenwick took Joyce to San Francisco for a brief visit, believing that a change of scene would do her sister-in-law a world of good. Joyce only became more despondent, and begged to return to Denver. Peggy complied with her wishes, but not before she made other arrangements.

The letter posted, Luke went back to meditating on immediate plans. He was in the midst of heavy thought when the telephone interrupted him.

"Hello?" Luke said as a question, as he feared the caller would address him in Dutch.

"Mr. Luke Phenwick?" the man's distinctive voice asked at the other end in perfect English.

Luke breathed a partial sigh of relief. "Yes, this is Luke Phenwick. Who is this?"

"This is your brother."

"John Adam?"

A somewhat annoyed laugh came from the other end. "I rather imagined you would ask that. Had I meant John Adam, I would have said your *twin* brother."

"Hayden? Is that you, Hayden?" Luke sounded incredulous.

"Hooray, you remembered me," Hayden replied sarcastically. "Will you see me?"

"Of course I will," Luke exclaimed. "With open arms. Believe me, I'm sorry I mistook you for John Adam, Hayden. It's just that you were the last person I ever expected to hear from in Amsterdam, of all places."

"May I come up?"

"By all means. Room four-twelve. Don't mind the lift; it makes noises." Luke stared at the telephone after hanging up. Hayden in Amsterdam! Yet why should it seem so extraordinary? Of all the Phenwicks, including his sister Peggy, Hayden was the most unpredictable and by far the most adventurous of any of the family he had ever known. He had heard stories of the late Millijoy Phenwick, but he was certain that Hayden could well top her for audacity and unceremonious mettle. The brothers had never been particularly close, but they had always remained on good terms.

The tall, unusually handsome man had what seemed to be affected mannerisms as he stood in the open doorway. Luke extended his hand and Hayden shook it. Then, with an air of making himself at home, the younger brother sauntered into the hotel room as if he were on an inspection tour.

"You're looking well, Luke," Hayden said off-handedly.

"As are you, Hayden. Fact is, you look years younger than when we last met," Luke commented as he observed his brother. "Married life must agree with you, not to mention fatherhood."

"I manage to survive despite the bonds of matrimony and parenthood," Hayden returned as he went to the window to casually observe the scene below.

"Are you miffed because I mistook you for John Adam?"

"Not in the least. My childhood was fraught with mistaken identity. Frankly, I never did think I so greatly resembled you and John Adam. But that may only be my opinion."

"Are Olga and the family traveling with you?" Luke felt obliged to force a conversation.

"I deposited Olga in London with Daniel Charles and Louise," Hayden replied. "Belinda and Cornelius remained in San Francisco, where they're to be shuttled between the Duvanes, their grandparents, and sister Lola. Frankly, I was of the opinion they should be put into private boarding schools and leave it at that."

"You should enjoy your children while you can, Hayden. Won't you take a seat?"

"Mind if I pace for a while?" Hayden returned. "I can organize my thoughts better and talk more freely while moving about—not that speaking has ever been a difficulty for me. As to enjoying the children, I was ill-disposed to marriage in the first place, and even more so to fatherhood. Still, one conforms to conventions occasionally, if only for the sake of appearance."

"I detect underlying problems in your statements."

"Perhaps. I suppose you had heard that Olga is verging on dipsomania, hadn't you?"

"Dipso—?"

"Poor dear has a drinking problem, to put it

86

politely," Hayden filled in. "But being married to me, that doesn't come as a surprise. I don't believe there has been a truly alcoholic Phenwick woman in the past. At least it's a point of some distinction."

Luke had questions, but he decided it would be propitious not to ask them. His brother had always been a convoluted puzzle to him. "Perhaps Daniel Charles and Louise will be able to help her."

Hayden made a sardonic sound that suggested Luke was mistaken. "Lola sends her love, of course, as does Peg."

Taking that to mean he wished no longer to discuss Olga, Luke persisted in light conversation about their immediate relatives and their families.

"Have you ever gone out in one of those little boats with the motors they drive through the canals?" Hayden asked when he had tired of speaking of the family.

"Can't say that I have."

"I did the last time I was in Amsterdam. It's great fun. One can hire a boat and drive it oneself," Hayden said.

"Why did you mention that?"

"There is a man down below who has been leaning against that lamppost, reading a newspaper ever since I've been here," Hayden observed. "At least he has pretended to be reading. No, stay where you are, Luke. As much as I hate to admit it, I suspect he mistook me for you and followed me from the train station."

"Why do you suppose he did that?"

"I'll tell you later," Hayden replied. "There is a place to rent boats such as I mentioned, at the end of this street. I will distract our friend below while you go there and arrange for a boat. Then I'll lose him and join you in fifteen to twenty minutes."

"I don't understand."

"Nor do I completely at this point," Hayden said. "Just do as I tell you. Take a heavy coat and work

87

at being inconspicuous. I'll meet you as promised."
He went directly to the door and let himself out.

Luke puzzled the situation for a few moments before it occurred to him that Hayden was dead serious about what he said. From the window he watched Hayden move out into the street and pause to light a cigarette before he walked in the direction of the palace. The man by the lamppost hesitated a few minutes before he followed.

Filled with urgency, Luke left the hotel, hailed a taxi and instructed the driver to take him to the boat landing at the end of the street.

With the boat's motor running and an extra can of petrol in reserve, Luke watched as his brother came suddenly into view, casually walking as if he were on a sight-seeing tour. Even as he climbed down the steps to the boat, Hayden displayed no urgency or anxiety.

"Scoot over and let me drive this thing," Hayden said as he got in beside Luke. "Occasionally look unobtrusively back and see if we've been followed. 'Unobtrusively' is the key word. I believe I managed to elude him, but I could have been mistaken."

"I see no one."

Hayden veered the boat out into the canal. "I have a map of the canals in my pocket. I hope we won't get lost."

"Can you tell me what this is all about?"

"Dear brother, I thought you could enlighten me."

"Well, then, will you explain what you're doing in Amsterdam?"

"Shortly, Luke, shortly. Just sit back and relax like you did this sort of thing every day of your life."

Sit back and relax? Luke thought. That was an impossibility.

NINE

"I became curious when Joyce told me, during her visit to San Francisco," Hayden said about ten minutes later, "that on two different occasions men had been to your house in Denver inquiring about you . . . and about Oliver. They were routinely told that you were in Washington, D.C. with your military position and that Oliver had been missing after being lost on a hunting trip to the Rockies. Naturally, since I've always been extremely fond of my nephew, the news concerning Oliver distressed me. That's when Peggy explained to me that he was actually in Germany on a secret mission. Unwittingly Joyce and Peggy had led the queryists in Denver to San Francisco. Fortunately they weren't led to me. I did a bit of investigative work, learned a thing or two about what you were up to—and from Xan, what Oliver was doing—and decided it would be best to make the trip. Olga's condition seemed excuse enough to travel."

"Are you making more of this than there really is, Hayden?"

"I doubt it.

"About three months ago, give or take a week, I was approached in my office at Medallion West," Hayden related, "by a man who was organizing money interests to invest in European industry. It seems the Phenwicks at Medallion in Boston had been contacted and they would not participate in the venture if we in San Francisco would not. I presume that is how my name was acquired."

"What sort of investments?" Luke questioned.

"In a word, armaments."

"Armaments?"

"I spoke with Uncle John about the matter in Boston," Hayden continued, "and he told me that he had heard of a group of financiers who had joined together as a means of easing the economic situation throughout the world, men of power who actually pull the strings behind world events. To simplify it, the Phenwicks have been chosen to participate in the power struggle. I can give you no further details at this time, because that is all I know. But I expect to know more before I return to San Francisco."

"How does this involve me?"

"You're a Phenwick, aren't you?"

"Yes, of course, but Medallion in Denver is hardly noteworthy in contrast with Medallion in other places," Luke said.

"I doubt it is Medallion, Denver that has involved you, Luke, rather that it is a curious chain of circumstances that has placed you in an awkward position. I came to Amsterdam to find you. I must know precisely why you're here."

"As a Phenwick and as a representative of the U.S. military," Luke replied, "several meetings have been arranged for me to attend with prominent

90

industrial and military persons in different places in Europe. I quite frankly was mystified as to what it was all about until just now. Although I'm still not clear on what is transpiring, I begin to see a hint of light."

"Do you have such a meeting set up here in Amsterdam?"

Luke thought a moment. "I have a meeting set up."

"Your reflective pause causes me to suspect there is something unusual about this meeting."

"I never realized you were so perceptive, Hayden."

"There are many things you haven't realized about me, Brother. Most of them are unimportant." Hayden lit a cigarette. "It's cold out here, isn't it?"

"Yes, quite."

"Are you going to tell me about this Amsterdam meeting?" Hayden swerved the boat and went into another branch of the canal. "I may be able to assist you."

Luke pondered the idea. While he had never been as close to Hayden as he had been to his twin, he had gained tremendous respect for his younger brother and did not at all feel slighted that Hayden had been selected to take over Medallion West when their father retired. In fact, over the years, Hayden had adroitly given assistance that kept Medallion, Denver from going under during financial crises. "I am to meet with a Baron von Klootz—Conrad von Klootz and his—"

"Have you suddenly developed dry-mouth?"

"No. I was going to say, Baron von Klootz and his—well, his son," Luke managed to say.

As they went under a small bridge, Hayden slowed the boat and pulled it over to a small landing. "Just hold onto that post for a few minutes."

"Why've we stopped here?"

"Luke, it's Oliver, isn't it?"

Luke turned away.

Hayden grabbed his brother's chin and forced his face back to him. "Isn't it?"

"Isn't *what?*" Luke was trembling.

Hayden did not release his hold. "I love Oliver. I believe I love him more than I love my own children —I'm certain I do. I know Oliver is in grave danger—and I suspect you may be, too. Xan told me about Baron von Klootz. I forced it out of him. Now I want to know the truth, Luke, because I want to help you."

"How can you—?"

"You've always had a tendency to underestimate me in the past, only to discover in the final analysis that you had been mistaken. That is neither here nor there; the past is over."

Luke's eyes had become liquid and he had extreme difficulty in controlling his emotions. "Both Joyce and I have nearly gone crazy with worry ever since Oliver left."

"When is the meeting set?"

"Tomorrow at two-thirty—in a restaurant."

"Why in a public place?"

"Baron von Klootz thought it would be best. His son is in the military and on leave before taking on a particular assignment," Luke explained.

"*His* son?"

"Frederick von Klootz was accidentally killed in a hunting accident," Luke continued. "Young von Klootz had been trained for a special mission— what that is, I don't know. Frederick's death made an enormous hole in the plans. Von Klootz let it be known only that his son had been wounded and was recuperating at an undisclosed place. Xan learned of the incident, as only Xan learns about such things. He saw a picture of Frederick and saw an amazing likeness in it to Oliver. I'm certain you can fill in the rest of the pieces."

"I see. Why was this particular meeting set up?" Hayden persisted.

"Conrad von Klootz had matters to discuss with me," Luke replied. "And I suspect, from what you tell me, they may have to do with this international financial situation. But you see, I have the feeling that von Klootz isn't in with the people who have contacted you; rather, in opposition to them."

"Why do you suspect that?"

"I can't say. It's just a feeling I have, which could mean that Oliver is in far more of a powder-keg position than we thought he possibly ever would be," Luke said. "There, that is all I can tell you."

"Very interesting. What are your plans for the evening?"

"To see our distant cousin perform in the ballet," Luke replied. "Peggy may have told you about Letitia Phenwick. I'll have supper with her afterwards."

"Good. I will contact you first thing tomorrow morning," Hayden said. "Better still, meet me at the boat landing at nine o'clock. Be aware that you may be followed and do your best to shake whomever it may be. Now release that post and I'll go ahead to the first substantial landing I can find and let you out. You can take a taxi from there."

They did not speak again until they reached the next landing.

"Trust me, Luke."

"I do, you know I do, Hayden. And I'm glad you're here with me. I can see where matters could get difficult." Luke shook his brother's hand.

"Go on back to your hotel room."

Hayden watched as Luke climbed to the street, then he leisurely guided the boat back into the middle of the canal and went without turning back to where the boat had been picked up.

"I'm sorry I can't attend the party after the performance," Letty said when she and Alexandria arrived at the dressing room. "I have other plans."

Alexandria was in the process of removing her dress. "What sort of plans?"

"With a gentleman. A Phenwick gentleman," Letty said coyly.

"Have Tim and Charlie arrived from London after all?"

"No. My, that was an eager expression. No, this is another Phenwick gentleman."

Alexandria went about her business, seemingly unconcerned. "Do I know him?"

"You've met."

"Not the one we accidentally met on the street?" Alexandria asked. "What is he doing in Amsterdam?"

"He had free time, so he came to see us perform, as he promised he would," Letty replied.

A knock came at the dressing room door the two girls shared. Alexandria slipped into a robe to answer it. The stage doorman stood outside with two wrapped bouquets of flowers.

"Looks like you both hit it lucky tonight," the man said in broken English. "Funny, too, closing night and all."

"One for you and one for me," Alexandria announced as she placed the wrapped flowers at Letty's place.

"Mine must be from Cousin Luke. It's the sort of thing I would expect him to do," Letty commented as she pulled into her tights. "Let me open mine. I've never received flowers in a dressing room before."

"Red roses," Alexandria said as she opened the wrappings.

"What did you say?" Letty called from where she was tugging into the costume.

"Red roses. I got red roses."

"Maybe that means you're going to become a Phenwick woman," Letty replied teasingly.

"What did you say?"

Letty crossed to the dressing room table. "I said maybe you're destined to become a Phenwick woman.

Red roses are supposed to be an indication of it. You recall my telling you about finding the rose in my egg basket that time."

"That's silly. Why would I become a Phenwick woman?" Alexandria laughed. "I think that's a lot of foolishness anyway." She examined the card. "All the card says is, 'Love, A.'"

"There, you see, A stands for Adam." Letty pulled at the paper. "Oh, what lovely tulips! Aren't they gorgeous?"

"I'm partial to my red roses, despite whatever meaning you want to read into them."

"There's no card in mine, just an empty envelope. Luke forgot to include the card. Isn't that funny?"

"I'll go get something to put them in. It'll only take a minute," Alexandria announced as she dashed out the door.

When Letty crumpled the paper to discard it, a piece of writing paper fluttered from it to the floor. The writing was in German, and from what little she knew of the language, she was unable to make head or tail of it. Thinking it something accidentally included by the florist, she started to throw it away with the wrapping. Then a curious thought came to her and she folded it and tucked it into her bodice before she continued dressing.

Alexandria returned a few minutes later with two containers filled with water. She arranged the roses in one and the tulips in the other. Then, when she saw that Letty was preoccupied with preparations, she checked through the wrapping paper.

"Did you lose something?" Letty asked, seeing that Alexandria appeared to be frustrated.

"What? No. Just trying to straighten up this mess," Alexandria replied. She deposited the paper in the waste receptacle and went about dressing.

The performance that night was extremely well received. Both Letty and Alexandria were given special ovations.

"I'm glad I saved the wrapping from the flowers," Letty said as she removed her costume at the end of the evening. "I'll see if Cousin Luke won't take me by the hotel to drop off the tulips. They'll wilt if I have to carry them all evening. Would you like me to take your roses, too? That way you won't be detained from going to the party with the count and the new countess."

"That will be kind of you, Letitia," Alexandria replied. "I was wondering what I would do with them. I wish they could have been presented to us from the stage."

"There'll be time for that, Alexandria."

Carrying both bouquets of flowers, Letty was the first to reach the stage door, with Alexandria directly behind her. Luke was waiting.

"I'll see you back at the hotel after the party," Letty said after Alexandria had greeted Luke and seemed anxious to leave.

"Yes. And you have a wonderful time, Letitia." Alexandria embraced Letty and kissed her cheek.

"Be careful of the tulips Cousin Luke sent me," Letty warned as Alexandria squeezed.

"Tulips?" Luke questioned. "But I sent you roses, Letitia."

Alexandria stood frozen for a moment, a look of shocked surprise filling her face. "Roses?"

"I must have been mistaken about you being destined to become a Phenwick woman, Alexandria," Letty joked. "I hope you don't mind if we stop by the hotel to deposit the flowers before we go to supper."

"Letitia, was there—?" Alexandria started to ask, quickly changed her mind and departed.

"Was there *what*?" Letty called after her.

Alexandria kept on moving without looking back.

"I was having a game with you, sending the roses and signing them with an *A*," Luke explained as they walked toward the street.

Letty's hand absently went to the piece of folded paper at her bosom before she stared in the direction Alexandria had gone. "It's a short walk to the hotel, if you don't mind, Cousin Luke."

"Not at all."

TEN

"**Will you come up** to the room with me, Cousin Luke?" Letty asked as they reached the hotel. "It'll only take a short while to put these flowers in water. I'm sorry the roses weren't for Alexandria. It would be so wonderful if she were meant to be a Phenwick woman."

"It might look better if I were to wait for you down here," Luke said.

Letty practically pulled him to the lift. "Please, Cousin Luke, I insist you come with me."

"Is something wrong, Letty?" Luke asked as they got in the elevator.

"A man has been following us," Letty whispered. "I caught a glimpse of him as we walked away from the theater. He was standing just outside the main entrance when we got into the lift. He's wearing a black hat and a dark gray topcoat. I couldn't get a good look at his face."

"Very observant of you, Letty. Holy cow! I reckon I'm just not used to this sort of thing."

"What sort of thing?"

"Being followed."

Letty quickly unlocked the door. Once inside the room, she found a wastebasket made of metal. "This will have to do until I can get more appropriate vases. I'll have to go out in the hallway and fill it with water."

"Let me do that for you," Luke offered; "you just tell me where to get the water."

"I think I'd better do it. You stay here." Letty hurriedly darted out of the room, leaving the door ajar. She had to use the water tap in the bathroom to fill the container. A little water splashed over the side as she went back to the room. Entering, she shut the door firmly behind her.

"Let me take that," Luke offered. "You should have let me do it for you in the first place."

"The man in the black hat and gray topcoat passed me in the hallway," Letty said. "He pretended to be preoccupied, but he did look directly into my face. I believe I would recognize him again."

"Are you certain you're not letting your imagination carry you away?" Luke questioned with a lighthearted chuckle. "You've not been reading any of those new mystery novels, have you?" But he had difficulty containing a tremor of fear.

After placing the flowers in the container, Letty went again to the door and suddenly jerked it open. There was no one outside. Upon closing it, she went to where Luke was standing. "Do you read German, Cousin Luke?"

"Fairly well. My maternal grandmother was German," Luke explained. "John Adam and I were given a sizable gift of money from our grandmother if we would learn her native tongue. Come to think of it, I believe Hayden also got in on that, but I don't know about Peg and Lola. When my son was small in Denver, we hired a Prussian governess for him. Why did you ask?"

Letty fished into her bodice and produced the piece of paper she had found in the tulips. "Can you read this?"

Luke studied the paper and stared questioningly into her face. "It appears to be a rhyme of some sort, the kind that children recite. It doesn't really make a lot of sense. Thirteen sailor boys in a boat without a sail, used their hands for oars and paddled safely to shore."

"Is that the exact translation?" Letty asked.

"Basically that's what it says. Of course it doesn't rhyme in English. Where did you get it?"

"I just found it. It's nothing." Letty blinked. "This paper was in the package with the tulips. The flower vendor must have accidentally put it there. I think we'd better go for supper. I'm terribly hungry, and I'm tired, so I don't want to stay out late."

"Come along then," Luke said. "I've a busy day tomorrow, too."

Letty had reached the door before she recalled that she had left the paper with the nursery rhyme on the dresser. Making an excuse to go back and get a scarf, she put the paper in the drawer with her lingerie and, scarf about her neck, joined Luke.

As they left the hotel, both Luke and Letty looked about for the man in the black hat and gray topcoat, but if he was waiting for them, he was well hidden.

Georges LeVeque, Tiziano Spolini, Madame Roselle Ivanovich and Vladimir Popkin were in the party with the newly married count and countess, Alexandria, Laura Donnally, Worth Bassett and Jeremiah James, as well as six of the dancers from the company. It was more a closing-night affair than it was a wedding party, since few of the guests knew Philippe and Monique. As parties go, it was fairly dull, and most of the guests were exhausted from the performance.

"I find it peculiar that you came all the way to

Amsterdam from Paris to be married," shrewd-eyed Roselle Ivanovich said as she sat opposite the principal celebrants.

"We wanted to be with Alexandria for the occasion," Philippe replied, playing the role of the grand host.

"How thoughtful of you," Roselle returned. "Alexandria is a very sweet child, and most talented. I am proud of her, as you both surely must be."

"You're not Russian, are you, Madame Ivanovich?"

"Why do you ask that, Count de Marco?"

"Your name. You've obviously taken your husband's name, the masculine form," Philippe replied. "Were you Russian, you would simply be Madame Ivanova."

"And were I to translate it into English," the spidery older woman said, "I would simply be Rosie Johnson. The thought of being Rosie Johndaughter doesn't appeal to me. And it is quite true, I am part Hungarian and part French and—well, dear Count, I have no pedigree. Ivanovich is a name of strength for me."

"Do not try to win that argument with Roselle," Vladimir Popkin inserted. "We have been through it countless times. She has a most stubborn and determined mind."

"Vladimir!"

"You see?" Vladimir rose from his place beside the grand ballet mistress. "Excuse me, I will mingle."

"An extraordinary man, Popkin," Philippe commented.

"At least since we've returned from America, he has not drunk as much as he used to," Roselle commented. "Poor dear, he was so out of his element in Savannah. I didn't realize how it had driven him to drink."

Six instrumentalists were playing popular music at one end of the room. Only a few people were dancing.

"May I have the honor of dancing with my new stepdaughter?" Philippe questioned when he observed Alexandria sitting with a distant expression. "Alexandria?"

"If you like, Philippe," Alexandria replied. "But only one dance."

"Do you mind, my dear?" Philippe said to Monique.

"Not at all. I am pleased to see that you two get along so well," Monique replied and turned her attention again to Roselle.

"I am not particularly good at social dancing," Alexandria admitted.

"This is a waltz and I have a strong lead," Philippe boasted. "We must see to it that you learn social dancing."

"I've never much had the occasion in the past," Alexandria returned.

"I have plans for you, Alexandria," Philippe said as they reached the dance area and he put his arm about her waist.

"Oh, that's a relief," Alexandria responded, misunderstanding his meaning. "I thought they were to have been in with the flowers."

"I beg your pardon?"

"Wasn't there to have been a paper with the flowers that were sent to me?" Alexandria questioned.

"Wasn't there?" Philippe scowled. "No, no, keep dancing. We must appear as if we are enjoying ourselves. I was assured that it was to have been included with the tulips."

"Why couldn't you have just given it to me tonight?"

"I could have." Philippe glanced about before he continued. "It was of no great importance. The paper was merely a means in code by which you would be identified to the agent in Berlin. It was stupid of me to trust that Dutch florist."

"The envelopes got mixed up on the bouquets

sent to Letitia and me," Alexandria explained. "When we got that sorted out, the card I mistakenly thought was for me was actually for Letitia, and the other envelope was empty. I thought the message had been included with the wrappings, but I went back to the dressing room and searched about."

"I believe we can safely assume the florist blundered," Philippe said. "I'll write out another for you later." He swept her across the floor in a more energetic movement.

Vladimir Popkin, tall and craggy-looking, had stood by an open window smoking for several minutes, watching the others. His enigmatic expression was difficult to interpret. He appeared a bit uncomfortable in formal attire. Curiously his attention went to Laura Donnally, whom he had watched on other occasions but to whom he had said little in the past.

Disappointed that Letty had not attended the party, Laura found herself uncomfortable with the others, who spoke mostly languages that were foreign to her. She had spent some time in conversation with Jeremiah James, but Worth Bassett seemed to resent her intrusion. She pretended to understand and cut that short.

"Madame Donnally, do you mind if I join you for a few minutes?" Vladimir Popkin asked as he presented himself in as grand a manner as he could muster.

"Mr. Popkin, I would be honored," Laura replied. "Most honored because you speak English, and my best French is hardly passable with real French people."

"Americans are so unlike Europeans," Vladimir observed as he sat opposite her. "In Europe we learn a smattering of many languages almost of necessity. There is not that need in the United States."

"You're not European, are you? I mean, isn't Russia in Asia?" Laura asked awkwardly.

"It is, but I have been international most of my life," Vladimir returned with a hearty laugh. "We have many friends and acquaintances in common, Madame Donnally. It is strange that we've never spoken at length previously."

"Well, there's Letty and Jeremiah," Laura said. "And, oh, dear, I forgot about your keen friendship with Tommy Phenwick."

"Thomas and I mutually appreciate each other's talent," Vladimir stated. "I met another Phenwick cousin through Tommy several years ago. The fact is, I went to visit him in San Francisco just prior to forming an alliance with Madame Ivanovich."

"I confess I don't know my Western cousins, other than for Peggy."

"I was alluding to her brother."

"Oh? One of the twins?" Laura asked.

"Remarkable! Even he said that his twin brothers are always spoken of first," Vladimir said. "No, I was referring to Hayden Phenwick."

"I confess I've never met Hayden, but I did meet one of his twin brothers—Luke, it was—in London just recently," Laura related. "Luke is a marvelous person."

"Hayden only mentioned his brothers in passing to me." Vladimir adjusted himself in the uncomfortable chair. "Being tall can be a distinct disadvantage when attempting to conform one's body to fashionable furniture. Will you be traveling with the company, Madame Donnally?"

"No. I'm returning to the United States in two weeks," Laura answered. "I'll go back to London from here. Since Tiziano—that is, Signor Spolini— well, I no longer have personal reasons to remain in Europe."

"The artistic world is alien to you, isn't it, Madame Donnally?"

"Quite, although I find it terribly interesting."

"You will do well to get out of Europe, Madame," Vladimir said. "Things will be difficult here before long. I knew few of the Phenwicks in Savannah; still, there must be others of the family scattered about who are not among the affluent elite."

"It seems there are Phenwicks everywhere these days," Laura commented. "However, I find that a curious question."

"Just merely passing the time, Madame, that is all. May I get you something to drink?"

"Thank you, no. I'm going to excuse myself shortly and return to my hotel."

"May I offer to see you there?"

"I can find my way satisfactorily. Thank you all the same."

"Then permit me to see you to a taxi."

Laura stared into Vladimir's amazing face and she suspected what was behind his motive. She allowed him to see her to a taxi.

Letty was sound asleep when Alexandria returned to the hotel room. Since there were two single beds, Alexandria did not fear awakening her sleeping friend. Fatigue made her body ache. The performance was exhausting; the party afterwards had really been too much for her endurance.

After disrobing, Alexandria felt the need of a warm tub. Despite the lateness of the hour, she prepared herself in a bathrobe and went down the hallway to the lavatory facilities that were shared with other guests. Truly, she didn't care if she fell asleep and spent the rest of the night in the water.

Letty awakened with a start shortly after Alexandria left the room. She turned on the light and, seeing her friend's things, realized she had returned. Getting up for a glass of water, she noticed that Alexandria's purse was open on the dresser and a folded piece of paper was about to fall out of it.

When she went to adjust it, the paper fell to the floor. On impulse, she unfolded it and, although she couldn't read the words, she could tell that it was the paper she had earlier placed among her lingerie.

Examining the lingerie drawer and finding the paper she had placed there, she compared the two to determine that the words written on each were identical. Hurriedly she put the one back in the drawer and the other in Alexandria's purse, and as quickly she got back into bed and pretended to be asleep.

ELEVEN

Luke Phenwick had difficulty sleeping that night.
After tossing about restlessly, he arose early. He
wished that he had got a better look at the man in
the black hat and gray topcoat. Letty had attempted
to describe his appearance, but she could not be
specific.

Dismissing thoughts about the mysterious man
from his mind as best he could, Luke wished he
knew how to locate his brother. He wondered how
Hayden had occupied his time the previous night.
Standing at the window as Hayden had done the
day before, Luke stared down into the street. A few
people were moving about as if bent on destinations
of importance. No one was simply milling about.

When the sky brightened with dawn, Luke decided to go for a walk. Fresh air would help remove
the grogginess that had come over him, and he
dared not attempt to sleep for fear he would miss
his appointment with Hayden.

Nearly two hours later, lost and confused, Luke

hired a taxi to drive him back to his hotel. As the vehicle pulled up to the building, Luke spied a man in a black hat and gray topcoat at the hotel entrance. He managed to convey to the driver in German that he had changed his mind and wished to go somewhere near the boat landing to get breakfast. As the taxi moved away from the hotel entrance, the mysterious man in the black hat observed, and then tried to hail another taxi to follow it. He was out of luck.

Anxiously, Luke had the driver leave him out a short distance from his ultimate destination. Then he took the driver's recommendation of a small restaurant that catered to fishermen and others who worked on the water. The food was satisfactory and tasty. He lingered over coffee.

A tall man in fisherman's attire, with a beard, and a pipe firmly between his teeth, entered the small establishment and sat at a table next to where Luke was seated. He nodded.

The weathered-looking face, with heavy brows half-hiding the eyes, looked congenial enough. Since he appeared to be seeking a conversation, Luke decided that it could do no harm if the man could speak German.

The voice was guttural when the man replied in the affirmative. "I speak German. My grandmother was Prussian."

"What a coincidence; so was mine," Luke exclaimed. "Would you mind if I brought my coffee to your table?"

"Please do," the rugged-appearing individual said. "You're not Dutch. You're not drinking chocolate." He laughed.

"I'm an American." Luke introduced himself.

"We don't see many Americans in Holland. Are you here on a visit?"

"I'm traveling, yes." Sitting close to the stranger,

Luke observed a faintly powdery look to his complexion.

"Why do you stare at my face?"

"Was I staring? Sorry. My name is Phenwick—Luke Phenwick."

"I'm—Hans. You wouldn't be able to pronounce my last name. Hans is enough. I have heard that Americans are friendly, but one doesn't see people who go about introducing themselves as readily as you do. Not that Amsterdam is unfriendly, but we tend to be more cautious."

"You don't speak like a fisherman."

"Did I say I was a fisherman? You assumed from my costume that I am a fisherman, but I could be a foreign agent in disguise," he said playfully, then looked cautiously about him.

"A foreign agent? Are you?"

"Do you think I would admit it if I were?"

Luke laughed. "No, of course not. Are you?"

"I might be. Do you think I am wearing a disguise?"

"No. I didn't mean to give that impression."

"But I could be wearing a disguise," the man said, waving a piece of cheese. "And I could be a foreign agent. You accept my German with an accent because you think I'm Dutch."

"Are you having a game with me?" Luke questioned.

"You are naïve, Luke, and that could get you into trouble. You give too much information about yourself and do not listen. That could be dangerous. You can't trust people, not here, not now."

"What are you getting at?" Luke was becoming nervous.

"Think back to the start of our conversation. What is it that we have in common?"

"Nothing that I know of." There was annoyance in Luke's voice.

"Ah, but we both have grandmothers of the same

national origin. Had you been clever, you would have pursued that—then I wouldn't have had this game with you." He laughed, glanced around him again, then spoke in English. "A disguise must be fairly good when it fools one's own brother."

"Hayden?"

"Shh! Hans, if you please."

"Why have you gotten yourself up like that?"

"It's part of a ploy. Actually, I was afraid you might be followed to the boat landing, and I didn't want anyone to see that there were two of us who looked somewhat alike," Hayden explained.

"The man who followed me last night from the theater was at the hotel entrance this morning," Luke said. "Do you know what that is all about?"

"Was he wearing a black hat and gray topcoat?"

"Yes."

"It was the same one I saw yesterday," Hayden commented. "That means I am going to have to purposely lure him away if your meeting this afternoon is to have the privacy you desire. Come, let us pay for breakfast and go for a boat ride."

The two brothers spent an hour and a half riding through the canals, exchanging as much information with each other as seemed to be necessary.

As they were returning to the boat landing, a group of Dutch sailors were seen walking along the canal.

"What is your curiosity with the sailors?" Hayden asked.

"Nothing. They reminded me of something," Luke replied. "Letty found a paper last night with a nursery rhyme on it. It was something about thirteen sailors who used their hands to paddle a boat that was without a sail. It was hardly more than a silly little limerick."

"Do you intend to see Letitia again today?"

"I made no plans to do so."

After docking, it was arranged that Luke would

remain in that area for thirty minutes while Hayden removed his disguise and went to Luke's hotel to entice the person who had been tailing Luke onto a wrong track.

"Why was it necessary to meet here in Amsterdam?" the tall blond young man with the almost white mustache asked. His hand went to an itching sensation at his cheek where the tissue was healing from his recently received wound.

"People will know you're Prussian without your calling attention to that scar, Frederick. You must not be self-conscious about it," Baron Conrad von Klootz said. "And you must appear more relaxed. We are merely father and son on a Dutch visit. I am known here."

Conrad von Klootz did not lean heavily on his cane when he walked in public, but his limp could not be concealed. As the two entered the hotel lobby, the baron pointed with his cane toward the restaurant and they went in that direction.

"Ah, Baron von Klootz," the maître d' exclaimed upon recognizing the familiar face.

"You see, Frederick, I am known here," Conrad commented.

"I have your table waiting, Baron. How tall and handsome your son has grown," the stately maître d' remarked.

"You remember Frederick, then," Conrad said.

"I would know him anywhere."

"I am honored," the youth inserted. "My father cannot stand for long periods of time, if you don't mind."

"Of course; I wasn't thinking."

"Remember, no display of emotion whatsoever, Frederick," Conrad advised as they took seats. "We will wait until our guest arrives to order, if you don't mind."

Baron von Klootz polished his monocle as he

111

observed the maître d' retreat. "I am glad he has put us in a dimly lit corner. We are liable to be observed, but do not let that disconcert you. But be careful."

Within five minutes of their arrival, Luke Phenwick was shown to their table. The young man rose and clicked his heels.

"You will forgive my father if he does not rise, Herr Phenwick."

"Your—your father?" Luke questioned weakly.

"May I present my son, Herr Phenwick," Conrad said in introduction. "This is Frederick von Klootz. I might add that he is Corporal von Klootz now."

The youth extended his hand. "I am pleased to meet you, Herr Phenwick. My father has told me much about you." The handshake was held a trifle too long, but it could not be avoided.

"You may sit now, Frederick," Conrad ordered as he extended his hand to Luke. "I trust you were not followed here."

"No, I wasn't." Luke sat stiffly in the chair opposite Frederick.

"And did you have a pleasant crossing from the United States?" Conrad continued.

"It was pleasant enough. My wife isn't in the best of health. She is still very emotional over the loss of our son," Luke said, directing his attention to the baron.

"He was lost on a hunting trip, wasn't he?" Conrad questioned. "But, my friend, if you have faith, he will be safely returned to you. Like yourself, Major, my son will escalate quickly in rank in the Prussian army. One purchases commissions. Who knows, one day before long, Frederick may outrank you."

The waiter came and they ordered.

"Shall we get to the business at hand?" Frederick asked.

"There is time, my son," Conrad said. "But now

that you have brought the matter up, this is as good a time as any."

"I have not been able to make any concrete arrangements for financial transactions," Luke stated. "I have, however, managed to open an account in Zürich into which one million dollars has been placed."

"One million dollars is but a pittance when it comes to the vast expenses of military operation," Conrad commented.

"I am aware of that, Baron," Luke said. "I have spoken with my brother Hayden and he has agreed to match the amount because of the great love he had for my missing son."

Frederick knocked his water goblet, but managed to catch it before it spilled.

"Why are you so clumsy, Frederick?" Conrad asked.

"It is the light in here, sir," Frederick returned. "Your brother must have a very great love for your son, Herr Phenwick, to be so generous. I should suspect that, for a man to love his nephew so much, his nephew must love him equally as much."

"What do you know of uncles, Frederick?" Conrad scolded. "You've never had any."

"True, but I've read about such relatives."

"Ah, the things they fill these young people with in the name of education," Conrad commented with a laugh. "We will only be in Amsterdam until this evening, Herr Phenwick; therefore, this will be our only meeting. There is an envelope beneath your napkin. Put it on your person as unobtrusively as possible. I do not believe we are being watched, but I cannot be certain."

As Luke managed to get the envelope into his inside coat pocket, the waiter brought the meal.

"I was hoping I would have more time to spend with you and—and your son, Baron," Luke said later.

"That is impossible. Frederick must get back to his military life," Conrad replied. "I only trust it was not a mistake bringing him along on this trip."

At the close of the luncheon, a tall, severe-looking man with sharp features entered the restaurant and demanded to be shown to Baron von Klootz's table. The maître d' objected, but the man, with a militant manner, noisily insisted. The table was pointed out to him.

"Be careful," Conrad warned, "this could be trouble."

"Have no fear, Father," Frederick said soothingly.

The man approached the table briskly and clicked his heels. "Baron von Klootz. I am Major Rittenburg of the Prussian army. My papers." He flashed papers rapidly before the baron. "This is nothing to be alarmed about. I have come with word for Corporal von Klootz. If you will excuse us for a few minutes, I wish to speak to him in private."

"What is this all about, Major Rittenburg?" Frederick asked.

"This is for me to relate to you in private. This way, if you please." He made a sharp about-face and waited for the young man to rise.

"I must obey my superior officers," Frederick remarked. "I shall return shortly."

"What do you suppose that is all about?" Luke questioned.

"I don't know, but Frederick will be able to take care of himself. I have great confidence in him, Major Phenwick, great confidence. You must have the same."

"It is not easy, you know."

"Yes, I am certain it is not. But at least you know your son is still alive. Watch that they are not followed."

"You are suspicious of everyone, aren't you, Baron?"

"Suspicious of everyone and everything, Major."

114

Luke observed the two departing men until they were out of sight.

"This way," Major Rittenburg said as he nudged Frederick's arm. "I have taken a room."

The young man did as he was told.

The older man closed the door to the room firmly behind him and bade Frederick to go deeper into the room.

"Neither of us is in uniform, Corporal von Klootz, so I doubt that any unusual attention was attracted to us. Why are you here in Holland?"

"I had permission to travel with my father."

The older man lit a cigarette. "Have you heard of me, Corporal von Klootz? Is the name Major Rittenburg not familiar to you?"

"No, sir."

"But you will remember it." He paced, circling fully around Frederick as he looked him up and down. "There is suspicion about you, Corporal von Klootz."

"Suspicion, sir? What sort of suspicion?"

"That your identity is not what you claim it to be," the other said. "That you are simply posing as Frederick von Klootz, who was actually killed. Is that not so?"

"It is not true. I am Frederick von Klootz."

"I think differently." He put a monocle to his eye and looked the youth up and down. "Have you ever heard of Oliver Phenwick?"

Frederick's face tightened and he felt the increase of his pulse. "No, sir."

"Do not lie to me!"

"I am not lying, sir."

Again he circled the young man. "Oliver Phenwick is the son of Major Luke Phenwick, with whom you were having luncheon. Did you not know that?"

"I knew Major Phenwick had a son. He is missing from a hunting trip. Is his name Oliver?"

The interrogator held the cigarette between his

fingertips and again scrutinized Frederick. "I believe you are Oliver Phenwick."

"No, sir, I am Frederick von Klootz, sir."

A contemptuous laugh. "It might be to your advantage if you are Oliver Phenwick."

"I am not, sir."

The officer made an abrupt about-face and made a larger circle of the room. Frederick stood with his eyes directly ahead, his body stiff.

"Aren't you curious why it might to be your advantage for you to be Oliver Phenwick?"

"No, sir, because I am not that person."

"Who is Peggy Phenwick?" He snapped his fingers.

"I do not know, sir."

"Is the name Joyce Phenwick not familiar to you?"

"No—no, sir."

"Why do you hesitate?"

"Did I hesitate, sir?"

Pause.

"I know beyond any shadow of a doubt that you *are* Oliver Phenwick, Corporal. And no amount of denying it will convince me otherwise."

"Then I shall continue denying it, sir."

"Aha! So you admit it!"

"No, sir. I don't deny it, but I don't admit it either. Unless you have proof to support your allegations, sir—which is impossible, unless I'm being framed for some reason—I cannot see that this interrogation is getting anywhere."

"The information I have is confidential, known only to me, your father and Baron von Klootz. It will remain private with you if you cooporate with me."

Frederick considered the statement. "What do you wish me to do, sir?"

The man stood directly before him. "Embrace me," he said in English.

"Do *what,* sir?"

"You *do* understand English. Embrace me. Put

116

your arms around me and embrace me as you did when you were a small boy." Again he spoke in English.

"I beg your pardon, sir?"

"Oh, Oliver! Oliver! It was a cruel trick to play on you, but I couldn't bear the thought of you being so close and not seeing you again. You were gone from Denver before I even was aware of what was happening. Well, damn it, if you won't do it, I will." With that he threw his arms about Frederick and embraced him.

"Uncle Hayden—?"

The man suddenly became erect and stepped back. "And if I am *not* your Uncle Hayden, you just gave away your identity."

"And what if I am really Frederick von Klootz and you are not Major Rittenburg. Haven't you shown me your hand?"

Hayden laughed. "But my disguise is only temporary, as is my role. I was only testing you, Oliver. They will be clever, even more so later on."

The laughter ceased and they stared at each other. Suddenly, as if on cue, they each rushed to the other's embrace.

"Oh, Oliver, Oliver! Take care of yourself. The next Major Rittenburg you encounter may be real."

"I'll remember that."

"We cannot stay away too long or they're liable to become suspicious," Hayden said.

"I agree. I am pleased that you did this. You scared the hell out of me, but I'm glad you did it."

While Hayden was upstairs with his nephew, Luke kept periodically looking to the restaurant entrance. He began to worry. He suddenly made a sound of alarm.

"What is it, Major Phenwick?"

"Someone just entered who may recognize me."

"Where?"

"At the second table from the entrance, to the

117

right of it. The young lady and the older man," Luke said without pointing. "It's Alexandria Muzakova, and I believe that is the man who recently married her mother."

"An odd arrangement."

Alexandria was facing the entrance when Hayden and his nephew returned. "Why, that's—"

"Yes? What is it, Alexandria?" Philippe asked.

"That young man. I thought I had recognized him."

"Do not stare so, Alexandria," Philippe warned; "you'll attract attention. I thought you were above flirting with young men."

"I wasn't flirting, Philippe. Merely curious."

"Oh-oh, there comes the boy and Major Rittenburg. I don't want that girl to see me with him," Luke stated.

"Your back is to her. Act as if you're in pain."

"I beg your pardon, Baron."

"Act as if you're in pain," Conrad said. "Major Rittenburg, may we prevail upon your kindness?"

"What is it?" Hayden asked.

"Major Phenwick has suddenly had an attack of something." Conrad stated. "Would you mind accompanying him to the kitchen before he becomes unfortunately ill here?"

"I'll accompany him," Frederick volunteered.

"No, Frederick," Conrad returned. "The major will assist the major, won't you Major Rittenburg?"

Hayden looked at each of the three. "Yes, of course. Let me help you up, Major Phenwick."

"I can rise on my own." Luke stared at the boy. "I am pleased to have met you, Frederick. We will meet again."

"There is no time for formalities, Major," Conrad interrupted. "An unfortunate display of illness could be embarrassing for all of us."

Hayden took a tight grip on Luke's arm and quickly led him to the kitchen.

"That young woman over there may have recognized Major Phenwick," Conrad advised. "I only pray it was not a mistake to put him into Major Rittenburg's hands."

The youth suppressed a smile. "I will pray along with you."

As Conrad and Frederick left the restaurant, there was no escaping the immediate presence of Alexandria and Count de Marco. Frederick stared straight ahead.

"There, you've had a closer look," Philippe commented. "You were mistaken, weren't you? That is Baron Conrad von Klootz and his son. I would know them anywhere."

"Yes," Alexandria replied, "I was mistaken. But I am curious about the other two men who were with them."

"Chances are, we will never know that—then again . . ."

Alexandria stared in the direction the baron and his son had gone. She recalled a party in London and the impression Oliver Phenwick had made on her. It was the scar on Frederick von Klootz's face that made her believe she had made a mistake, but she wasn't altogether certain.

TWELVE

"I don't need a taxi," Luke protested as Hayden steered him out through the lobby and into the street.

"I insist." Hayden opened the door. "Get in." He gave instructions to the driver to take them to a remote area out of the city.

"Now, see here, Major Rittenburg, I don't know what this is about, but I demand an explanation." Luke scooted to the far side of the seat. "Furthermore, I demand to know what reason you had to take my—that is, you took young Corporal von Klootz into private."

"Did you know that your brother has become a master of disguises?" Hayden asked in German.

"My brother? What does he have to do with—" Luke leaned toward the other as they rounded a corner. "Hayden?"

Hayden laughed. "My years of enthusiasm for the theater, opera, what have you in the art world, have given me an extensive education, Luke. I sup-

120

pose I could have been an actor, had I wished to pursue such a career."

"What was that all about at the restaurant?"

"I wanted to see Oliver," Hayden replied. "I'm afraid you've made a great mistake, brother, as far as the boy is concerned." He glanced at the driver. "I will discuss the entire matter once we reach our destination."

The drive took about twenty minutes. The brothers spoke little during the ride. The land was flat, colored by fields of tulips, newly sprouted crops and windmills. Hayden pointed out a particular windmill near an old farmhouse and directed the driver to it. When they reached the destination, he instructed the driver to return for them in precisely one hour.

The mid-afternoon sky was laced with drifts of clouds. The sun was bright and the visible sky was clear cerulean. They walked over a path through tulips waving in the pleasant breeze.

"I'm fond of Holland in the spring," Hayden commented.

"Do you mind explaining what this is all about?" Luke asked, his annoyance not concealed.

"We're about a year too late," Hayden said.

"Too late for what?"

"To help avert a war."

"Why do you say that?" Luke appeared perplexed.

"Even if we poured the entire Phenwick millions into European industry, it would be far too late to bolster the economy. That is what Baron von Klootz wants," Hayden stated. "But he is old-fashioned, still living and thinking in the Victorian era. The grandeur of the monarchies has become tarnished, corrupted, rusty, and unfortunately in a sad state of decay. The same labor revolution that we have experienced in the United States exists in most European countries. Oh, they are fighting it as we did, but I fear it is inevitable. Basically von Klootz is resisting change, progress, modernization."

"How do you know all of this?" Luke asked.

"I have put my mind to discovering what precisely is going on," Hayden replied. "Xan has filled me in on much of this. War cannot be avoided, but to what extent it goes, that possibly might be checked. I want you to return to the United States as soon as possible, via London, where you will pick up my wife and see that she gets safely back to San Francisco. I want you to do no further negotiating with Baron von Klootz."

"But I've made a promise," Luke said.

"Then you will simply have to delay fulfilling it," Hayden stated.

"And what of Oliver?"

"That is a worry, isn't it?" Hayden thought a few moments. "Oliver is in the Prussian army now."

"He's an American citizen."

"That, Luke, may be difficult to prove at this time," Hayden said. "Fact is, he has become Frederick von Klootz. All of his papers verify that. But as Frederick von Klootz, he may be of great advantage to us. I will have to give that strong consideration."

"If I'm to return home and take Olga with me," Luke asked, "what are you going to do?"

"I will meet Xan in Edinburgh, Scotland next month," Hayden replied. "For another thing, I am going to assume a remarkable impersonation."

Luke laughed. "You amaze me, Hayden. Who are you going to be this time?"

"You."

"What?"

"In this instance it would be best if I were actually John Adam, but I'm not. I've spent a lifetime trying to maintain my private identity and not be mistaken for either of my twin brothers. You'd be surprised how often I am taken for you when John Adam and I are together. I will have duplicates made of your papers. There is a place here in Amsterdam I can have it done without raising suspicion."

"What do you expect to accomplish by doing that?" Luke questioned.

"First, I hope to save Oliver's life," Hayden stated. "As for the rest of it, that will have to develop in time. Now I want to know all the people you have met while in Paris and in Amsterdam. You'll have to make a list for me, as well as anyone outside of the family with whom you've dealt in London."

"That will be relatively simple, since I encountered few people other than at the American consulate in London," Luke replied. "I don't comprehend what you intend to do, Hayden."

"Don't worry about it." Hayden looked away before he quickly turned back and snapped his fingers. "Who have you met in Amsterdam?"

"Actually, only Letty Phenwick and you in your various disguises," Luke answered.

"You forgot to mention Baron von Klootz and his son."

"Well, you knew about them."

"You can't assume that I would know everyone you might have had the slightest brushes with."

"The hotel people," Luke added.

"And in Paris?"

"Again the hotel people, but I wasn't particularly friendly with them because of my inadequate French," Luke replied. "I accidentally encountered Letty shortly after I arrived in Paris."

"Was she alone?"

"Yes. No, her friend was with her when we first met—the one who was in the restaurant this afternoon," Luke said. "Her name is Alexandria Muzakova."

"Did you have conversation with her?"

"I basically asked her directions. Then last night,

123

I saw her briefly at the stage door of the theater when I went to meet Letty."

"I want you to concentrate on making that list of people for me, Luke. It is vitally important. And now I want you to tell me everything you discussed with Letty Phenwick and try, if you can, to recall exactly what you said to Alexandria Muzakova."

During the remainder of the time at the windmill, Luke told his brother all he could remember. By the time the taxi returned to pick them up, he had related about as much as he could.

The LeVeque Ballet Company remained three days in Amsterdam, where adequate rehearsal space was available. Rehearsals were called for all three days, but they were not as intense as they had been prior to opening in that city. The company had more free time than they had previously had, although they conscientiously maintained rigorous exercise periods and individual workouts.

Luke left Amsterdam the following day after his meeting with Baron von Klootz, which gave Hayden time to have duplicates made of his identification papers. Once Luke was gone, Hayden unobtrusively moved his things into the room at the hotel his brother had previously occupied. From the window, he could see the man in the black hat and gray topcoat below near the lamppost, which assured him that Luke had left without being detected.

Once settled into the room, Hayden called Letty's hotel and asked that she have lunch with him. She explained that she had planned a late lunch with Alexandria and that she was uncertain what time her friend would be able to meet her. Hayden suggested a restaurant where he could meet Letty, and Alexandria could join them there when she was available.

"Luke? Is that you?" Letty asked shortly after

124

two, when she joined him at a flower stand near the restaurant where they were to dine.

"Can I have changed in appearance so much overnight?" Hayden asked, assuming his brother's faint midwestern accent. "Holy cow, I didn't take a good look at myself before I left the hotel room, but I think it's the same me."

Letty laughed. "I can see that it's you. There's just a little something different about you. Maybe it's me. I got more rest than usual last night. Maybe my vision is clearer."

"Do you have any idea how long it will be before Alexandria joins us?"

"Perhaps forty-five minutes," Letty replied. "She was busy seeing the count and her mother off."

"Maybe, since it's such a pretty spring day, we can just stroll around a bit," Hayden suggested.

"I like that idea," Letty said brightly. "I like walking along the canals."

"So do I." Hayden offered his elbow and she accepted it.

"You know that note I told you about finding in the tulips you sent me?" Letty asked as they began to walk.

"About the thirteen sailors?"

"Yes. I got home before Alexandria last night, and when she arrived, I was sleep. Shortly after, she went into the hall bathing facilities and I awakened. While getting a drink of water, I discovered a duplicate of the note about to fall from Alexandria's handbag. At first I thought it was the one I had shown you, but that one was tucked away where I had put it. I later recalled that Alexandria appeared as if she were searching for something after the two bouquets arrived at our dressing room. I suspect it was that paper."

"If it was, where did the duplicate come from?"

"I don't know. It's a mystery."

"Did you mention the incident to your friend?" Hayden asked.

"No. I thought about it, but a kind of fear came over me," Letty admitted. "I can't really explain what it was, but I got a very tingling sensation and I just couldn't bring myself to ask about it. You seem taller."

"Perhaps your heels are shorter," Hayden said lightly. "Or maybe I'm just standing more erect than usual. After all, I was in a hurry when I first bumped into you and Alexandria in Paris. I have a tendency to lean forward a bit when I'm rushed. Shall I slump?"

"No." Letty laughed. "I'm certain it's just my imagination. What do you make of the situation about the duplicate notes?"

"I really can't make anything of them at this point. However, I'm glad to know about them. Do I perceive a bit of melancholia in your face, Letty?"

"What a thing to ask!"

"You don't have awkward suspicions about Alexandria, do you?"

"No. Goodness, no. I dearly love her. She's my best friend in all of the world. Of course, there's Jeremiah."

"Jeremiah?" Hayden drew a blank look.

"I told you all about Jeremiah last night, don't you recall?"

"Oh, yes, Jeremiah." But Luke had forgotten in their conversation about the mention of the young black dancer. "It slipped my memory that you had discussed him. I'm afraid I was a bit preoccupied at that particular time. I see a twinkle in your eyes. You're fond of Jeremiah, aren't you?"

"We're very close." Letty hesitated. Something wasn't quite right. She thought over the conversation she had had with Luke the previous night. "I don't expect to see Jeremiah again until we reach Berlin."

126

"Perhaps we should go toward the restaurant before we wander too far astray," Hayden suggested. "While I was in London, I had quite a chat with Timothy Phenwick, who, I might add, has intense emotional feelings about you. He confessed to me that he was very much in love with you, Letty."

"I'm fond of Tim, but I have to admit I'm not truly in love with him," Letty replied. "If I were, I'm certain I would think about him far more than I do. Jeremiah is more in my thoughts than Tim is."

"Do your two young men know about each other?" Hayden asked.

"I've spoken to each about the other. I just thought. You're not anti-Negro are you?"

"I beg your pardon? Anti-Negro? Whatever brought that up? As a matter of fact, I have several very good friends who are black," Hayden said.

"In Denver?"

"Actually, those I knew best were in San Francisco, where I was raised. Does your mind have a tendency to wander? We were speaking about your friend Jeremiah, and suddenly you ask such a peculiar question."

"It was just a thought I had." Letty looked up. "Isn't this where we were headed?"

"To be sure. Now it's my mind that appears to be wandering," Hayden said. "Shall we go find a table?"

Once they were seated and instructions given to show Alexandria to their table, Letty sat quietly studying Hayden's face. "Cousin Peggy once mentioned to me about the singular handsomeness of the Phenwick men. Naturally I thought she was prejudiced about her brothers. But in looking at you, I can see she was accurate."

"I don't blush easily, Cousin Letitia." Hayden glanced away from her intense expression. "Shall we have a glass a wine while we wait?"

"I thought you said last night that you didn't drink."

127

"Only on extremely rare occasions, a glass of wine."

"And I said I don't take wine on any occasion."

"Now I recall."

"Do you?"

"I beg your pardon."

Letty smiled. "Tell me more about your brother—not your twin, the other one."

"Hayden? Didn't I tell you enough about him last night?"

Letty looked away as the waiter came and Hayden ordered a glass of wine.

"Won't you tell me about Hayden?" Letty asked.

"We don't see much of each other. I really know little about him."

"Don't you?"

"See here, young lady, there's something on your mind."

She stared directly into his eyes. "You're not Luke, are you, Hayden?"

"I'm not—?" He laughed. "I suspect you have a stray feather somewhere in your bloomers, Letitia."

"Luke forgot to tell you about Jeremiah, didn't he?"

"I—that is—"

"Neglected to tell you that he was a dancer—and that he is a Negro," Letty continued.

"A *what?*"

"May I know why you've exchanged places with Luke?" Letty asked as the wine arrived.

Hayden took time to drink before he eyed her with an expression that varied from shock to good humor. "As my sister Peggy would say, you are indeed a Phenwick woman, Letitia. I see I have to work on my impersonation more. To my knowledge, you are the only one who knows that Hayden Phenwick is in Amsterdam. For all intents and purposes, Hayden Phenwick is no longer here and is returning to San Francisco once he gathers up his wife in London. Furthermore, no matter who

128

else you think I might be, I beg of you to think of me only as Luke." A sudden thought occurred to him. "Did you happen to mention to Alexandria Muzakova that Hayden was in Amsterdam?"

"I don't believe I did. We haven't spoken much since yesterday. She's been busy with her mother and the count."

"Did you tell her much about Luke?"

"Little or nothing. She knows that Luke is Oliver's father, and quite frankly, Alexandria was very much impressed by Oliver."

"I must ask that you not reveal my identity to your friend—to no one. That is most imperative."

"But I trust Alexandria implicitly."

"Do you? Even after finding the duplicate of the German nursery rhyme?"

"What are you suggesting?"

"Only that something irregular has happened," Hayden replied, "and it is wise to be cautious. I will tell you this: that I fear Oliver Phenwick is in grave danger and I wish to do all I can to help him. Please cooperate with me, Letitia."

"But I love Alexandria—"

"And Oliver Phenwick is one of the dearest persons in the world to me. Trust me." There was such sincerity in Hayden's expression that Letty took his hand and squeezed it in spite of the conflict of emotions going through her.

"I'm sorry if I've detained you from luncheon," Alexandria said a few minutes later when she arrived. "It was kind of you to ask me to join you, Major Phenwick."

"It was gracious of you to accept, Miss Muzakova." Hayden held the chair for her. "I am honored to be joined by two such extraordinary beauties. Since we are destined to be friends, I would be pleased if you would address me as simply Luke. And may I call you Alexandria?"

"By all means." Alexandria appeared to be in a

129

gay mood. "Speaking of unusual things, I just had an experience."

"How so, Alexandria?" Letty asked.

Alexandria had been concealing her left hand, which she suddenly brought forward and in which was a long-stemmed red rose. "As I was coming this way, I stopped for traffic, when a man came up behind me and told me that I had dropped this rose. I assured him he was mistaken, and he said that it must have been meant for me and insisted that I take it. Have you ever seen anything so lovely? Or smelled a rose so exquisitely fragrant?"

Letty had sprouted gooseflesh and was unable to reply for a few moments.

"It is superb," Hayden commented.

"Whether it was meant for me or not, it's mine now," Alexandria stated.

"Did the man say anything else?" Letty asked.

"Nothing of importance. Then he just sort of disappeared."

"Disappeared?" Hayden asked.

"When I looked up from examining the rose, he was gone." Alexandria played her hand over the flower. "The rose brightened my day, after going to the railway station with Mama and the count."

"Farewells can be tiring," Hayden commented.

"Well, it's done with, thank goodness," Alexandria commented. "You know, Luke, I thought I saw you yesterday while I was in a restaurant with my new stepfather."

"I was in the country yesterday," Hayden said.

"The man's back was mostly to us. I can see your shoulders aren't quite as broad as his, and I would judge you are slightly taller than he," Alexandria related. "He was seated with Baron von Klootz and his son, who bears a remarkable resemblance to your son, Oliver, as I recall him. The man I mentioned suddenly seemed to have an attack of some sort and another, taller man, very Prussian looking,

130

with a monocle and all, assisted him from the room. Oddly, they went out through the kitchen."

"Who is Baron von Klootz?" Hayden asked. "Are you familiar with him?"

"No, certainly not. My stepfather, Count de Marco, recognized him. Philippe, that's the count, doesn't see eye to eye with Baron von Klootz, apparently, since he made no effort to speak with him."

"So you found my son attractive, did you, Alexandria?" Hayden asked as a means of changing the direction of the conversation.

"Did I say 'attractive'? I found him interesting-appearing, but I will admit I thought he was extremely handsome."

"And that, coming from Alexandria, is quite a statement," Letty interjected, "since she rarely makes comments about men."

"I have said that Tim, Charlie and Augustus Phenwick are very good-looking, Letitia," Alexandria admitted. "I simply don't gush over men because I don't permit my thoughts to be occupied with them."

"Why is that, Alexandria?" Hayden asked.

"My romance is with ballet, Luke, if you must know."

With that, Hayden directed the conversation into a discussion of the LeVeque Ballet Company and the arts in general, on which he was well informed. The conversation over luncheon remained in that vein and the three thoroughly enjoyed themselves.

"Luke isn't at all what I imagined he would be," Alexandria said later that day when she and Letty returned to their hotel room. "He struck me as being quite different when we bumped into him in Paris that night."

"He was a stranger then," Letty replied. "People always are much different once you get to know

131

them. Like everyone, Luke has two sides to his personality."

"I was impressed by his extreme good looks," Alexandria candidly admitted. "And he has such a wonderful mind and knowledge of so many different things."

"It isn't like you to speak like that, Alexandria."

Alexandria looked away. "Have you noticed how perfectly fresh this rose still seems to be? I'd better get it in water."

Letty watched as Alexandria went off to get water. She found the change that had come over her was quite amazing.

THIRTEEN

Over the next three and a half months, the LeVeque Ballet Company fulfilled its tour commitments with ever-increasing success. After leaving Amsterdam, Alexandria was given one of the principal roles, and whenever she performed it, she received unanimous praise from audience and critics alike. By the time the company danced in Berlin, she was paired with Jeremiah James for an exotic and spectacular pas de deux, for which both received tremendous acclaim.

Letty, too, danced feature roles, for which the response was ecstatic. But when Letty was compared with Alexandria, the latter was singled out as a truly great artist. Letty achieved technical perfection but she seemed to lack that quality which sets the artist apart from the technician. In a sense that was nit-picking, and Madame Ivanovich was the first to discredit the critics for not knowing their pinkies from their kneecaps. Her preference had always been toward Letty.

During the tour Alexandria performed her clandestine liaison work of passing coded information, a process which required merely that she receive the messages and deliver them at the next performance stop to a party who identified himself to her with a prearranged password. The messages always came to her dressing room, usually with flowers. The following morning she would have breakfast in a café near the theater, where the recipient would appear, give the proper password and the information would be passed.

At the end of the three-and-a-half-month tour, the company returned to Paris for a final seven performances.

While the LeVeque Ballet was traveling about, Hayden Phenwick was kept extremely busy gathering information on his own. He checked out Alexandria's background and that of Monique and Philippe de Marco. Further, he investigated the backgrounds of Tiziano Spolini, Georges LeVeque and Worth Bassett, as well as that of Baron von Klootz.

That first week in July was comfortable in Paris, but the temperature was rising. Tension was in the air. There were an increasing number of political rallies; discontentment grumbled everywhere.

Arrangements were made for the ballet company to stay in the same hotels it had occupied when last in Paris. They were not actually scheduled to perform before the second week of July. The plan was that the dancers were to return to London after Paris for a hiatus until September, a time to holiday. Both Letty and Alexandria were looking forward to the rest; it had been an extremely grueling tour.

"Mon dieu! Hayden Phenwick! Of all people!" the thunderous voice called as Hayden made his way toward the Champs Elysées. He cringed at the mention of his name. "Hayden Phenwick! Wait up!"

Hayden glanced back to see several persons behind him, a crowd in motion. Then he observed one figure towering over the rest and recognized the unmistakable face of Vladimir Popkin. He had no choice but to let the pianist catch up with him.

"Vladimir Popkin! You're the last person I expected to see in Paris!" Hayden exclaimed.

"No, my dear friend, you are the last person I ever suspected of seeing here." Big arms wrapped around Hayden in a bear hug. "I insist you join me for a drink."

"Something cool and soothing but nonalcoholic," Hayden said. "I've signed a temperance pledge."

"You haven't!"

Hayden laughed. "Figuratively speaking, that is. I have to keep my mind alert, so I actually don't imbibe before late night, and then just enough to relax."

"In here," Popkin instructed. "They're certain to have something acceptable to your abstinence." His arm about Hayden's shoulders was persuasive.

Hayden was actually relieved to get out of the crowd, where their conversation might be overheard. They found a table in an isolated spot.

"What are you doing in Paris, Vladimir?" Hayden asked while they awaited the refreshments.

"I play the piano with the LeVeque Ballet Company," Popkin replied. "It is not a particularly demeaning career; it only seems that way."

"Does that mean Madame Ivanovich is also with the company?" Hayden questioned.

Vladimir nodded, then shrugged. "She is good to me; I don't always return the favor. But it is so good to see you, old friend. My face looks like a very busy road map, but yours is just as handsome as it ever was. You never seem to age."

"But I do age, Vladimir," Hayden said, then leaned forward as if he wished Popkin to examine the age lines in his face. "I must take you into my confidence."

135

"You know you can trust me, Hayden. I often think about you and number you among my very best friends, if not the one I most admire," Popkin exclaimed. "We must spend time together, just the two of us."

"My time is pretty much taken up, Vladimir," Hayden said. He paused while the waiter served the drinks. "I am in Europe on most secret and confidential business. The fact is, I have assumed my brother's identity for the occasion."

"Your brother's identity? How can that be?" Vladimir questioned.

Hayden explained the situation as precisely as he dared without revealing the full purpose of his mission. "So you see, you must refer to me as Luke Phenwick, or Major Phenwick. Only my distant cousin, Letitia, knows my true identity. And she, too, is sworn to secrecy."

"You have my word, Luke, as your very good friend that I, too, will be sworn to secrecy. How can I help you?"

"I was hoping you would ask that." Hayden smiled. "I greatly can use your assistance."

"After this week, I will have the rest of the summer to do whatever you wish of me," Popkin volunteered.

"Good. I am at the Leanore Hotel, a second-rate establishment, but sufficient to my needs," Hayden related. "Can you meet me in the lobby there at midnight tonight?"

"Tonight? I will make arrangements. You can count on me." Vladimir drank.

That same afternoon, shortly after Alexandria had unpacked her things, she received word that Count de Marco was sending an automobile around to pick her up. She put a few things in a small bag and left a note for Letty, saying that she would return the next day.

Alexandria's attitude had changed somewhat with

the notoriety and acclaim. She had become more concerned with her appearance. With money at her disposal, she purchased fashionable clothing to replace the plain and simple outfits she had worn in the past. Where she had previously chosen dark and drab colors, she selected pastels, basic colors, and occasionally, vivid and shocking colors. She used to wear berets and scarves over her head; now she sought elaborate and conspicuous hats with broad brims and decorations to various extremes. Attired in a cool lavender-and-blue dress with a chiffon skirt that bellowed out and a light blue straw hat with a large lavender cabbage rose, her appearance was stunning. So much so, that Monique, who was waiting in the automobile, did not at first recognize her daughter.

"Alexandria? Is that actually you?" Monique qeustioned.

"I love your incredulous expression, Mama. It pleases me to see you so amazed by my appearance," Alexandria said as she slid onto the seat beside her mother.

"I am overwhelmed by the change in you," Monique exclaimed and called to the driver to start.

"What is this all about?" Alexandria asked as she settled back to enjoy the ride. "I confess I'm surprised to see you here."

"I came without Philippe knowing it," Monique replied confidentially, and made certain the glass was tightly closed between them and the chauffeur.

"Is something wrong, Mama?"

"Philippe doesn't take me into his confidence about certain matters," Monique explained, "but I have learned how to eavesdrop on his conversations with others. I believe every wife should know what her husband is up to—one way or another. I must ask you several personal questions. You may answer them as you see fit, Alexandria, and what you say will remain between us."

137

"You sound terribly serious, Mama. And I thought this was to be a holiday."

Monique took her daughter's hand. "Have you considered marriage, Alexandria?"

"Marriage?" Alexandria tensed. "I've always considered that I was married to my dancing."

"Oh, do be practical. I'm not speaking of devotion to one's career," Monique stated. "Surely you have the normal excitement stimulated by the presence of men. Every young woman your age has."

"I ignore most men, Mama."

"Why?"

"Because of my dancing. I am an artist. I am devoted to ballet."

"Absurd! Well, be that as it may, I asked the question to see if there was any man in particular who had attracted your interest."

"No one—not really."

"The way you say 'not really' makes me suspect that there is someone," Monique observed.

"Charles Phenwick seems passively interested in me. I met him in London. He's Letitia's distant cousin. His brother is quite infatuated with Letitia."

"It is interesting that you mention Charles Phenwick," Monique responded and cast a glance at the back of the chauffeur's head. "I will reserve comment about that until later. But I suspect Charles Phenwick is not the man who has magnetized your interest."

"Quite perceptive, Mama. I am artistic, not a romantic."

"Have you ever had an affair with a man?"

"What a question, Mama!"

"Don't get all huffy with me, Alexandria."

"I have never permitted such a relationship," Alexandria confessed. "I have ideals."

"Doubtlessly brought about by your attitude toward my profession."

138

"Your former profession, Mama. You're a happily married countess now—aren't you?"

Monique flipped her hand to dismiss the subject. "That is neither here nor there. Philippe has plans for you which may involve an intimacy."

"Then I will have no part of them," Alexandria affirmed. "The idea is totally repulsive to me."

"Oh, don't be so puritanical with me, mam'selle!" Monique fired back. "You delight in the fame you've acquired, don't you?"

"As a ballerina, yes."

"You wouldn't have received that were it not for Philippe. He bought you the position of prima ballerina."

"I'm not a prima ballerina yet." Alexandria laughed, then her expression changed. "What are you getting at?"

"Philippe has a special assignment for you," Monique explained. "Later he wants to arrange a marriage for you."

"That's ridiculous! I'll have no part of an arranged marriage. And that is final."

"Don't be too hasty with such statements, my child. He wants you to marry into the Phenwick family."

"To do *what?*"

"I have not overheard how he plans to arrange that. Yet the fact that Charles Phenwick has an interest in you, may prove to be to your advantage."

"How could it possibly?" Alexandria asked, a singular curiosity coming over her.

"Those are details that will have to be worked out later," Monique said. "Philippe has recently acquired a Swiss chalet near Zürich. We plan to spend most of the rest of the summer there."

"Are you changing the subject, Mama?"

"I merely wanted to advise you about what you are to expect from Philippe." Again Monique held

139

her daughter's hand. "Please keep an open mind about this, Alexandria, and try to cooperate as best you can. Ideals, morals, principles, all of that, are meant to be broken. Actually, if one doesn't deviate from such things, one never knows if they are really right for them, or if they are only just so many words and thoughts fed to them by someone else."

Alexandria laughed. "Forgive me, Mama, but your rationalization amuses me. And considering the source, I have every right to be amused, don't you agree?"

Monique laughed, too, but she felt a tiny stab of hurt.

When Letty arrived at the hotel room, she was surprised to find Alexandria's note. Shortly after she had unpacked and was wondering how she would occupy her time that evening, she received a call from Hayden. She readily accepted his invitation.

With plans for a leisurely bath and a quiet stroll about the city that afternoon, Letty was again interrupted by an urgent call from Jeremiah James.

"Can you give me an hour, Jeremiah?" Letty asked over the telephone.

"No more than that," Jeremiah replied. "Worth is busy until six, so I'm not being chaperoned."

"Chaperoned? What a peculiar word to use."

"Is it? I'll explain when we meet. I'll bring a blanket along and we can find a shady place in the park," Jeremiah said. "Don't be more than an hour, Miss Letty, please."

Letty stared at the telephone after she put it back in the cradle. She hadn't heard such urgency in Jeremiah's voice in a long while. Plans for a leisurely bath were changed to a quick bath. Later she hurried with final preparations to leave, motivated by an unexplained sense of urgency.

FOURTEEN

The park along the Seine was green and cool. Many people were out despite the fact that it was a weekday. Little attention was given to the young black man and the pretty white girl as they walked hand in hand until they found a spreading chestnut tree with an umbrella of unoccupied shade. Jeremiah spread out the blanket.

"What was so important, Jeremiah?" Letty asked as she arranged her skirts around her.

"You know that Alexandria and I have become quite friendly because we are dancing together," Jeremiah explained. "I consider her to be quite a cool person, not warm like you, but I have thought of her as a friend."

"What about Alexandria?"

"Worth and Count de Marco were chatting one day last week," Jeremiah said, "and I overheard Alexandria's name mentioned in their conversation."

"You shouldn't have listened to their conversation," Letty scolded. "What did they say?"

"I only heard that Count de Marco had purchased Alexandria's way into solo spots with the ballet company, which Worth arranged," Jeremiah related.

"Cousin Laura bought my way into prominence with the company," Letty admitted. "And certainly Worth Bassett was instrumental for your career rising as rapidly as it has. Such things are arranged."

"I'm aware of that, Miss Letty," Jeremiah returned, "but I heard them making plans for her to become prima ballerina—if—"

"If?"

"If she carries out a task they have for her to perform."

"What sort of task?"

"I didn't hear that," Jeremiah said. "I accidentally made a sound at that point, which they overheard. I pretended to be nonchalantly going about my business as if I was just passing through, but I did hear that it had to do with something or someone in Berlin . . . someone she had passed information about at the time we were dancing there."

"Passed information?"

"I distinctly heard that, but I don't know what the information was or who it was about," Jeremiah admitted. "Then there were some other things that didn't make any sense to me at all. They said something about thirteen sailors. I couldn't make any connection with that."

"Thirteen sailors?" Excitement shivered up Letty's spine. "Are you certain it was thirteen sailors?"

"Positive, Miss Letty. Does it mean anything to you?"

"No. I mean, it has a familiar ring to it, but it doesn't mean anything to me." Letty took a moment to collect her thoughts. "I'm curious why you referred to Worth Bassett as your chaperone."

"Sometimes I feel as if he's my jailer; that's what it's like. I have no privacy when I'm not dancing or

142

rehearsing or Worth isn't occupied," Jeremiah explained. "He doesn't like me to have friends of my own and he's very much against me seeing you too often. Yet when I speak of having a life of my own, he threatens me with my position in ballet. I know I wouldn't be where I am today without Worth."

"Do you love dancing, Jeremiah?"

"It's all I ever think about."

"Then it appears you will have to conform to Mr. Bassett's dictatorial wishes, won't you?"

"Yes. I've thought about that. I really don't have a choice, do I?" Jeremiah suddenly brightened. "Worth is planning to take me to perform in the United States in the fall or winter. Mama and Daddy will get to see me dance then."

"That's important to you, isn't it, Jeremiah?"

"Oh, yes, very important. They won't know me."

"Then you must do whatever Mr. Bassett wants of you. Everything in life has a price." Letty paused. "I want you to keep your ears open, especially if you ever hear Alexandria Muzakova's name mentioned. I fear she may be asked to pay a price she isn't ready to pay."

Alexandria listened to Philippe de Marco's proposed scheme, anger tensing every part of her. He spoke with a smile as he explained what he wanted, doing his best to soothe and coerce her into seeing the advantage to her in carrying out such a plot.

"There is a witness who claims he actually saw Frederick von Klootz killed and even checked his pulse to verify the fact," Philippe said in the solitude of the spacious library in his Paris château. "The validity of the man's character has not been absolutely proved; that is why we must ask you to do this."

"What is so important about Frederick von Klootz?" Alexandria asked.

"His identity—that is, of his impersonator, if that

143

is the case—may have a very important American connection," Philippe replied. "And it is imperative that we have that information as soon as possible. Time is now of the essence. I can explain no more than that."

"And if I refuse to do this?"

"How badly do you wish to become a prima ballerina?" Philippe countered.

"Ah, the inevitable price! Is nothing sacred?"

"Are you religious, Alexandria?"

"Suppose I try, and fail to get the information you want?"

"That is a possibility. Still, if you make the effort, it will be a mark in your favor." Philippe lit a cigarette. "If, however, you refuse to even take on the assignment, I regret to inform you that your position with the LeVeque Ballet Company will not be what it has been in the past."

"But you told me that all that was required of me was to pass information," Alexandria objected.

"That was then, Alexandria. Now you are involved."

"But we have a written agreement."

"True. I cannot dispute that, and it will be upheld for as long as you're alive," Philippe said with threatening overtones.

"As long as I'm alive?"

"Think about it, Alexandria." Philippe inhaled and let smoke slowly curl out of his mouth. "Why don't you take a stroll about my lovely garden, dearest Alexandria, and think the pieces of your puzzle through. It will be to your greatest advantage to cooperate to the fullest—and in time you will be an international celebrity. Take your time, Alexandria."

Alexandria was fuming as she left the library. She thought of all the things she wished she had said, and on consideration, decided it was best that she hadn't. She was involved, he had said, and now he was trying to involve her even more.

By the time she reached the garden, Alexandria had worked herself into a lather of pink rage. She wanted to scream, to escape, to die.

Water was gurgling from a dolphin-shaped fountain. Golden carp were swimming in the pool below, and pastel water lilies floated on the surface among their large round pads. Serenity seemed to spill with the flowing water. Alexandria put her hand in the water and, thinking she had food for them, the fish swam to her. As if the gentle afternoon breeze had brought it, she suddenly felt surrounded by a very sweet fragrance. The wind fluttered her chiffon skirt. The fish touched her hand with their lips. She jerked it from the water.

"They won't bite you. They want something to eat."

"What? Who—?" Alexandria turned with a start, since she thought she had been completely alone in the garden, as Philippe had promised she would be.

"The fish won't bite. There's a container of food for them over there. They'll eat it out of your hand."

"You're too well dressed to be one of the servants," Alexandria said as she went to the container. "Philippe assured me that I would have solitude in the garden."

"Am I disturbing your solitude? Forgive me if I am."

Alexandria held her hand with the food in the water and watched as the fish took it. "Who are you?"

"I'm a friend, Alexandria."

"How do you know my name? Did Philippe send you out to spy on me?"

"No, Philippe de Marco didn't send me. As to knowing your name, I've known it for a long time, Alexandria. It's a very pretty name, one to which I've been partial."

"Is that sweet fragrance your cologne?" she asked.

"No, not really. But it came with me."

"That's an odd statement."

"You'll find I'm notorious for making odd statements."

"Why did you say you were my friend?"

"Because I am. Don't I look friendly? I believe I do."

"Why do you look familiar to me?" Alexandria questioned.

"Examine my appearance more closely. Don't you recall the day in Amsterdam you were rushing to have luncheon with Letitia and her cousin?"

"The rose! You're the one who stopped me and said that I had dropped that remarkable rose! Why, do you know it kept its form as a fresh bud for days?"

"Yes, I'm well aware of that."

"How did you know I was going to meet Letitia and Luke?"

"Luke? Oh, yes, her cousin."

"I know I didn't mention their names to you. Did you follow me?"

"I have a way of learning information. You see, I've known Letitia for a long time, even back in Savannah."

"You know facts, but this entire incident doesn't make much sense to me," Alexandria remarked.

"Maybe I'm all in your imagination, just as that rose may have been. You might think of me in that way, if you like."

Alexandria shook her head. "Are you having a game with me?"

"Life, you will find, Alexandria, is a game that you've come to earth to play. It must be played according to the rules, but it must also be enjoyed for the game that it is. And since we're having a game, let me suggest that you become quiet for a

moment and say the first name that comes to your mind."

"What kind of game is that?" Alexandria appeared to be impatient. "Oh, very well." She closed her eyes. "The only name that comes to mind is the one Letitia has mentioned from time to time."

"Which is?"

"Adam." Her eyes flashed open. "Adam Truff?"

"Beautiful! You win a gold star!"

"You're Adam Truff?"

"That's the name I've answered to for years and years . . . and years." His laughter was the breeze.

"But Adam Truff isn't a real person. I mean, Letitia said that he was some kind of spirit or something like that."

"What else did Letitia tell you?"

"That Adam Truff had chosen her to become a Phenwick woman," Alexandria said. "I laughed when she told me, the idea was so preposterous. Yet I know she has been accepted by her family as a Phenwick woman. I quite frankly could never see what all the fuss was about."

"Alexandria, I do not have the power to remain visible to you over a long period of time. So I will tell you that you, too, have been chosen, and that it is necessary for more reasons than I can explain that you go to Berlin as Count de Marco has asked you to do. I will be nearby. Once a girl is chosen to become a Phenwick woman, I stay around to see that the promise is fulfilled."

"I don't believe this is happening to me," Alexandria exclaimed. "I must be dreaming."

"Alexandria, if you find one of my special roses in your room in the chateau, will you try to believe—just a little?"

"Well—I—" Alexandria glanced down at the water. When she turned back, she found herself alone, with the exception of the lingering fragrance of roses.

As if shot from a cannon, Alexandria ran toward the house, raced up the stairs to the second floor, where her assigned room was. The door flew open with her touch, and she felt as if she were catapulted into the room. She stopped short as she beheld the red rose placed on the bolsters at the head of the bed.

"I have to believe in him; I must."

"There, you see."

"Adam Truff?"

There was no reply.

"But why me?" Alexandria asked aloud.

Alexandria thought of Peggy Phenwick, of Louise and Evelyn, those grand ladies who were known as Phenwick women—of Letitia. There was something about each of them that was unique and set them apart from others—well, like Laura Donnally, who was born a Phenwick but was not chosen to be a Phenwick woman. How strange!

Nearly an hour later, Alexandria left her room and descended the stairs. As she did, she sensed a difference in her stature, certainly in her attitude. She had never given much thought to the subject of faith, but at that moment, the word came to her.

Rapping firmly against the library door, Alexandria waited for permission to enter.

"Ah, Alexandria, you've returned," Philippe exclaimed.

"So I have, Philippe. You have a most attractive garden; I might even call it mysterious."

"Mysterious?"

"Perhaps I should say I felt as if I had had a mystical experience while I was in it," Alexandria said, taking command of the situation. "Have you put in writing that I am to become a prima ballerina?"

"Then you agree to take on this assignment?"

"If you have an agreement in writing."

148

Philippe studied her. "You've changed, Alexandria. Something inexplicable has come over you."

"It is the effect your garden had on me, Philippe." She laughed.

"There is one other matter I wish to discuss with you, Alexandria," Philippe said offhandedly, as if it were of little consequence. "I'd like you to consider the prospect of marriage—that is, a marriage arrangement with a member of a prominent American family."

Recalling her mother's earlier words, Alexandria smiled. "The idea is appalling to me."

"But if the prize is right—?" Philippe questioned.

"The prize?" Alexandria laughed. "I'm willing to listen."

As she braced herself to listen, Alexandria again became aware of the scent of roses.

FIFTEEN

During their time together the previous night, Letty had related to Hayden the information she had received from Jeremiah as well as observations she had made concerning her best friend. Still she had to admit that it was difficult for her to feel the same as she had about Alexandria, now that she suspected her of involvement in a questionable conspiracy. Hayden found the data interesting, but he made no analytical comment about it and appeared to pass lightly over it.

That day was noticeably warmer and far more humid than the previous day. Worth Bassett wore a lightweight suit of white cotton. His appearance was always immaculate, and it annoyed him that the summer attire wrinkled as easily as it did. An Italian straw hat with a pale blue band about it shaded the afternoon sun from his eyes. People about him seemed to be suffering from the sudden change in the weather. He managed to look cool after he dropped Jeremiah at rehearsal. Since he had little planned that day, he decided to visit the Louvre museum. Aside from viewing the paintings, he scrutinized the people, which amused him in a bizarre way. A sensuous expression played over his well-structured face from time to time, and his eyes often reflected the stimulation that beauty aroused in him.

"Are you an admirer of Degas?"

Worth glanced into the face of the tall man who stood beside him. "Pastels generally leave me with a bland reaction, don't you know. Still, I think Degas has captured some interesting balletic poses."

"I have to agree with you," Hayden replied. "I tend to be a bit of a classicist myself."

"One wonders which of the modernists and contemporary artists will become the classics of the future," Worth commented. "Genius in art is rarely recognized in an artist's own time." It did not occur to him until that moment that they were conversing in English. "I say, you're not British, are you?"

"No, I'm an American."

"I didn't think Americans were that interested in the arts," Worth said. "I've visited America several times, but I can't say that I found the people extremely stimulating. Actually, I thought they were quite banal and uninteresting for the most part."

"Perhaps you simply haven't met the right Americans," Hayden suggested. "My countrymen, for the most part, are pretty much basic."

"Plebians, that's what they are. Oh, I say, no offense, old fellow, just my personal observation." Worth chuckled.

"I won't continue the pretense, Mr. Bassett; I know who you are," Hayden stated. "I attended the ballet in Amsterdam and you were pointed out to me."

"Ah, are you a lover of the ballet, too? I don't believe I got your name."

"It's Phenwick . . . Major Luke Phenwick."

"Not one of the Medallion Phenwicks, are you?"

"Very much one of the Medallion Phenwicks, Mr. Bassett."

"How very interesting—and curious, since I have been anticipating another trip to the United States for the express purpose of becoming acquainted with your family," Worth remarked. "The only Phenwick I've heard much about is a chap in San Francisco. Hayden is his name."

"My brother. I have two brothers, John Adam, my twin, and Hayden. Your interest in the Phenwicks whets my imagination, Mr. Bassett. Are you an industrialist?"

"Some people think me a dilettante because I dabble in so many different projects, don't you know," Worth replied. "The fact is, I'm an investor of sorts. My association with the ballet and the arts in general is pretty much of a sideline with me. One does need an avocation, rather. Naturally, since the beginning of the industrial revolution, as they call it, I've involved myself in various ventures. Actually, I arrange for investment backers in various projects in which I am concerned."

"International projects?" Hayden asked.

"Quite so. I've not got a toehold in America yet, but that is to be my next conquest. Do you have a few minutes, Major Phenwick? I would like to have a chat with you."

"I believe I can spare a bit of time."

The two men found a lounging area and sat comfortably back.

"You were saying, Mr. Bassett?" Hayden began.

"Basically what I am up to is getting large investors together," Worth said. "I foresee a time when all wealth will depend upon joint financing, with the exception of families such as yours, Mr. Phenwick, who are enormously wealthy from years' of accumulation. Wealth is the real power behind everything; therefore, if the extremely affluent merge their resources with others like themselves around

152

the world, they manipulate the strings of destiny, actually are in control of everything."

"Even to the extent of arranging wars?"

"Precisely. Such a group can establish governments and topple them just as easily," Worth went on. "Everything is a matter of economics. Monarchies are defunct because they no longer control wealth. And even imperialist governments are beholden to the privileged few for necessary financial backing."

"I have heard of such a thing. My brother Hayden is far more into that sort of business than I am."

"I've not been unaware of your brother, Major. I say, he's a bit of a dilettante in his way, too, so rumor has it."

"Hayden concerns himself with many different matters."

"I should very much like to meet him one day, don't you know."

"Hayden has a tendency to be elusive, Mr. Bassett. Does your organization invest in any one specific government or country?"

"Not at all. That is wherein lies our strength," Worth related. "We invest wherever we see expansion and progress. That is why we—that is, I am, most interested in establishing strong relationships in America. We're already firmly represented throughout Great Britain, Germany, France, Belgium, Spain. To be perfectly candid, we are the financiers behind revolutions."

"Quite an ambitious undertaking, isn't it?"

"Far greater than you can imagine, Mr. Phenwick. But enough of that. I'll eventually speak in more precise detail about it with your brother." Worth altered his position. "I don't know whether you are aware of the fact, but I have a young American protégé, a black dancer, Jeremiah James. His fam-

153

ily was once slaves to the Phenwicks of Savannah, Georgia."

"I know of Jeremiah. He is a very close friend of my cousin Letitia Phenwick."

"Quite so." Worth smiled broadly. "Jeremiah is enormously talented, don't you know. The critics have gone simply wild over his performances. Quite a natural talent, he is. I only mention him by way of getting to another topic."

"Which is?"

"A group of ladies who have the distinction of being known as the Phenwick women."

"Many of the ladies in my family, but not all of them, are known as Phenwick women, my sister and sisters-in-law, for instance."

"I see. And your wife?"

"Yes, quite so."

"Obviously, persons like Letitia Phenwick, who are born into the family, have a distinct advantage to acquiring the title," Worth continued. "But the others, such as your wife and sisters-in-law, are then products of arranged marriages?"

"Arranged?" Hayden mused over the question. "In some cases there has been a kind of arrangement, such as with my brother Hayden and his wife, the former Olga Duvane. It is one of the least successful of the Phenwick marriages."

"If a person wished to go about to create such an arrangement, how would they manage it? That's a hypothetical question, of course."

"Of course." Hayden studied the intense expression in Worth's eyes. "I suspect you have something less hypothetical on your mind, Mr. Bassett."

"Most perceptive of you, Major." Worth laughed artificially. "I have a very close colleague, with whom I have many business interests, who has recently remarried and has become the stepfather of a most enchanting and talented young lady—a rare beauty, if I do say so, rather."

154

"There are several eligible young Phenwick men. Perhaps if I were to get to know the young lady in question, I might be a better judge of her qualities," Hayden said. "My own son would be of marriageable age. Unfortunately he went on a hunting trip in the Rocky Mountains and became lost. My wife still holds hope that he will return, but I confess I fear he will never come back to us. Alas, poor Oliver. That's my son, Oliver. My cousin Daniel Charles of Medallion London has three strapping sons. There's a possibility. Who knows, perhaps we can form some sort of arrangement. But of course I would want to meet the young lady first, perhaps take her out for the evening and become well acquainted with her. I assure you, if I like her, I'll do whatever I can, everything in my power, to see that she is introduced to the proper Phenwicks. And who knows, we may be able to do other business, Mr. Bassett. But for now, the time is growing late and I have an appointment. It's been pleasant chatting with you. Do you have a business card?"

Worth searched in his inside coat pocket for a card case. "You can reach me at this number mornings and early evenings. And it has most decidedly been my pleasure to meet with you, Major." After shaking hands, Worth watched as Hayden strode away from him and out of sight.

Both men were of the opinion that it had been a most beneficial conversation.

There was a change of plans. Alexandria would appear in only the first two performances by the LeVeque Ballet Company in Paris. Worth Bassett sent word around to Hayden inviting him to attend either of the evenings, but he replied that he had previous commitments.

"But why are you going to Berlin?" Letty asked when Alexandria explained why she would only dance two nights.

155

"My mother and stepfather wish me to accompany them on a business trip," Alexandria contrived. "I'll only be gone for a week or so. I will see you back in London. Philippe wished me to summer with them in Zürich, but I don't think I could take them for that long a period of time."

"Wasn't Georges LeVeque disturbed when you said you would be away?" Letty asked.

"Count de Marco holds substantial influence over Monsieur LeVeque, Letitia. All arrangements have been made."

Worth Bassett was relieved that Hayden had not attended either of the performances in which Alexandria danced, because she was technically imperfect in each and her timing was badly off.

Too many things were on her mind, Alexandria rationalized, for her to give her full concentration to her dancing. The idea of the Berlin trip bothered her, and she felt she was being forced into it against her will. The only thing that kept her in the least bit positive were the words of Adam Truff. Even that disturbed her, since she couldn't for the life of her imagine what possible reason he could want her to go to Berlin.

The day after her last performance, Alexandria caught the early-morning train to Berlin. Letty saw her to the station. They parted affectionately, yet there was an underlying tension between them, an uneasiness.

"I hope you will enjoy yourself, Alexandria," Letty said before the train was about to leave.

"I hope I will, too," Alexandria returned. "Wish me luck."

"Luck?"

"That's only an expression." She kissed Letty again and got aboard. The train wasn't crowded and she found a compartment in which only one other lady was seated. The heavyset woman was nodding.

After the train started to move and Alexandria

waved from the window, the conductor collected her ticket. She made herself comfortable and watched with eager anticipation as the train moved out of Paris and passed through the rural countryside.

The heavyset woman opened her eyes, blinked and reached into her bag for a peach. "Would you like one, Fraulein? A peach. It's very good, very ripe and juicy."

"Thank you, no. I eat sparsely, and never between meals," Alexandria said.

"Not me. I eat whenever I feel like it, and that is most of the time." She rolled with laughter.

Alexandria could see that that was the case, but she didn't mention it.

Her peach devoured, and her face mopped with a soiled handkerchief, the heavyset woman glanced up at Alexandria. "Don't think it forward of me, but you are Alexandria Muzakova, aren't you?"

"How did—?"

"I am clairvoyant. I hear voices and get messages from the spirit world. Frau Hauser is my name. But I confess I only used my psychic powers to locate you, Fraulein, because I knew you were to be on this train. I stood in three different compartments before I decided that this was the one in which you would be. And I was correct."

"I do not understand, Frau Hauser."

"How I do it is unimportant. It is a gift," the woman replied. "As to knowing you were to be on the train, I was given instructions to relay to you."

"To me?"

"It was important that you did not receive them until you were aboard the train. I am only going as far as Frankfurt, but that will give me sufficient time to explain what you are to do in Berlin."

Alexandria wore an incredulous expression. A few moments later Frau Hauser relayed the instructions she had been given.

SIXTEEN

The girl was fifteen; she looked younger. Her prettily shaped face, round rosy cheeks and light blond hair gave her an almost Scandinavian appearance. Pale blue eyes had a dreamy quality to them. The older man beside her had similar coloring and facial structure, but his were not as delicate. Still, there was a marked resemblance between the two.

"It's like trying to find a mustard seed in a box of sawdust," the man muttered in German.

"We will find her, my father," the girl replied as she scanned the faces of those alighting from the train at the Berlin railway station. "She has dark hair, and she's supposed to be very pretty. I wish we didn't have to do this."

"Now, now, Romula, you have a task to do and you must perform it without emotion, is that clear?"

"Yes, Father," Romula said. She thought a moment. "But I know Lieutenant von Klootz is as much a German as I am."

"And you're a quarter Swede," Joachim Holtzer returned.

"I asked him if he would help me with my English lessons, and he said he only knew a few words. Doesn't that prove something?"

Joachim shook his head. "Romula, I see you have romantic notions about Lieutenant von Klootz, which you must immediately purge from your head. We're nothing but peasant stock, and Frederick von Klootz is the son of nobility. Only in fairy tales does Cinderella marry the prince."

"I know Freddie only thinks of me as a child—"

"Which you are."

"But I feel as if I'm betraying a friend."

"A friend? For all we know, he may be the enemy," Joachim speculated. "Now I'll hear no more of this talk. There! That must be her."

"No, Father, she doesn't walk like a dancer. That one is not graceful enough," Romula said.

"You're not saying that because she is a beauty, are you?"

"No, Father." Romula looked up, then quickly lowered her head. "That is her, the one in the blue-and-lavender dress, with the big hat. She is confused and doesn't have her bearings, but she walks like a dancer."

"I think you're right," Joachim exclaimed. "And she's even more of a beauty than the other one. If I were only a young man again."

Romula glanced at her father and covered her annoyance.

"Fraulein Muzakova?" Joachim asked as he held his hat and looked every inch a peasant paying respects to royalty.

"Yes," Alexandria replied.

"I am Joachim Holtzer and this is my daughter Romula. We've come to meet you," Joachim explained. "My wife and I run a bakery shop not far from here. It is a short walk. We live above the shop. You will come there until other arrangements can be made."

"How pretty you are, Romula," Alexandria said in German. "Can you be more than thirteen?"

"I am fifteen, Fraulein."

"You are large boned," Alexandria observed, "but you have the looks of a very young girl. I don't mean to offend you by saying that."

"This way, Fraulein," Joachim instructed as he picked up Alexandria's valise.

Alexandria put her arm about Romula, but the girl jerked away from her. Alexandria simply smiled and dismissed the matter from her mind. Taking the attitude of a tourist, she looked around as they walked to the bakery shop in silence.

Frau Holtzer was a large woman who very much resembled Frau Hauser, who was on the train as far as Frankfurt.

"Of course I resemble Gertrude Hauser," the large woman stated; "she is my sister. I used to call her my little sister, but that only has to do with her age. You can sleep with Romula. And if she kicks you, she will sleep on the floor."

"I wouldn't want to deprive Romula of her bed," Alexandria said. "Surely there's a hotel nearby where I can stay."

"If you play your part right, Fraulein Muzakova," Anna Holtzer stated, "you won't have to worry about finding a hotel." She laughed much as her sister had on the train. "We are a Christian family, but we know what goes on between young men and young ladies. But then, you know all about that sort of thing, don't you, Fraulein, your mother being—"

"Frau Holtzer!" Alexandria interrupted. "I don't believe there is any need for you to mention my mother in this or any other conversation. I think it would be best if I were to immediately find a hotel room."

"No, no, I apologize, Fraulein," Anna exclaimed. "I didn't mean any offense. I regret if you are offended. You must stay here one night. Romula can tell you everything about Lieutenant von Klootz."

"If I am to pretend to accidentally meet him," Alexandria asked, "why must I know anything about him?"

"It is well to know something about one's adversary," Anna replied.

Alexandria refrained from reacting aloud to the woman's statement. She turned to the girl. "Will you show me to the room, Romula? I would like to freshen myself."

Romula led the way up the stairs to the top floor of the building. The day was particularly hot and Alexandria felt the need of a sponge bath, at least.

By the time Joachim carried the two buckets of water to the third-floor room, Alexandria had removed most of her clothing. She remained behind the protection of a large stand mirror. The man tried to peer around it, but Romula cleared her voice so loudly that Joachim merely scampered from the room.

"My father considers himself to be quite a romantic," Romula commented as she closed the door firmly behind him. "I believe his imagination is overactive; at least, something in him is. I think he is basically harmless."

"Would you mind running the wet cloth over my back, Romula?" Alexandria asked after she had washed all the places she could comfortably reach.

Reluctantly Romula did as she was asked.

"Why do you dislike me, Romula?" Alexandria asked.

"I do not dislike you."

"I think you do. Is it because of what I have come to Berlin to do?"

Romula thought before she nodded her head.

"Do you like Frederick von Klootz?"

"He is my friend."

"How did that come about?"

"I was told to go and make friends with him, to get to know him," Romula explained. "He is very nice, and not at all what I imagined he would be. But I will tell you this; he is not an American and he is the real Frederick von Klootz."

"Would you say that even if you knew it weren't true?"

Romula stared at Alexandria. "Yes."

"You must like him very much."

"He thinks I am only a child."

"But you *are* only a child, Romula."

"I'm fifteen. Aunt Gertrude was married when she was fifteen."

"Are you in love with Frederick?"

Romula hesitated. "I like him very much. And he likes me—as a friend, that is all."

"Then you are lucky to have his friendship."

"I should have lured him into bed with me, that's what I should have done," Romula stated. "Then he wouldn't have thought I was a child."

"Have you ever been to bed with a man?"

Romula blushed. "No. But I've seen boys without clothes on—my cousins. And I've got things pretty well figured out."

Alexandria laughed. "You're more experienced than I am, Romula; the only unclad male bodies I have seen have been statues in museums." Her attitude changed. "I am here because I was told I had to come; it's completely against my will."

Romula stared, uncertain whether to believe her or not. "Freddie is to meet me at the zoo tomorrow morning. I will not be there. You will be. What will they do to Freddie if they discover he is an impostor?"

"I don't know." Alexandria began to dress. "Do you think he might be an impostor?"

"No."

"Even if you did, would you admit it?"

"No."

162

"Then that must be why I was brought here."

"If you discover he's an impostor, will you tell on him?"

Alexandria turned to face the girl. "I—I don't know."

"Please don't."

"But you said you didn't think he was an impostor."

"I don't. Even if you discover that he is, please don't tell, Fraulein Muzakova, please don't tell!" Tears had come to Romula's eyes.

"Do you imagine that you are in love with this man?" Alexandria asked.

Romula shook her head. "No. No. But I do like him very much—and I'm afraid."

"Afraid of what?"

"That you will like him very much, too." Romula burst into tears.

Going to the girl, Alexandria paused before she put her arms about her and held her head to her breast. "Oh, dear Romula, I must tell you that I am impervious to men. My love is dancing. I simply don't have time in my life for romance. Maybe we will have to share your Freddie's friendship, but you needn't worry about me falling in love with him. That will never happen."

Alexandria ate dinner with the Holtzers, then she and Romula went for a stroll around the neighborhood. The evening was still very hot and uncomfortable. They returned home early. Each sponged off before retiring to the goose-feather mattress.

"Good night, Romula."

"Don't you wish to talk any more tonight?"

"No, Romula, I suddenly feel very tired."

The zoo gates opened early during the summer months. Children swarmed over the grounds, talking to the animals and playing amongst themselves. A large number of military personnel wandered about the zoo, which was an inexpensive form of entertainment. Most of the soldiers and sailors were hardly more than boys themselves, and they delighted in joining in the children's games.

"Freddie, come over here and I'll show you what my aunt Mathilde looks like," a youth called as he pointed toward the chimpanzee cage, "except that Aunt Mathilde is homelier." He laughed.

Oliver motioned the other away. "I'm waiting for someone."

Two other soldiers made mocking sounds.

"There is a name for older men who go out with children, Freddie," another soldier teased.

"I'm not an older man."

"You're older than that child we saw you with last week."

"We're only friends," Oliver wished he could go to another location away from his buddies. He checked his pocket watch. That was the third time in five minutes. It was ten-fifteen, and Romula had promised to be there at ten o'clock sharp. He paced.

The other soldiers wore government-issued uniforms, but Oliver's had been especially tailored for him, cut to accentuate his handsome figure. Although he outranked his friends, he had accidentally run into them and they had earlier teased him about his sudden advance in rank. Their jeering didn't bother him.

"Excuse me. Do you by any chance speak French?" Alexandria asked as she approached Oliver. "I speak some German, but French is easier for me." She was wearing a simple white cotton dress and a large white straw hat with a white ribbon on it.

"I speak a sufficient amount of French," Oliver replied in that language. "Are you in Berlin on holiday?"

"Just for a few days, and I don't know a soul," Alexandria said, adding a touch of pathos to her voice. She could not look directly at Oliver in the beginning, for fear embarrassment would cause her to blush. When she did finally get a good look at him, she gasped.

"What is it?"

"Oh, you look so very much like an Ameri—I mean an Englishman I once saw—in London," she said in English.

"I beg your pardon," Oliver replied in French, "I speak very little English. I recognize the tongue, but it is foreign to me. Are you French?"

"Partly. My name is Alexandria Muzakova."

Oliver stared at the familiar expression he saw in her face. "Oh. Excuse me, I am Lieutenant Frederick von Klootz."

"Are you alone, Lieutenant?"

"I am waiting for someone."

"Oh." Alexandria sounded disappointed. "If you'll point me in the direction of the lions and tigers, I'll go, and disturb you no longer."

"You're not disturbing me. I mean—the fact is, I'm waiting for a little girl—just a child." Where had he seen her face before? "Perhaps her parents wouldn't permit her to come. I'll wait another fifteen minutes; then I'll give up on her."

"If she's just a little child, you had better give her longer than that," Alexandria said. "Excuse me; I'll go see the lions and tigers. They're my favorite."

"Enjoy them." Oliver watched the swish of her backside as she sidled away from him, obviously conscious that he was watching her. Suddenly he snapped his fingers. "The restaurant in Amsterdam! No, it couldn't be the same—or could it?"

"Are you talking to yourself, Freddie?" one of his friends asked as he came up behind him.

"Just trying to memorize my English lesson," he replied in German. "I find English a most difficult language."

"As do I, Freddie. Come on with me; I'm going to see the elephants."

"No, I'm waiting for someone."

"You shouldn't have let the one you just had get away."

"What are you talking about?"

"The lady in white." He whistled. "Maybe she's by the elephants."

Oliver examined his watch again. He snapped his fingers again. "At the home of Cousin Daniel Charles in London, the night I met Baron von Klootz. No, impossible! It can't be the same girl. Or can she be?" He checked his watch again and looked toward the zoo entrance. There was no sign of Romula.

Ten twenty-seven. Another three minutes wouldn't make that much difference. The girl simply was not going to be there. Resolutely Oliver headed in the direction of the lions and tigers.

SEVENTEEN

Oliver used his hand to shield the sun from his eyes before he located Alexandria at the tiger's cage. He hesitated a short distance from her, appraising her loveliness. Surely he would have recalled such a beauty, had he seen her in the past. He admired exquisite women, about whom he entertained unrepressed fantasies. Still, his fantasies actually held little reality for him. Priding himself in being a young gentleman of honor and distinction, certain aspects of his experience had been limited. Baron von Klootz would not disapprove of him taking a mistress, and in fact encouraged the idea, provided the right one could be found. But the older man had cautioned that women had a way of weakening a man's vulnerability and that Oliver must guard his identity at all costs.

Alexandria turned her attention from the animals. She hadn't intended to enjoy watching them, but she found herself fascinated by them. Oliver glistened in the mid-morning sunlight. A sting of excitement went through her as she glanced over at him before she returned her presumed interest back to the animals. Yet as that sense of anticipation increased and caused a startling reaction within her, she could barely focus her attention on the stately cats. There was no shadow, but she felt his presence as he neared.

"Fraulein Muzakova," Oliver said, speaking in German, "you seem lost in observing the tigers."

"What? Oh, Lieutenant von Klootz, I wasn't aware that you had come this way." Alexandria tried to control the tremble that shook through her as she assumed a nonchalant attitude. "There are triplet tiger cubs in the next cage down. I don't believe I've ever watched cats as intently as I observed those. My mother has a plain house-cat named Hermione, but I must say I've never found cats particularly interesting. The tiger cubs are magnificent. You must come and see them." She wanted to reach her hand back to take his. She didn't. In her mind, she tried to imagine how Romula would act under the circumstances.

"Hermione is an odd name for a cat," Oliver commented. "I would like to see the tiger cubs."

"There are two female cubs and one male," Alexandria pointed out.

"How can you tell?"

"One of the attendants told me." Alexandria laughed. "You see how the females seem to surround the male? They're instinctively protecting him. The male's face is rounder. He looks like a little boy. The other two have longer faces."

"You must enjoy animals," Oliver commented, "to be so aware of them."

"I enjoy beauty, and all things of nature are beautiful to me," Alexandria replied.

"You knew I would come to find you if Romula didn't arrive, didn't you?" Oliver said as he stood close to her.

"Romula? Oh, the little girl you were waiting for," Alexandria remarked as if searching her memory. "Did you give up on her?"

"One cannot spend the entire day waiting for another," Oliver stated. "Life is too short to simply wait around with nothing to do. I detest waiting."

"Are you impatient by nature?"

"Not necessarily. Have we met before?" he asked.

"We've not met, Lieutenant," Alexandria replied, "but we happened to be in the same restaurant in Amsterdam several months ago. My escort pointed you and your father out to me."

"My—my father. How did you know—? Oh, yes, of course, my father, Baron von Klootz. I did not know that my father was so well-known or so conspicuous. I recall the occasion, but I must confess I don't remember seeing you, Fraulein Muzakova."

"You were preoccupied in conversation. I thought perhaps you might have recognized me from that time, since I received the impression that my face was familiar to you," Alexandria said. "Of course, your face was familiar to me and I have to honestly say that, upon recognizing you a short while ago, I blatantly made a point of speaking with you."

"Are you always so forward, Fraulein?"

"Not always. See how the female cubs are washing their brother."

Oliver watched the tigers with curious interest. "Do you care to see the other animals?"

"One doesn't come to a zoo if one doesn't desire to see the animals," Alexandria returned lightly.

"May I accompany you?"

"I would be pleased if you did, Lieutenant."

"My friends call me Freddie."

"And mine call me Alexandria."

For the next fifteen minutes, the two strolled about, casually observing the animals.

"You say you're traveling alone, Alexandria?" Oliver questioned. "Isn't that dangerous?"

169

"For a young lady?" Alexandria asked. "I don't think about danger. Actually I was in Berlin only a few weeks ago. I'm a ballerina, and we danced here. At the time I didn't have the opportunity to see much of the city, so I've come back on holiday. Originally my friend was going to accompany me, but at the last minute she decided to stay in Paris."

"She?"

"Letitia is my dearest friend in all the world. I'm extremely fond of her."

"When you said friend, I thought perhaps you meant a gentleman," Oliver said.

"No." Alexandria walked away to admire the peacocks.

"Surely you must have many gentlemen friends, Alexandria," Oliver remarked as he caught up with her. "A beauty such as yourself must have gentlemen falling all over themselves seeking favors."

Alexandria laughed off the statement. "As with yourself, Freddie, I suspect women must find you quite interesting."

"Do you find me interesting?"

"At the moment you remind me of that peacock with his tail-feathers fanned out—and I think he is most interesting," Alexandria commented. With a toss of her head, she changed the subject. "I met different people while I was dancing in Berlin. I stayed with some friends last night, but I had to share an uncomfortable bed with a rather large woman. I resolved during the night that I would take a hotel room today. Unfortunately, when I checked at the hotels this morning, I was told to come back after noon. There seem to be an unusual number of visitors in Berlin at the present time."

"Probably military people," Oliver replied. "I've been recently transferred here. No more did I arrive than I was given a holiday. I suspect what it must mean, since I must let my superiors know where I am at all times."

"What must it mean?" Alexandria asked.

Oliver studied her pretty face, the exotically shaped eyes, the sullen yet so kissable lips. "It means that I have limited freedom and that I can do whatever I wish for the next few days."

"And what do you wish to do, Freddie?" Alexandria asked as her attention was held on his sensuous face.

"What does any man wish to do?" he said with a shrug. "I mean, to enjoy himself."

Alexandria felt herself being magnetically pulled toward him. Her lips parted as she stared at his mouth before she quickly turned her head away. "Do you have the time?"

"The time for what?"

"The time of day. I don't want to miss out on finding a hotel room," Alexandria replied, her eyes twinkling excitement, the likes of which she had never known before.

Oliver held his attention on her as he fumbled for his pocket watch. "It is nearly eleven-thirty."

"I can spend a little while longer viewing the animals," Alexandria said.

"May I go with you to find a room?" Oliver asked. "We can share lunch together, if you don't mind."

"I would like that, Freddie."

They sauntered about the zoo for another fifteen minutes, then they left to locate a hotel.

The conservative-looking man behind the hotel desk glanced at the young couple over his pince-nez and made a point of repositioning it a notch or two lower on his long nose. "I have had one cancellation. It is the only room available, and quite suitable for two."

"Oh, we—"

Alexandria nudged Oliver. "May we see it, please?"

The deskman looked from one to the other before he slammed the palm of his hand against the bell.

"I would not deliberate too long, if I were you. Rooms are at a premium."

"He thinks we're together," Oliver whispered as they followed the bell captain.

"If it is a double room," Alexandria speculated, "he might not rent it to me alone."

"Even if you pay the price?"

"Even then. My experience with hotel employees is that it offends their sense of something or other not to have rooms used for the purpose they were intended."

The room was large and airy. Comfortably furnished, it had a private bedroom and a small terrace.

"Do you have luggage?" the deskman asked after Alexandria assured him that they would take it.

"I'll have to send for it," Alexandria replied.

"You both must register," the deskman said. "That is a specific requirement."

"But I—"

"You sign first, Freddie," Alexandria stated.

Oliver appeared embarrassed as he wrote his name.

"Ah, von Klootz?" the deskman questioned. "Not Baron von Klootz?"

"The baron is my father," Oliver replied.

"Had I known that, I would have shown you an even nicer room, with far better accommodations."

"I thought you only had the one room available," Alexandria commented before she wrote her name.

"The other room is for special guests. Just let me know where to send for your luggage and I will see that it is taken care of. And yours, Lieutenant?"

"I have a small bag at the railway station, but I'm not—"

"I'm certain the gentleman can have it sent for, too," Alexandria inserted. "Have you a dining room? I only had a light breakfast, and all that walking about has created an appetite."

"The bell captain will show you the way. Shall I let you have the other suite I mentioned?"

"The one we saw will be sufficient," Alexandria replied. She took Oliver's arm as they went to the dining room.

The young couple was shown to a linen-covered table near a window overlooking a small garden. A single red rose was in a crystal vase in the center.

"You amaze me, Alexandria."

"Sometimes I amaze myself," Alexandria replied.

"Do you realize what you've done?"

"I've taken a hotel room with you."

"But you don't know me from Adam."

Alexandria was in a giddy mood, quite unlike her. "Oh, I'm certain I could tell the difference between you and Adam."

"Adam?" Oliver's attention briefly went to the red rose. "That was merely a figure of speech. You know what I'm saying, don't you?"

"That I don't know you, and only a short time after we've met, I've placed you in an awkward position." Alexandria frowned briefly before the smile returned to her face. "When I left Paris, I told my friend that I wanted to have an adventure in Berlin."

"And why have you singled me out, Alexandria?" Oliver asked with an intense expression in his eyes.

Alexandria swallowed hard and tried to cover it over by glancing out into the garden. "Do you think I purposely singled you out, Freddie?"

"You said you recognized me from that day in Amsterdam."

Alexandria glanced back at him. Her eyes fell to the rose between them. She put her hand to it. "Lovely, isn't it?" Her eyes darted back to his. Her lips trembled before she spoke. "I found you extremely attractive in Amsterdam, and I find you even more so now, Freddie. I trust my candid reply doesn't offend you."

173

"Not in the least."

The waiter came for their order. They asked him to return, since they hadn't had the opportunity to read the menu. The man stepped back and appeared to be uninterested while they made up their minds.

"My father is to come to Berlin next week," Oliver said after they had ordered. "I am anxious to see him."

"Baron von Klootz?"

"Of course, Conrad von Klootz is my father. Why do you ask in that peculiar way, Alexandria. Do you think me an impostor?"

"Goodness, no!" Alexandria replied, sounding very much like Letty. "That thought never crossed my mind. Why should you ask such a question?"

"When a young lady is as forward as you seem to be, Alexandria, one wonders if there is an ulterior motive behind her aggressiveness," Oliver replied. "And one might suspect that she is out to prove or disprove some matter. If you like, I'll show you my papers, which are all quite in order."

"Why have you suddenly become angry?"

"I'm not angry, Alexandria," Oliver stated. "About a year ago I was in a hunting mishap, during which time I was badly wounded. Rumor was spread that I had been killed. There was even a man who swore that he had checked my pulse and found that I was dead. But as you can see, Fraulein, I am very much alive. Because of the rumor of my death and my father's political affiliations, there have been those who have attempted to prove that I was an impostor. Is my own word and that of my father not enough?"

"I am sorry I caused you to become so defensive, Freddie." She put her hand to his. "I'm pleased you told me this. I certainly don't want to be thought of having ulterior motives."

"Forgive me, Alexandria. I am sensitive about this point."

174

Alexandria glanced away from his intense expression. Her eyes focused on the image of a man seated two tables away. He smiled as he reached for the crystal vase in the center of the table and gently raised the red rose as if in a toast to her. She graciously smiled and turned back to Oliver.

"Let us enjoy each other," Oliver said as he let his hand curl about hers.

"Yes, indeed, Freddie."

EIGHTEEN

From the moment Alexandria first saw the man known as Frederick von Klootz at the zoo, she was impressed by his resemblance to Oliver Phenwick, to whom she had been briefly introduced in London months before. Often, during those days they spent together in Berlin, when she was extremely close to him, she would study his remarkably handsome features, stoic, sensuous, exciting. Comparing Freddie with the memory of the Oliver whom she had met, she concluded that the face she had become fond of was more angular, less round than the American's from Colorado. The scar on his left cheek, explained as a Prussian military tradition purposely inflicted while fencing, gave Freddie an aggressively rugged appearance. The mustache added a touch of maturity. Alexandria wanted to believe with all her heart that Frederick von Klootz was not an impostor.

When did it happen, that precise magic moment when physical attraction, mutual admiration and various other aspects of two people harmonize and evolve into love? Alexandria honestly believed that she had resisted emotionally reacting to Oliver, that she had objectively gone into the situation as if it were some sort of clinical experiment, one from which she had intended to remain detached. As she sensed that mysterious something inside her, that ultimate response of another human being, she rationalized that her reactions were different than they had been in the past because it was the first time in many, many years that her time, thoughts and energy weren't completely absorbed in dance and the attitude of being an artist. Perhaps it was the first time she had ever permitted herself to truly relate to a man.

Lying shirtless that warm summer day, his hands clasped behind his head, Oliver turned his focusless upward gaze to Alexandria, skimpily attired, as she was positioned beside him on her side, with her head propped against her hand, hair cascading over her wrist. He was aware that she had been scrutinizing him in silence for nearly fifteen minutes, her index finger occasionally drawing little lines on his chest. He certainly had not intended to become emotionally involved with any woman, and he had set out to prime himself to only have physical encounters with women, no attachments, no involvements. That was what Baron von Klootz had advised him to do and why the older man from time to time had suggested the idea of a mistress. Over the years of growing up, Oliver had rarely discussed such matters with his parents. Joyce, his mother, had always hoped that her son would eventually fall in love and that his wife would become a Phenwick woman. She had been a sustaining force in his life, and part of her romantic nature was reflected in her son. Luke had always been proud of Oliver and as close to him as he could possibly be. There was a beautiful father-and-son mutual admiration and love between them in a conservative way. Each was proud of the other.

It was, however, Hayden Phenwick who had always been outgoing in his devotion to his nephew. Hayden had persistently demanded and gotten a show of physical affection; and Oliver was the one person in the entire world to whom Hayden totally related in an absolute loving way. From the first time he had beheld Oliver as a baby, the uncle was convinced that they were kindred souls and that from the beginning of time there had been an altruistic love that joined them in an interminable series of lifetimes.

Hayden had always encouraged Oliver to enjoy life, injecting the boy with his philosophy that life was not without reason and purpose, and there were many lessons to learn through it, but that above all, life was meant to be enjoyed. Yet all things need balance, and pleasure and enjoyment of all kinds required being in proper perspective. How often Oliver had thought of his uncle's words during his sojourn in Germany. And how very often he had wished that Hayden was nearby with whom he could converse as he had done for hours on end during his years of growing up. He wondered what Hayden's reaction would be to Alexandria, not only to his relationship with her, but to the fact that he believed he had fallen in love with her over such a short period of even knowing her.

"What are you thinking, Freddie?" Alexandria asked at last, after she had lowered her face to kiss his bare shoulder.

"About you and me and all that has happened in just a few days," Oliver replied. His eyes were smiling, but there was a touch of pathos in them. "I don't believe I've ever known such moments of happiness. I was thinking, too, of my parents and especially about my uncle, the one I have been so very close to. And I was wondering what we were doing

178

here in this place and time, and how long this all can last. Will it only be a dream to hold in memory while I endure the agony of war?"

"War?" Alexandria leaned forward. "Give my your arm. I want you to hold me." She snuggled into his embrace. "Why is there so much talk about war?"

"On the twenty-eighth of June," Oliver explained, "Archduke Francis Ferdinand, heir to the Austrian Empire, was assassinated in Sarajevo, the capital of Bosnia. He was killed by a Serb. Frankly, I don't believe the Serbian government was behind it at all; rather that it was precipitated by the powers in control as a means of triggering off a major conflict. The armies have begun marching. That is why I am here in Berlin, just awaiting orders. For all I know, this could be our last day together."

"No!"

"Or we could have several more days and nights like this," Oliver explained. "There's little chance that I will remain in Berlin for long."

Alexandria recalled statements made to her at the Café du Clair by the fanatical student, Guy Croisant, concerning war, and she vaguely recalled the crux of what he had recited by the philosopher Nietzsche. At that time, war was a nebulous, distant unreality which did not directly involve her. Now, convinced that she was deeply in love with Frederick von Klootz, the gross reality of war was as close to her as his breath was at that moment. She trembled and her entire body shook with fear. "Oh, God, just let these moments last forever!"

Oliver kissed her, pulling her face to his.

"I wish I could ask you to marry me, Alexandria," Oliver said softly, "and that we could escape to some distant place, maybe another planet, and live in complete love and serenity forever."

"I wish that were possible too," she sighed. "I do love you more than I can possibly express in words, Freddie. I never knew what love was before. I will

179

probably never know it again as I do at this moment. I hadn't meant for this to happen. I never thought it would. Yet it's part of the ambivalence of my nature, being an extremist and torn between two opposing emotions. I actually feared falling in love because of this very reaction I'm having now. Yet if I had to choose between my love for you and my love for ballet, I want to say that I would select you; but I wonder if that is only because I am so tightly entangled with you at the time that my point of perspective is out of balance."

"We are in a hopeless situation, Alexandria. War—and it will be ultimately declared—is about to snatch us apart. Time, space, situations and people will come between us. It is inevitable. Even if we both survive the war, what atrocities will occur to mar our lives, even our love, we cannot begin to guess. Love itself, I think, is forever; that is, the emotion or the force of love—if it is indeed a cosmic force, as Uncle Hayden used to say."

"Who?"

Oliver felt himself turn crimson. "My uncle, the one of whom I'm so very fond. His name is actually Hyman," he fumbled, "but I call him Hayman."

"I thought you said Hayden."

"I mumble sometimes."

Alexandria rolled over onto her back, with Oliver's arm still about her. She wanted to believe that she had not heard correctly. She closed her eyes and decided to take a desperate measure. "I could never possibly marry you, Freddie, war or not. And it's not that I don't love you; you must believe that. You see, I have been chosen to marry into a prominent family. I am to become a Phenwick woman. I know what you must be thinking. How could I come to Berlin and fall in love with you, if I knew all along that my destiny was being arranged? The fact is, I've only met a few Phenwick men; there's none in particular—it's simply that I know

180

what I've been chosen to be." She paused. "Aren't you curious to know what a Phenwick woman is?"

"No. I don't want to know," Oliver replied. "What we are and what we have at this very moment is actually *all* we really are allowed to know. We cannot live in the past or project into the future; what was, will never be again, and what will be, will depend on what happens in the ever-present *now*. If we know, enjoy, love each other beyond this moment, then that is a reality we will have to face when it happens. As to your becoming a Phenwick woman, that is something with which you must deal at another time."

Although Oliver usually managed to affect a German accent when he spoke words in English, which were few and far between, Alexandria was aware that he clearly pronounced the *W* in both Phen*w*ick and *w*oman. She wanted to believe that he was simply imitating her pronunciation. "Let's don't talk about it, Freddie. Make love to me and don't talk about anything but that."

Oliver was about to raise himself to give her a kiss, when there was a rap at the door. He gave her a quick peck. "Who is it?"

"The bellman, Lieutenant von Klootz. I have a message for you."

"Couldn't you have called me on the telephone?"

"I was asked to hand-deliver it," the voice responded from the hallway.

A puzzled exchange of expressions before Oliver rose and went to the door. He opened it enough to receive the message and to hand the deliverer a gratuity. Standing just inside the door, he read what had been given to him. He placed the folded paper in his pocket and stepped to where his shirt was hanging over a chair.

"What is it?" Alexandria asked as she watched him buttoning his shirt.

"I have orders to report to my commanding officer immediately," Oliver stated. He examined himself in the mirror. "No, I must change these trousers; they are far too wrinkled."

"Is it *that* urgent, Freddie?" Alexandria called as he went into the bathroom after removing his trousers. The message he had received fell from the pocket. She got up. "Freddie?"

"Military orders are always urgent."

Alexandria picked up the fallen paper. She read: "Meet me at the Rathskeller in Kinderstrasse as soon as possible. Major Hans Rittenburg." She placed the paper back in his pocket. As she considered the words, she thought they didn't sound like official military orders. Still, it was signed by a major.

"I expect to return in an hour or two," Oliver said after he was fully dressed and ready to leave. "Will you be waiting for me?"

"You know I will be, Freddie," Alexandria replied. She reached her lips for his and kissed him with all the emotion that was churning within her. "Hurry back to me, please, hurry back to me!"

"I will, my love. Have no fear."

In a moment Oliver was gone. A terrible sensation of apprehension stabbed at her solar plexus. The pain was so great that she wanted to cry. A few moments later, she resolved to dress and to go out to find the Rathskeller in Kinderstrasse.

It was still daylight out, but evening shadows were moving in as Oliver strode from the hotel. Alexandria was still very much in his thoughts, but even more paramount in his consciousness was the anticipation of meeting Major Rittenburg.

"Freddie!" a feminine voice called to him as he was about to step into the street. "Freddie! Wait a minute!"

He turned back to see Romula Holtzer running toward him. "Romula?"

"I was waiting to see you," Romula said between gasps.

"I've urgent business, Romula."

"Aren't you happy to see me, Freddie?"

"I'm always pleased to see you, Romula. But I haven't time to talk now."

"But you must listen to me," Romula begged. "They will kill me if they ever discover I've told you this."

Oliver slowed his stride. "What is it, Romula? What are you talking about?"

"It was not accidental that we met when we did," Romula confessed. "I purposely sought you. Just as it was not coincidence that I did not appear at the zoo the other day and Alexandria Muzakova did. My family has been assigned to disprove that you are Frederick von Klootz. When I insisted that that was your real identity, Fraulein Muzakova received a similar assignment. She is in Berlin for the sole purpose of discovering who you really are."

"Are you certain of this?"

"Yes."

"But you just said that you believe I am the real Frederick von Klootz."

"I do, because I want to believe that, Freddie. Even if I discovered you were not, I could not betray you," the girl said in all sincerity. "You must believe that."

"I do, Romula. Can we meet early tomorrow morning?"

"When? Where?"

"At six, near the zoo entrance."

"I will be there."

"Good. Now I must hurry. I have military orders." He took her hand and squeezed it. "Thank you, Romula, for the information—and for being my friend."

"I will be waiting for you tomorrow morning," Romula called as he rushed ahead.

Grim-faced, Romula stood in a sheltered doorway and watched until she could no longer see the man

183

she so greatly admired. Tears wanted to come, but she fought them.

Remaining there for some time, her thoughts in complex confusion, and watching night fall on the city, Romula was about to leave when she saw the distinctive walk she had recognized that day at the railway station. She stepped back into the shadows and waited until Alexandria passed her. On a hunch, Romula followed at a cautious distance behind the dancer as she turned into Kinderstrasse.

NINETEEN

Candles were in glass bowls in the darkly lit Rathskeller, which was in the basement level of an old building. The room reeked of beer and old smoke. An elderly man was playing an accordion and several German soldiers were drunkenly singing. The establishment was not especially crowded, but it was noisy.

As Oliver climbed down the stairs, he scanned the faces for one that might be familiar to him. He recalled his last meeting with a Major Rittenburg in Amsterdam, when the man turned out to be his Uncle Hayden in disguise. Was there another *real* Major Rittenburg? He had to be extremely cautious, as Hayden had previously warned him.

Stein of beer in hand, Oliver wandered among the soldiers and finally decided to sit and wait in a secluded corner where he could observe but not be forced to participate with the rowdy group. He knew these men were aware that it was only a matter of time before they would be in active duty in combat and that their drunken celebration was a means by which they thought they could relieve the ever-increasing anxiety and sheer fear of war.

As he sat in contemplative silence, Oliver considered what Romula had told him about Alexandria. He experienced deep hurt, emotional turmoil because of the love he was certain he had for the dancer. Never before had he felt such a pain or emotional anxiety as that caused by the knowledge of the possibility that Alexandria had simply played with his feelings. Yet there was the chance that Romula, because of an obvious attachment she had established with Oliver, might have contrived the information she gave about Alexandria to make him suspicious of her.

"The light is dim in here, Lieutenant," the voice said from a space beyond where Oliver was seated. "I suspect you are in deep thought."

"Major Rittenburg?"

"The same. Won't you join me?"

Oliver went toward the sound of the voice. He clicked his heels and saluted. "Lieutenant von Klootz reporting, sir."

"Drop formalities, Lieutenant. You will only call attention to my presence here, which I wish to avoid. I have been watching you. Won't you sit?"

Oliver adjusted himself in the chair and squinted forward to get a better view of the man with whom he was speaking. The candlelight was weak and flickering low, as it needed to be replaced.

"We will not remain here, Lieutenant. Although I doubt we will be overheard, I prefer a place of greater privacy. However, we will leisurely finish these steins of beer and be congenial."

"Do you have instructions for me, Major Rittenburg?"

"There is time for those, Lieutenant. I like your caution, Lieutenant. It is good you recalled our last

186

meeting in Amsterdam, and the warning I gave you then."

Oliver breathed a sigh of relief.

"Do not let down your guard, Lieutenant. I still may be testing you."

"Not when you say that, sir, if you will pardon my saying so," Oliver returned. "I'm so happy to see you again."

"We will see more of each other when we get in better light," Hayden replied.

"Your message said it was urgent you see me," Oliver said.

"Most urgent. Let us finish our beer then and leave."

Alexandria had intended to enter the Rathskeller, but she decided against it at the last minute and positioned herself across the street from the entrance, in an inconspicuous place. Romula stopped a short distance farther down the street. Both young ladies saw the emergence of Major Rittenburg and Lieutenant von Klootz. As they walked down the street in a brisk military manner, Alexandria began to follow them, remaining a reasonable distance behind.

When Romula perceived what was happening, she decided to intercede. "Alexandria!" she called. "Alexandria Muzakova!"

Fearing that Oliver might overhear the shouts, Alexandria fell back and turned to recognize Romula approaching her.

"You passed me a moment ago," Romula lied. "I didn't recognize you at first. Where have you been? We've missed you."

"I'm busy now, Romula. I haven't time to chat," Alexandria said, hoping to dismiss the girl as quickly as possible.

"My father sent me to find what information you had discovered," Romula continued.

"I have learned nothing unusual as yet," Alexandria returned. "At the present time, you may tell your father, I am convinced that Lieutenant Frederick von Klootz is who he claims to be, that he is authentic. I will speak with your father tomorrow. Now you must forgive me, Romula, if I rush on. We'll speak at another time."

Romula could see that the two men had disappeared from sight. "Yes, we will do that, Alexandria. Have a good evening."

Alexandria hurried forward, but she could find no trace of the men.

"Hotels are at a premium these days," Hayden commented as they entered the cramped room he had taken. "I am fortunate to have one at all, arriving in Berlin on such short notice as I did."

"Why *did* you come?" Oliver asked.

Hayden went to the door and put his ear to it. Suddenly he jerked it open. No one was outside. He turned and opened his arms to embrace his nephew. "Oh, Oliver, it is so good to see you again!"

"And you, Uncle Hayden."

"We must not use names. These walls may be paper thin. I have nothing to offer you, but we must speak."

Oliver sat on the bed. "Isn't it risky disguising yourself as a German officer here in Berlin?"

"Risky but necessary. I have come to take you back with me."

"What?" Oliver was shocked. "I don't understand."

"Baron von Klootz is fighting a lost cause. His resistance movement is destined to defeat before it even begins," Hayden replied. "Word has reached me that Russia intends to mobilize her troops in a matter of days, perhaps as early as tomorrow. France feels the threat of invasion from the Kaiser, and, because of the tremendous debt France has to Russia, she is being called in to assist. Once war is declared, it will be impossible for you to get back to England, much less to America."

188

"Is it as immediate as all that?" Oliver asked.

"As it is, rather than going immediately to Paris, where trains will be closely watched," Hayden explained, "we must go to Hamburg and cross into Denmark and go via the North Sea to England."

"Why such a circuitous route?" Oliver asked.

"Although I have arranged to have papers for you," Hayden replied, "you have the distinct appearance of a Prussian officer. If you are picked up, there could be an intense interrogation. Besides, there is too much suspicion already around you."

Oliver explained the situation with Alexandria and what Romula had told him.

"So that is what she is up to," Hayden remarked. "I have been suspicious of Alexandria Muzakova's actions for sometime. I never dreamed they involved you."

"They involve me even more than you can know," Oliver confessed. "I have fallen in love with her. Even knowing what I do about her, I cannot stop the intense emotional feelings I have."

"Love? You're far too young and inexperienced to know what love is, Oliver."

"I love you."

"Of course you do. But I am your uncle. You've loved me from infancy because I've loved you. That is a completely different kind of love than that which is expressed between lovers. It was your cousin Letitia who first became suspicious of Alexandria— and they are the best of friends. Alexandria has told Letitia that her only true love can be dancing."

"I honestly believe she has changed," Oliver replied. "I don't believe she can be pretending the feelings she has for me any more than I can manufacture the emotions I have for her."

Hayden thought the situation through. "Unless Alexandria reveals herself as a German agent, she, too, may have difficulty returning to Paris, since she is a French citizen."

"Then if I leave Germany, which I think may present many problems," Oliver said, "we must get Alexandria out with us."

"How do you propose to do that?"

"Simply by taking her with us."

"Impossible."

"Why?"

"First, the papers I have for you declare that you are an American citizen," Hayden explained. "If Germany declares war on France, as is inevitable, any French citizen would immediately be in jeopardy. It is too risky."

"I could marry her," Oliver stated. "Then she would technically be an American citizen by virtue of that arrangement."

"Preposterous! First and foremost, you would have to reveal your true identity to her, perhaps exposing yourself to even greater danger. No, that would be an impossible situation."

"Alexandria has received a red rose. She believes she has been chosen to be a Phenwick woman," Oliver said.

"How do you know that she has?" Hayden asked. "Merely her word for it? Remember, she has been a good friend of Letitia for a long while now, and Letitia undoubtedly told her about the tradition of the red rose. If Alexandria suspects your right identity, she could have mentioned that as a means of forcing you to reveal yourself."

"I just can't believe that Alexandria has not been honest in expressing her love for me," Oliver stated.

"Of course you can't, because you're far too close to the situation. You can't as yet honestly detach yourself from it," Hayden insisted. "Romantic emotion is the greatest instigator to disillusionment there is. I know. I've found myself in that situation more than once, and I know how distorted and confused my reasoning was because of it. But that realization only came in retrospect. I'm not being unsympathetic, Oliver, only brutally realistic."

"What do you suggest I do?"

"Simply tell Alexandria that you have been called to active duty," Hayden said. "I've already given you that opportunity by arranging this meeting today. There is a train tomorrow evening for Hamburg at six. You will meet me at the railway station by five-thirty. I will have your papers at that time. We will travel to Hamburg as soldiers, then make a transformation and become an American uncle and nephew who have been on holiday. Alexandria will have to use whatever connections she has to get out of Berlin. If you really care for her as much as you claim you do, I suggest that you advise her to leave Germany at the earliest possible time."

"What would happen if I were unable for any possible reason to meet you at the railway station tomorrow evening?" Oliver asked.

"Then, unless I could make the necessary arrangements, you would find yourself very much involved in war as a German officer," Hayden stated. "In which case, you may be called to act as— well, I won't even suggest that at this time."

Oliver again embraced his uncle. Their relationship had always been extremely physical. This time, however, he hugged much tighter than he ever had in the past. "Uncle Hayden, I'm scared! I've never admitted that before, but now it is true and I can't deny it."

"You must be at the railway station tomorrow evening. I wish it were tonight, but certain circumstances cannot be avoided." Hayden held him powerfully close in silence for several minutes. "Now I think you must leave, Oliver. I have business to arrange."

The farewell verged on being tearful until Oliver was able to gather his emotions, hold himself tall and leave without looking back.

191

Alexandria took the announcement that Oliver was to go into active duty as calmly as she could under the circumstances. "I don't want to eat. I don't want to go out anywhere. I just want to stay with you and hold you for as long as I can," she said.

Oliver kissed her as if clinging out of desperation. "If only we could escape and find a different life. You, too, must leave Berlin tomorrow, Alexandria. You're a French citizen."

"Don't talk. Just hold me and make love to me."

"Alexandria, marry me! Please marry me. At least if you do, you will be a German subject. I'm certain my father will be able to help you to get back to Paris if he knows you're my wife."

"Do you love me that much?" Alexandria asked, her mouth practically touching his ear.

"Words can't express the depth of my love." He kissed her again and would not allow her to pull her head away, as if his passion was meant to suffocate her.

Alexandria turned away from him. "I can't marry you, Freddie, not now. We may deeply love each other, but we don't know that much about the other. Maybe I've deceived you—or you've misrepresented yourself to me in certain ways."

"Alexandria—"

"No, let me speak. I want you to know that I honestly love you as much as any person can love another," Alexandria said. "I didn't believe this could ever happen to me. I certainly didn't plan it in any way. But it has happened."

"Is being a Phenwick woman so very important to you?" Oliver asked after he had kissed her again.

"Not at all. If I could only know your complete love for the rest of my life, I would be absolutely satisfied, Freddie. I know that." She kissed his hand and did her best to control the trembling within her. "I came to Berlin for an express purpose; I was sent here to acquire information."

"About what or whom?"

"I cannot tell you that, Freddie. It isn't important, because I cannot and do not want to disprove what I came to do."

"You speak in riddles," Oliver said.

"Because that is the only way I can speak at this time." Alexandria threw her arms about him and clung as tightly as she could. "Just love me, Freddie. Just hold me and love me. Let this be a night that neither of us will ever forget."

Oliver knew then and there that he had to return with Hayden. He reasoned that once he was in London and Alexandria was there—providing they both made it—he could reveal his true identity to her and it wouldn't make any difference as far as Baron von Klootz was concerned. Then, perhaps, he could propose to her again and she would accept.

"Just love me, Freddie . . . please, just love me."

TWENTY

Oliver was fully awake the next morning at four-thirty. The room was excessively warm. Shirtless, he went to the terrace, where he gathered his thoughts. Even with what Romula had told him about Alexandria and her awkward admission that her reason for being in Berlin had not turned up proof of what she was after, he felt no diminished sense of love for her. If anything, he had awakened that morning with even a greater consciousness of love for her. He was actually surprised and perplexed by his own reactions.

By five-thirty Oliver was dressed and ready to leave. Identification papers were always on his person. He had little else with him except for one change of clothing. As he stood in the dawn-dark room, he gazed down at Alexandria's sleeping face for several seconds before he bent to softly kiss her. She stirred but did not awaken. Again, at the door, he stared back at the sleeping beauty. A singular thought hit him: what if this were the last time he

194

was to see her? He tried to shake the thought from his head, but it persistently remained.

Downstairs, as he walked through the lobby, an uneasy sensation came over Oliver as if it were a foreboding of disaster. He left his key at the desk. It clattered with a hollow emptiness. The nodding desk clerk glanced up, bobbed his head to acknowledge the act and made no comment.

Tension hovered in the early-morning air as Oliver walked through the streets. It was July thirtieth. As he passed a newsstand, he read the bold print that exclaimed that Russia had mobilized her armies. Fear jabbed at him. His steps accelerated as if he were racing against time. There was no traffic, few pedestrians. Was it his imagination, or had that germ of anxiety spread?

Romula was waiting at the zoo gates. Although her dress was plain and lightweight for the weather, she wore a large-brimmed hat that shadowed part of her face. "Freddie, I'm so glad you didn't keep me waiting."

"Is something wrong?"

"Why do you ask?" Romula questioned.

"I sense it." He stared down at her. "Why are you wearing a hat? I've never seen you wear one before."

"Don't you like it?"

"I can't see your face."

"You wouldn't want to see my face this morning," she said.

"Why?" On impulse he lifted the brim of the hat. Even in the still-dim morning light, he could see a large bruise on the left side of her face, and her eye was swollen. He lifted the hat from place. "Who did this to you?"

"It is not important," Romula replied.

"But this is terrible," Oliver exclaimed.

"Don't touch it. It's very tender. I'll live through it."

195

She tried for a smile. "Information was forced from me and I was punished."

"Tell me about it," Oliver coaxed, putting his arm about her. "You must tell me."

"Someone saw me speaking with you last night," Romula related. "They also saw Alexandria Muzakova follow you from the hotel and me follow her. I distracted her attention long enough for you and the other soldier to lose her after you left the Rathskeller."

"Alexandria followed me last night?"

"Yes. When I reached home, my parents and two men were waiting for me," Romula explained. "It was one of those men who had seen me earlier. They accused me of warning you against Alexandria Muzakova. I denied it. Then I was forced to admit that I—well, that I liked you very much and that I had strong feelings for you."

"You have? I mean, you did tell them that?"

"Only after they hit me several times and I could no longer tolerate the pain. But no matter what they did to me, I stood firm in my belief that you are not an impostor, Freddie. If Fraulein Muzakova tells them differently, I may be in serious difficulty. I don't think she will. I could see in her face that she is in love with you *too*."

"In love with me *too?*" Oliver took her hand. "I am fond of you, Romula, but this is not the time for either of us to think seriously about love. We are friends and we always shall be friends."

"Do you feel only friendship for Alexandria Muzakova?" Romula asked.

"I cannot answer that," he said.

She sighed deeply and stared at the ground. "You have already answered it. I must get back. I will be discovered missing, and I don't want them to come looking for me and find me with you. It was very risky for me to come here this morning." She started to leave.

196

"Romula—"

"What is it?" she asked as she paused but did not look back.

"Thank you, dear friend." He stepped toward her.

"Don't touch me, Freddie. People may be watching."

"Can't I walk a little way with you?"

"No. It is best if you did not."

The rumble of moving vehicles could be heard approaching.

"Please, go your way, and I will go mine," Romula begged. She walked away from him as quickly as she could.

A parade of army cars clattered by where Oliver was standing. He observed until they had passed, then he looked in the opposite direction, but he could see no sign of Romula. There were things he had meant to say to her, questions he had wanted to ask. The meeting had been too short, yet he felt he had learned all that he was to know. Anger rose inside him as he thought of what they had done to Romula. He perceived that what had happened was far worse than what she had disclosed.

Oliver stopped in a restaurant for coffee and a roll. His stomach was churning with emotion, and he mistook it for hunger. The buzz of conversation in the restaurant dealt primarily with the Russian mobilization of her armies. Speculation was that war would be declared within five days.

Leaving the restaurant, Oliver went directly to the hotel. No sooner had he stepped inside than he was confronted by an army lieutenant, who was with two other officers.

"Lieutenant von Klootz?"

"Yes, sir."

"Major Kramer wishes to speak with you."

"Now?"

"Now. You will come with us."

"Can't I even go to my room and get my things?"

"We have your belongings, Lieutenant. You will come with us immediately." The young man's attitude was officious.

"Can you tell me what this is about?"

"I can tell you nothing, Lieutenant." He motioned for the other two men, and the four went outside, where the automobile was waiting.

Major Kramer was a short, thin, baldish man with dark-rimmed glasses and a brush mustache. He sat at a large desk in a building that had been taken over by the army. Beady eyes glanced up at Oliver before the little major motioned with his head for the other soldiers to stand back. "Come forward, Lieutenant von Klootz." He took a metal case from his pocket. "Would you like a cigarette, Lieutenant von Klootz?"

"No, thank you."

"Don't you smoke?"

"Yes, occasionally."

"Good. Then, I suggest you take a cigarette." Major Kramer held the case toward Oliver. He struck a match and put it to the cigarette, waited until it was lit, then blew it out. His words were measured. "Lieutenant von Klootz, you have been under intense surveillance for some time now, for several reasons."

"I have been, sir?"

"For several varied and different reasons," Kramer replied. "We are now convinced that you are not an impostor. The man who claimed to have seen your dead body admitted that he had lied about the situation. He was your good friend, Herman Schnick." The corner of his mouth twitched with a sardonic reaction. "At least you *thought* he was your good friend. He was, we have learned, meant to have been your assassin. It was not the imperial government's doing, but that of a conspirator against your father. There is a full report here concerning that matter, which you may read at your leisure."

"Herman Schnick was meant to be my assassin?"

198

"He shot you. Alas, he is a poor marksman. The gun jammed after the first shot, so he merely presumed you were dead," Kramer recited without inflection in his voice.

"Why are you telling me this, Major Kramer?"

"It is to preface the dramatic disclosure I have yet to make." Kramer motioned for the other men to leave the room. When they had gone, he indicated for Oliver to take a chair, while he sat on the edge of the desk. "You have always been close to your father, Baron von Klootz, is that not so?"

"Since my mother's death several years ago, I and my father had no other close relatives. I am devoted to him, as he is to me," Oliver said.

"So we have been led to understand, Lieutenant." He gazed intently at the young man. "Then you are well aware of the fact that your father had been attempting to form a resistance movement among his aristocratic friends and associates to counteract the imperialist reign of our sovereign emperor, Kaiser Wilhelm."

"I was aware he was involved in such a movement," Oliver said, "but I had opposed it from the beginning, since I believed he and his peers would never be able to gather sufficient power to be any threat. As much as I love my father, I am only too aware that his philosophies and techniques are of another outdated era. Still, I pretended support, simply because he is my father."

"We have also discovered that about you, Lieutenant." Kramer stood and paced around the desk so he could approach Oliver from the opposite side. "I believe that is true. Are you loyal to Kaiser Wilhelm?"

"Yes, sir."

"I would not, in all honesty, expect you to answer otherwise." Kramer chuckled dryly. "It would have been a great tragedy if your father had had to

199

spend the remainder of his days in prison for treasonous behavior. Don't you agree?"

"What are you getting at, Major Kramer?"

"Frederick, your father has been killed."

"What?"

"Quite so. I realize that this is shocking news."

"I can't—I can't believe it. Who—who killed him?"

"For all intents and purposes, your father's death was an accident. You are now Baron Frederick von Klootz. And you have a choice to retain your title, your property and your wealth and join Kaiser Wilhelm with your full support, or you can rebel, attempt to resist the power of the Kaiser and lose everything—possibly even your life." Major Kramer took a cigarette and offered another to Oliver.

"Do you call that a choice? It sounds more like an ultimatum," Oliver replied. He refused the cigarette.

"Call it whatever you like, Lieutenant." Kramer rose again and paced as Oliver appeared to be attempting to control his grief. "We know that, from all exterior appearances, you have been supportive of your father and his colleagues in their resistance attempt, while in your heart you've known it would be a failure from the start. You can be of vast, valuable service to the government by assisting us to squelch this movement and any further attempts it may make. Agree to this, and you will immediately be raised in rank to Lieutenant-Major. Continue to prove your loyalty to the Kaiser, and I personally guarantee you will rise much higher in rank."

"My alliance is with the Kaiser," Oliver stated. "Since I foresaw the failure of the resistance movement initiated by my father and his colleagues, I persuaded him that I could be of greater service to them if I were in the Prussian army. It was a ploy. I purposly deceived my father because I believed in the long run that this was the best way I could help him when their movement proved to be unsuccessful."

"Very wise of you, Lieutenant von Klootz—if that is the truth."

"Do you question it?"

"I have an open mind. You must prove yourself—beyond the slightest doubt of your faithfulness to the Kaiser," Kramer said. "There is transportation waiting for you to take you to your home to attend your father's funeral. It will not only be a time to express your grief, but one in which you can convince his allies that you are still working with them. You must be back here in Berlin by the first of August."

"The first is only the day after tomorrow."

"Funeral arrangements have been made. It will take place tomorrow," Kramer announced. "You will return the following day."

"Very well, sir. I take that as an order," Oliver responded, certain that he had to play the role to the hilt.

"Let me advise you that you will remain under surveillance," Kramer stated, "for a considerable period of time. Your destiny is entirely in your hands. We will cooperate with you as long as you cooperate with us. You may go now."

Oliver stood and accepted the hand extended toward him. "Thank you, Major." He started. "Oh, there is one question."

"Yes, Lieutenant von Klootz?"

"My friend, Alexandria Muzakova—may I say goodbye to her?"

"There is not time for that, Lieutenant. Time is of the essence. Besides, Fraulein Muzakova is a French citizen and it is expedient that she depart from this country as soon as possible. She has been given instructions to do so."

"What was she told of me?"

"That you were arrested. It was necessary to make

her think that." Kramer's words were biting. "Alexandria Muzakova was not your friend, Lieutenant. Rather, she was your enemy and she conspired against you. That is all, Lieutenant. You may go now."

"But she—"

"That is all, Lieutenant."

Tears had welled in Oliver's eyes. He quickly saluted, turned about-face and determinedly walked from the room.

TWENTY-ONE

The large hands of the great clock at the railway station moved to five-thirty. Hayden examined his pocket watch and glanced around for his nephew. The insufferable heat made the makeup he was wearing itchy and uncomfortable. He went to the men's lounge to check the condition of his appearance, and returned at five-forty-five. Still there was no sign of Oliver. Boarding had already begun on the train destined for Hamburg. Could Oliver have gone aboard while he was in the men's room? Frantically Hayden went through the train, checking each compartment. There was no sign of Oliver.

Pushing his way back into the main waiting room of the station, Hayden circled around, desperately scrutinizing the crowd.

At six o'clock the train to Hamburg pulled out. Hayden watched as it eased down the track. He was about to leave the station when he recognized Alexandria Muzakova entering, and went toward her. She looked both bewildered and upset as she struggled with her luggage.

"May I assist you, Fraulein?" Hayden asked in German. "You appear to be having some difficulty."

"Oh, thank you very much, sir. I am really in a terrible state of mind. I must get out of Berlin tonight. It is most urgent," she stated.

"Where are you going?"

"To Paris. There is a train at six forty-five. I have been detained for hours."

"Detained?"

"I cannot explain."

"Not even if I told you about thirteen sailor boys in a boat without a sail who used their hands for oars and paddled safely to shore?" Hayden asked.

Alexandria's mouth dropped as she stared incredulously at him. "You know of thirteen sailors?"

"Didn't I just tell you?"

"They arrested him," Alexandria whispered.

"Arrested? Whom?"

"Lieutenant von Klootz. They told me that his father has been assassinated and that Freddie— that is, the lieutenant was arrested as part of a resistance movement on the part of his father and his associates," Alexandria explained. "I have been given twenty-four hours to get back to Paris. I don't understand all that is happening."

"Have you a ticket?"

"No."

"Then you wait here and I will get it for you." Hayden hurriedly went to the ticket window and exchanged the two tickets he had for Hamburg for transportation to Paris. It took more time than he had anticipated.

Alexandria warily waited, continuously looking about her as if she expected something to happen to alter her course. Periodically she wiped tears from her eyes as she thought of Oliver. She was certain he must think her responsible for his arrest. If only she could explain the situation to him. Now he might never know the truth, and that thought made her feel even worse.

"We just have time to make the train, Fraulein Muzakova," Hayden announced as he arrived with the tickets. "I have two sleeping compartments. We can ride together in one until it is time to retire."

"Are you going to Paris, too?"

"Yes."

"But you're a German officer, aren't you?"

"I am, from all appearances, at this moment. Leave it at that." Hayden gathered his luggage as well as Alexandria's and followed her to the train.

"This is a double compartment," Alexandria observed as they found the assigned space and Hayden put her luggage in place.

"You will have it to yourself, I assure you, Fraulein," Hayden said. "Now if you will excuse me, I'll place my own luggage in my compartment and return to join you later."

Alexandria could not relax as the train began to pull out of the station. Hayden had not given her the ticket and she feared the conductor would appear before he returned. She had done her best to put thoughts of Oliver from her mind, but they relentlessly kept leaping back at her. Her heart bounced to her throat when the rap came at the compartment door.

Hayden entered. He had changed from the military uniform to a business suit. "Forgive me for taking so long, Fraulein, but I suspect our ride will be more pleasant if I am not in uniform."

"May I know your name?"

"Major Hans Rittenburg."

"You met with Freddie last night."

"I did," Hayden admitted. "I fear it was essential that I share him with you for a short time. Actually, I wished to question him to verify your story. It is all a formality."

205

"To verify my story? Have I been watched while here in Berlin?"

"You have, Alexandria. You do not mind if I call you Alexandria, do you?"

"No, of course not."

"I know a great deal about you, Alexandria. I will be candid about that," Hayden explained. "I am not personally known to Count Philippe de Marco, but I know of him."

"How do I know I can trust you, Major Rittenburg?" Alexandria asked a few minutes later, after deliberating on the thought.

"You don't. I doubt one knows when they can trust anyone," Hayden replied. "Just as, I presume, Lieutenant von Klootz thought he could trust you. You played with his emotions, didn't you?"

"No. I will be perfectly honest with you, Major," Alexandria confessed; "I fell in love with Freddie. I never believed it possible of me."

"If you did fall in love with the gentleman," Hayden questioned, "could it be that you did not give accurate information about him to your contact in Berlin?"

"I told them that I believed beyond a doubt that Freddie was who he claimed to be."

"And there was never a question of doubt in your mind?"

"Very little."

"That causes me to conclude that there must have been some doubt."

Alexandria smiled. "I told him that I had been chosen to be a Phenwick woman, and when he repeated Phenwick woman, he pronounced the *w*s as *w*s, not as *v*s. That was noticeable to me because at one time, when I first was speaking English, I, too, had difficulty saying *w*s properly. Later, I realized that Freddie simply must have been repeating precisely what I had said."

206

"Undoubtedly the case. And there was nothing else that caused you to question him?"

"Only some statement that he made about a favorite uncle of his. I misunderstood the name he said at first." Alexandria turned her head toward the window and stared out as tears came to her eyes.

"Are you all right?"

"What will they do him, Major?" Alexandria asked before she turned toward Hayden.

"You are in love with him, aren't you?"

"More than you can possibly know."

"Enough to try to help him now instead of working against him?" Hayden asked.

"How can I—?" She changed. "Are you testing, Major?"

"I might be." Hayden examined his watch. "There is no way at this moment to know what has become of your Freddie, Alexandria, but we can go to the dining car and share conversation over dinner. It is early, but dinner is only served for a limited time."

"I'm not particularly hungry, but I suspect it is best to eat something, since it will be a long journey to Paris," Alexandria said. "I would be pleased to join you for dinner."

After they were seated in the dining car, and had ordered, Hayden asked, "This favorite uncle Lieutenant von Klootz mentioned, what was his name?"

"Hyman," Alexandria replied.

"And what did you think he had said?"

"Hayden."

"I see. Why ever did you think he might have said 'Hayden'?"

"Freddie greatly resembles a man I was once introduced to in London by the name of Oliver Phenwick," Alexandria explained. "And I know through my friend Letitia Phenwick that Oliver Phenwick has an uncle named Hayden. It's an unusual name, so I remembered it. From what I've heard about Hayden Phenwick, I would very much like to meet him someday."

"Perhaps that can be arranged."

During dinner Hayden got Alexandria to speak about ballet and her aspirations. It was a means of inducing her to get her mind from Oliver for a while. He even coaxed her into telling about Adam Truff and how she had been chosen to be a Phenwick woman.

"Do you believe in all that spirit sort of thing?" Hayden asked.

"I didn't. In fact, when Letitia first told me about her experiences with the red roses, I laughed at her statements, thinking them ludicrous. I've changed my opinion since."

"Just as you've changed your notion about falling in love?"

"Yes, that, too. I'm afraid my mind had been closed in the past about a good many things," Alexandria admitted. "Now I see things so differently. I'll be very happy to be back in London with Letitia. I have so very much to talk to her about."

"London?"

"I think I will be able to get my emotions sorted out there," Alexandria said, "especially once I get back to dancing. Why, do you know I have hardly exercised since I've been in Berlin? It'll take me weeks to get back into condition."

"And will that help you to forget about Frederick von Klootz?"

"I don't believe I will ever forget him—never." Alexandria sighed. "I never realized it could hurt so to be in love."

"Do you think Count de Marco will permit you to return to London?" Hayden asked after considering the subject.

"I have fulfilled what I was assigned to do. That was all I bargained for."

"And if he has another assignment for you?"

"I will decline to take it."

"And if he attempts to force you into it?" Hayden asked.

"I have a legal agreement with Philippe in writing."

"But suppose what he wishes you to do can be turned about in such a way that you can help Freddie?" Hayden baited.

Alexandria shook her head. "No, Major. You are clever. You're attempting to make me say something I may later regret." She stared into his eyes. They were eyes she thought she would never forget. "Your eyes remind me of Freddie's. Maybe I shouldn't, but I instinctively feel that I can trust you, Major."

"Why should you, Alexandria? Simply because I knew a code phrase?"

"I've thought about that. And that's not the reason," Alexandria replied. "There's just something about you that makes me feel comfortable. Some people are like that. Letitia is."

"Let me test you just to see how much you trust me," Hayden said with a smile. "Do you in your heart believe that the man you know as Frederick von Klootz and Oliver Phenwick are one and the same person?"

"It's a trap, isn't it? I can't answer your question."

"Or you won't?" Hayden suggested. "It doesn't matter if you trust me or not. One day you may." He laughed. "Dear Alexandria, let's speak again about ballet. You are much more at ease when you discuss that subject."

Why did she want to trust him? All her reason and rationality told her she must beware of this stranger.

After dinner Hayden escorted Alexandria to her compartment door and checked inside to see that the bed had been properly turned down.

"They will check our papers at the border," Hay-

209

den said as he stood at the door. "I don't foresee any problem, but one can never tell. I am two compartments down. Do not hesitate to call on me if there is trouble."

"I will. Thank you. And thank you, Major, for all you've done for me this evening," Alexandria said. "Despite everything, I believe I've enjoyed myself."

"Unless you have specific business in Paris," Hayden remarked in parting, "I suggest you go directly on to London as soon as possible."

"I must see my mother and Philippe, unless they've gone to Zürich already. In that case, I'll go immediately to London." Alexandria smiled warmly. "Thank you again, Major."

"Good night."

In spite of the lurching, swerving ride, Alexandria slept well, probably because she was in a state of emotional exhaustion. Her thoughts and memories of Oliver took her into sleep.

Although a thorough investigation was made at the border, Alexandria was not disturbed and slept through it. She did not awaken until the next morning when the conductor announced that they would be arriving in Paris within the hour.

After she had prepared herself, Alexandria was told that breakfast was being served in the dining car.

"If Major Rittenburg is going to have breakfast, I will join him," Alexandria told the conductor.

"Major Rittenburg is no longer aboard the train, mam'selle," the conductor said in French. "He left shortly after we crossed the border."

"By himself?" Alexandria inquired, a hint of fear in her words.

"I do not know, mam'selle."

"He wasn't arrested, was he?"

The conductor shrugged. "I was unaware that he left until I found the door to the compartment open and the space unoccupied. His bed was hardly touched. That is all I can tell you, mam'selle."

Alexandria didn't know what to think.

At the Paris railway station, Alexandria tried to call her mother by telephone, only to have a servant announce that the count and countess were in Zürich. Taking Hayden's advice, Alexandria immediately arranged to go on to Calais and for boat transportation to Dover.

Before sailing from Calais, Alexandria learned that the German army was approaching the French border and an invasion was expected at any time.

TWENTY-TWO

Deciding that she needed to spend a few days of quiet reflection before she got back full-scale into dancing, Alexandria took a room in a small hotel in Earl's Court, London. A depressed feeling enshrouded her, dreary gloom that seemed to make her feel lethargic. Her thoughts were largely about Oliver and their short-lived relationship. His face constantly arose in her memory. News that France had been invaded by German troops didn't penetrate her consciousness as she wafted about in a vacuum of dreary gloom.

On the fourth of August, the Belgian village of Vise was ablaze through the German occupation. The following day, a British vessel discovered a German mine-laying ship off the mouth of the Thames and sank it. Even then, the British went about life as usual. Alexandria only scanned headlines which told of such events: they might have been happening in a world completely remote from hers.

Two days later, Alexandria finally left her place of isolation and walked in Kensington Gardens and on into Hyde Park. The fresh morning air and manicured gardens had an uplifting effect on her spirits. She avoided people. Eventually she found a bench beneath a willow tree beside a lake, where she watched the ducks and swans. The placid setting somehow caused her to realize that she had to snap herself out of that mood, that the world was continuing and, as long as she was part of it, she had to participate in what was happening.

"It's time you went on, Alexandria." The words came with the scent of roses.

"I know . . . I know. But I can't seem to find the energy to do so," she replied before she looked to find the source of the voice. "If this is what love does to a person, I don't believe I ever want to fall in love again."

"Think of the beauty, not of the sorrow."

"There were beautiful moments, weren't there? But why can't they go on forever? Why did they have to end so soon?" she asked.

"Everything is transient; all things pass. It wasn't meant for you to linger in the arms of love at this time. But you have tasted the loveliness of passion. The memories will remain with you. They are inescapable. Now you must turn to the reality of today. I told you that you were to become a Phenwick woman, but yours will not be a marriage for love. In a sense, it will be a matter of convenience, especially for you. It will give you the prestige and position you will need. Do not look for marriage and love to go together for you; they won't. I can tell you no more than that at this time. Yet I must explain that what will happen will be for the best."

"How could I marry another man when I love Freddie so very much?" she questioned.

"You will discover the way. I have strong faith in that."

213

The fragrance of roses lingered but the image was gone.

Alexandria sat another fifteen minutes, mulling over the thoughts she had heard. Were they meant to imply that she would never see Oliver again? With a new curiosity, she considered her old attitudes about art and the responsibility of the artist. She concluded that she had been right in the first place; her full love must be for her dancing, her creative artistry. But she wished it could be different.

As she went toward a gazebo, Alexandria became aware of people around her, moving, breathing human beings. Children and nannies, old people, young people, all engrossed in the matter of living. She had contemplated suicide, but not seriously. Life was for a reason, and she had to know what that was. As if by magic, the will to live returned to her with enthusiasm. What was she doing moping around in a dream of yesterday? A decision was to be made, and she made it.

"I beg your pardon," the tall man said as he nearly ran head-on into Alexandria, while deeply involved with reading the newspaper.

"I'm terribly sorry. I wasn't watching where I was going," Alexandria apologized. "I have been temporarily blinded, but I believe my sight has suddenly been restored." She stared into his amazingly handsome face, where she recognized a familiar expression. "Do I know you?"

"Do you?" he asked. "My name is Phenwick."

"I knew it! There is something very distinguishing about a Phenwick face," Alexandria said awkwardly. "My best friend is a Phenwick."

"Many of my relatives are Phenwicks," he returned; "I can't say that many of my friends are. Is that being too glib? I like being unconventional."

"My name is Alexandria Muzakova."

"I'm Hayden Phenwick."

214

"You're Oliver's uncle!"

"I've been recognized as many and diverse things," he replied, "but rarely, if ever, by the distinction of being Oliver's uncle. The fact is, you are absolutely correct, young lady. Do you know my nephew?"

"No. I've met him just once," Alexandria explained, "but I know, through my friend Letitia, that he has an uncle Hayden." Suddenly excitement had come into her voice.

"Ah, then, you're cousin Letitia's friend, are you? Well, well. Fancy we should meet here in Kensington Gardens. Would you care for a cool glass of lemonade?"

"That would be pleasant, thank you."

Hayden had assumed the grand eccentric attitude he displayed in artistic circles. Always the actor, he enjoyed taking on different roles; and the façade he presented Alexandria at this time was practically the antithesis of the one he had shown her as Major Rittenburg. They sat in the shaded area and sipped lemonade.

"No, dear child, my wife is not in London," he said. "Mrs. Phenwick has developed somewhat of a problem and it was judicious of her to return to San Francisco. She missed the children. I saw Letitia just the other evening and she expressed her concern about you. Have you avoided seeing her since you've returned to London?"

"I've avoided everyone, I'm afraid, but I believe I'm ready to get back into the swing of things now," she explained.

"We must arrange to dine with Letitia, just the three of us," Hayden remarked as he examined his watch.

"That watch!"

"What about it?"

"Haven't I seen it before?"

"Not this particular one, I dare say. It is not

215

unique; there are many like it. I carry it because it is inexpensive and easily replaceable. London is notorious for pickpockets." He laughed and returned the watch to his pocket. "It is later than I thought it was, and I have an appointment shortly. May I walk you somewhere?"

"Just out of the park. I can find my way back to Earl's Court," Alexandria replied.

"Because of all this mess that is happening on the continent, with Germany and all, Letitia is staying with the Daniel Charles Phenwicks. You must at least call her and let her know you are well. She is deeply concerned about you, you know."

"I've been so neglectful. I'll get in touch with her this very afternoon," Alexandria promised.

Alexandria walked back to her hotel, a new energy in her step. Before freshening herself and changing into a cool summer frock, she called the Daniel Charles Phenwick house. Letitia was not in, but Mrs. Phenwick was expecting her for luncheon, so she was bound to be returning momentarily.

Alexandria would surprise her friend.

"Are you one of the ladies for luncheon?" the butler asked when he opened the door to Alexandria nearly an hour later. "I say, you're a bit early, but do come in. It's much cooler inside."

"Since I'm early," Alexandria said, "would it be permissible to go into the garden? I recall it from last time I was here."

The servant nodded consent.

"I can find my way, thank you."

The garden was as manicured-looking as when she was last there, but the summer atmosphere had taken away the bright freshness she remembered. Still, the roses were in full bloom, as were the dahlias and several other varieties of summer flowers. She strolled to the pond with the dolphin-shaped fountain and admired the bright water lilies

216

and water hyacinths. Had the whole Berlin experience happened since she was last there?

"Mortimer said you were here in the garden, Miss Muzakova," the soft masculine voice said, interrupting her reverie.

"Oh! Charles! You startled me."

"I was afraid I might, don't you know, but I've never been keen at subtly announcing my presence."

Alexandria ran her eyes over him, clad in a white summer suit and sparkling in the sunlight. He had previously struck her as being a handsome man in a conservative way. That Phenwick attractiveness was unique in itself. "You seem to have changed somewhat."

"I've lost a bit of weight," Charles replied. "I suppose at thirty, one should begin to lose his baby fat." He laughed. "I have tried to alter my appearance, as well as my attitude. I say, it's been a ruddy difficult job. Father has threatened to disinherit me if I don't marry soon. I don't know what he's going on about. I suspect he feels it time to kick me out of the nest. The change, you see, is all in preparation for making myself a suitable spouse. Augustus has been up to it, too. Do you find that humorous?"

"Interesting, if not humorous," Alexandria returned. She took a closer look at him.

"If Mum had her way, we three would remain her infants the rest of our lives," Charles said with a chuckle. "That being the case, I think it high time I got on with the business of matrimony."

"The business?"

"Of course, that's what it is," Charles replied. "You should remember me from the past. Cold-fish-Charlie I'm known as in some cicles, especially where ladies are involved. Cousin Letitia said she thought I would be a perfect mate for—well—" He caught himself and hoped he wasn't blushing too severely. "Well, for a—that is—an acquaintance of hers."

"Oh, she did, did she?" Alexandria responded light-

217

ly. "I won't dare guess who that might be." She glanced at the water lilies again to avoid the intensity of his stare. "So you think marriage is a business arrangement, do you, Charles?"

"The best marriages are always arrangements," he replied. "I've never been strongly romantic—not hardly, old girl. Oh, I do have my moments, don't you know, but they're only moments sometimes, with large intervals between. Cousin Letitia suggested that I would be ideal for a woman in the artistic-creative world who had her own interests and devotion to her profession. I'm surprised you didn't ruddy detect that in me on those picnics and motor outings we used to take with Tim and Letitia. Now, Tim is another matter. He is pure romantic from the word 'go.' Isn't it peculiar how brothers can be so different from each other?"

"Quite remarkable."

"I don't suppose you recall back last whenever it was," Charlie continued, "at the time my parents gave a lavish party. All of Mum's parties are lavish, so that's hardly a way of defining which party it was, you know. Anyway, there was one—and I'm certain you'd come down from Somerset at the time—when my distant American cousin put in a brief appearance. My brother and I had taken him to the club. What a physical specimen he was! And it's no wonder, the way he exercised and did all of that physical nonsense. Oliver was his name."

"Oliver?"

"The situation is, I've never been able to decide if Oliver is in the least bit romantic or not. I should think he might be."

"Why should that concern you?"

"No particular reason," Charlie replied. "Actually, I took Oliver as an example and I've been exercising as I watched him do. I've a long way to go, don't you know, but I've made a start."

"Why are you telling me all of this, Charles?"

"Why? I don't know, rather. It just struck me as the thing to do."

"Why?"

Charlie shrugged. "Perhaps I'm trying to impress you."

"Me? Whatever for?"

"You do make it a bit difficult for a bloke, don't you?"

Alexandria strolled toward the rose garden and waited until she saw Charlie's shadow blend with hers. "Charles, this friend of Letitia's—excuse me, 'acquaintance'—is she someone I might know?"

"I suspect she might be." Charlie reached to pluck a red rose and stuck his finger on one of the thorns. "Damn!"

"Careful, Charles! Roses do have thorns, you know."

"A truth that has been made painfully clear to me." He managed to disconnect the blossom from the bush. "I'm not much of a horticulturist. Ruddy all thumbs I am, when it comes to such things." He handed her the rose. "Be careful of the thorns."

"I've been warned. Thank you." Alexandria held the rose and admired it. "Is there something you are attempting to ask me, Charles?"

"Ask you? Oh, I say."

"Let me put it this way, since you appear to be all thumbs in more ways than one," Alexandria said as gently as she could. "Am I the 'acquaintance' of Letitia's you mentioned?"

"I—that is—well, as a matter of fact, yes," he stammered.

Again Alexandria walked away from Charlie and waited for him to touch her once more. She gazed at the rose and thought it ironic that it was red. She recalled the thoughts she had heard earlier that day in the park. She turned toward him. "I've thought of you over the months, Charles. As you know, I am devoted to my dancing. That is my life.

But I have considered the business of matrimony. Perhaps we should spend more time together and become better acquainted."

"Does that mean—?"

Alexandria smiled. "This is an extremely lovely rose, Charles. Thank you so much for giving it to me. The noonday sun is hot. I suggest that we go inside, where it is cooler."

"Alexandria—?"

"Yes?"

"May I take your hand?"

Alexandria held her hand toward him. "I would be honored, Charles."

His was a pleasant touch, mildly exciting, but sturdy. It wasn't Oliver's hand but it was warm and friendly and she received a sense of security from it. They went into the house.

TWENTY-THREE

"Alexandria! I can't believe it!" Letty exclaimed. "What has brought about such a change in you?"

"Have I changed, Letitia?" Alexandria asked. "I had an eye-opening experience in Berlin. I can tell you no more than that about it. But I did have the opportunity to be away from the world of dance long enough to take an objective look at myself. So much has happened in such a short time. And I realize now more than ever that there is little or no place in my life as an artist for romantic love."

"You're not in love with Charlie, then?" Letty asked, cocking her head as she scrutinized her friend. "Something strangely mysterious must have happened to you in Germany."

"It did." Alexandria turned away. "Maybe someday I will be far enough detached from it to explain everything. Now, you mustn't ask me any more questions about what happened. I can't tell you; it's too painful to do so."

"Alexandria—?"

"Whatever occurred in Berlin caused me to be realistic," Alexandria said. "I know now that if I were to marry for romantic love, I could become as obsessive about it as I have been about ballet. Two such obsessions would be in conflict with each other."

"So you've chosen to stick with your ballet," Letty concluded. "But why marry at all, if that is the case?"

"I will answer that at another time, Letitia. Now I must ask you to go. I'll never be ready in time for our luncheon with your cousin Hayden, not if I keep talking to you. I hope you understand. Please try. Hayden is sending around a car and I must be ready on time."

Letty was confused, but she knew Alexandria well enough to know that once she had made up her mind about something, there was no changing her. She quietly said goodbye and let herself out of the hotel room.

Alexandria paused a moment as she reflected over her conversation with Letty and her announcement that she had consented to marry Charles Phenwick. She wanted to have her things packed to move to the Academy at Somerset later that day. In a sense it was inconvenient having luncheon with Letty and Hayden, but she felt it important enough to alter her plans since it was the only time Hayden had available.

The front desk called to tell Alexandria the limousine was waiting for her. She hurried with last-minute details before she went downstairs.

The chauffeur, with his cap pulled low on his forehead, was a short man. He automatically opened the door for Alexandria and closed it behind her once she was seated. The automobile roared away from the hotel entrance at an abnormally fast speed.

Vladimir Popkin was standing at the desk telephone when he was distracted by the sound made by the limousine. He turned back to the telephone.

222

"What do you mean, Miss Muzakova is not in her room? I was sent to pick her up. Well, it isn't exactly a limousine, but it is a respectable automobile." He was told that Miss Muzakova had not five minutes earlier been informed that a limousine was waiting to take her to lunch with Mr. Phenwick. "Impossible! Mr. Phenwick sent me." He slammed the receiver down and swore in Russian. As a thought struck him, he dashed outside. There was no sign of the limousine. He turned to the doorman. "Did you happen to see in which direction that limousine went?"

The bored doorman pointed.

Quickly Vladimir got into the car belonging to Hayden Phenwick and drove in the direction the doorman had pointed. At one point along the way, he caught sight of the vehicle, but traffic became snarled and he was unable to keep track of it. He followed in the direction he thought it had gone.

"I can't understand what has happened to Alexandria," Letty said as she sat at the table.

"Nor do I," Hayden replied, "since I trust Popkin beyond a shadow of a doubt. Perhaps there was motor trouble."

"I have a queer feeling, Hayden. I think something is wrong," Letty remarked. "I just have a weird sensation all over me, like when I returned to Moss Grove before the fire."

Vladimir Popkin arrived at the restaurant a short time later and explained what had happened.

"Who would want to kidnap Alexandria?" Letty questioned.

"I can think of several persons who might," Hayden replied. "Can you manage to get back to Daniel Charles's house? Remain there. I'll go with Popkin to inform the police about what has happened."

"Yes, but what do you suppose—?"

"If I had any notion whatsoever, Letitia, I wouldn't

223

be so concerned," Hayden interrupted. "Just do as I tell you. I'll call there." He rose, placed money on the table and grabbed Popkin's arm. "Come along, Vladimir."

After reporting the incident to the police, Hayden took a few moments to converse with his friend.

"The doorman didn't notice a number on the car, did he?"

"Doormen don't usually notice car numbers without provocation," Vladimir replied. "I wouldn't, under the circumstances. What do you propose we do now?"

"Let us think this thing out," Hayden said. "I feared there might be some reprisal because of the incident in Berlin. I don't believe Oliver would be foolish enough to try to get Alexandria back to Germany, not with what's going on over there. There is the possibility that my disappearance from the train to Paris could have aroused curiosity, but in that case, why wouldn't they come after me? No, I think I thoroughly covered that."

"Who would want to abduct Alexandria Muzakova," Popkin asked, "if indeed she has been abducted? We may be only jumping to unwarranted conclusions that she was kidnapped."

"Who indeed?" Hayden pondered. "Think!"

"I am thinking, but my brain is weak and my imagination is on the verge of decay," Popkin replied.

"There is only one logical conclusion I can reach," Hayden said. "Her stepfather, Count de Marco."

"Philippe?"

"Do you know him well enough to address him by his first name?" Hayden questioned.

"I've known Philippe de Marco since we were students in Paris. When I was short of money, I would do odd jobs for him," Popkin explained.

"Why?"

"Why? Simply because we were good friends. There was a time when I could out-drink Philippe. I

224

invariably had to see that he got home, and I often found myself passed out in the room with him. It was through me that Philippe met Tiziano Spolini and Worth Bassett as well as others in the arts. Philippe has always been a dilettante in the creative world, but he enjoys the surroundings and the way of life."

"How did you react when you learned that de Marco intended to marry Alexandria's mother?"

"How did I react?" Popkin thought a moment. "Surprised is the first word that comes to mind, but I think shocked would be more to the point."

"Why so?"

"There have been rumors that Philippe's last wife did not die of natural causes," Vladimir related. "And there has been conjecture that Philippe himself may have arranged for her untimely demise—but only conjecture."

"Nothing was proven?"

"I doubt if anyone wanted to prove it. She was a woman with no family and, I suspect, came from a similar background as the present countess."

"It wasn't a matter of marrying for wealth, then," Hayden thought aloud. "Why?"

"Philippe has always had a darker, nefarious side to his life of which few people have known," Popkin said. "I tell you this in the strictest confidence; he has actually had contempt for most women, and has been known to use them notoriously. A woman of the streets, as it were, would intrigue him; and those with whom he has consorted, have disappeared. I believe in his heart he is a misogynist."

"If that is the case, why did he marry Madame Dupree?" Hayden questioned as he observed a sheepish expression on Popkin's face. "I believe you have something to enlighten me with there."

"Why do you say that?"

"You have stood on the sidelines, Vladimir, and

have observed," Hayden commented. "I know you see and hear more than you ever divulge."

Popkin looked away and wet his lips with his tongue. "Shortly after Madame Ivanovich and I arrived in Paris with LeVeque and Spolini, I encountered Philippe at La Petite Fleur Café, an insignificant establishment but convenient to where we were staying. At any rate, we reestablished our acquaintance of long standing. As always, Philippe was overjoyed to see me and insisted that I spend a weekend at his country château—without Madame Ivanovich. The reason for that was so that we could drink together as we had done in the past without Roselle's interference."

"And did you go?"

"Yes," Popkin admitted. "During that visit Philippe inquired several times about young ladies in the ballet company. Alexandria Muzakova was not then with the LeVeque group, but she had been interviewed and I knew that Spolini was impressed with her—more so than he was with Letitia, I might add. Later, after Miss Muzakova was a dancer with the company, Philippe again inquired about her. By then I had learned about her mother and her—shall we say, occupation."

"I see. Where is all this leading, Vladimir?"

"To the fact that within a week, Philippe again called on me and asked for an introduction to Georges LeVeque, stating that he would have gone through his friend, Worth Bassett, had he not been in Moscow. As you know, Miss Muzakova made an enormous and unexpected leap in prominence with the company, which almost coincided with Philippe's marriage to her mother."

"Ah, yes, I see the picture now. So there is no doubt in your mind that de Marco knew of Alexandria even before he met her mother. Where does that leave us?" Hayden questioned.

"I suspect, if Alexandria has been abducted,"

Popkin commented, "that it is to take her back to Paris—or to Zürich, where I understand Philippe and the countess are spending the summer."

"Why?" Hayden asked. "He could not have had righteous reasons if he abducted her."

"Could it be connected with what Alexandria did—or did not do—in Berlin?" Popkin questioned.

"Possibly. Or perhaps Philippe has some other assignment for her." Hayden considered the situation. "Yet for Philippe to have arranged such an abduction, he would have to be here in London, wouldn't he?"

"Not necessarily," Popkin responded. "He is enormously wealthy and can arrange for others to handle certain matters for him. I well know; I've been his errand boy in the past."

Hayden snapped his fingers. "We've overlooked Worth Bassett in all this."

"Meaning?" Popkin scratched his head. "Bassett is in Spain—Madrid, I believe—with Jeremiah James on a recital tour."

"But Worth Bassett has a home here in England, hasn't he?"

"Yes, a monstrous old place near Dover. I was there once years ago. I don't believe anyone has lived there in a long time. I can appreciate why that would be."

"Do you know where this house is?"

"I believe I could find it without too much difficulty," Popkin replied. "I drove there several times in the past. We went there last winter to examine it as a possible place for the ballet company to live. It was entirely out of the question."

"It's only a hunch, Vladimir, but my psychic senses are telling me that we should go to Bassett's house near Dover." Hayden suddenly brightened. "Dover, of course! Channel crossing to France."

Popkin was staring at a bearded young man wearing glasses, who was walking along the street.

"Did you hear me, Vladimir? What has captured

your attention?" Hayden followed Popkin's gaze. "Whatever has attracted you to that unkempt individual?"

"I recognize him. He is French. I have seen him at La Petite Fleur Café," Popkin explained.

"Call him over."

"Is that another hunch?" Popkin asked before he whistled loudly and motioned for the youth to come to the automobile. "Do you speak English?"

"A little," the youth replied, "but I converse better in French."

"We are both multilingual," Hayden said. "Are you from Paris?"

"Recently, yes."

"Your name?"

"Guy Croisant; I am a student—an impoverished student. I need money to return to France. I came here to organize support against the Kaiser."

"How badly do you need money?" Hayden asked in French.

"I will do anything for it."

"Anything?"

"Absolutely anything. I must return at once."

"Get in the car," Hayden ordered. "I will give you one hundred pounds if you will accompany and assist us."

Guy jerked the door open and slid onto the back seat. "I am your servant; use me."

"Guy Croisant, eh? What are you doing in this neighborhood?" Hayden asked after instructing Popkin to get on the Dover road as quickly as possible.

"I ran into a young woman I had met in Paris a while back," Guy explained. "We had tea yesterday afternoon. She is a dancer, and she gave me money for helping her to move some luggage. I was to help her move her things this afternoon, but she had a luncheon appointment first. But in lieu of a hundred pounds, she can move her own things."

228

"Were you an excessively handsome young man," Hayden remarked, "your eager attitude for money could get you into difficulty. Hurry on, Vladimir, I believe we're onto something."

TWENTY-FOUR

"Where are you taking me?" Alexandria demanded to know from the back seat of the limousine. "We're completely out of the city of London!"

The driver ignored her question. She tried to move the glass between the front and back seats. It wouldn't budge. She had tried the door handles, but they apparently could only be opened from the outside. The windows rolled down only about three inches to permit air to enter. Alexandria saw the sign pointing to Dover and fell back on the seat as the vehicle took a sharp curve.

The sky had become overcast and they appeared to be headed for a summer storm. Alexandria hit her fist against the glass partition, but it would not give. The car made another sharp turn. She hung on to brace herself and caught a glimpse of an arrow sign with the word "Bassett" on it. The limousine jolted over a curved, dirt incline. Weeds had grown in the path, indicating that it had not been regularly used. Suddenly a dark wall came into view, with an iron gate, directly ahead of them.

The chauffeur stopped the car and got out to open the gate. As he returned to the car, Alexandria tried for another look at his face; yet she perceived something familiar about his peculiar walk. Moments later the vehicle was pulling up to an ominous-looking mansion, and came to a sudden jolting stop near the front entrance. The place was badly overgrown with weeds and the shrubbery was in desperate need of pruning. Shutters covered the windows.

The driver removed his cap and used it to dust leaves from the front seat before he got out and went to open the door for Alexandria. For the first time she could plainly see his face.

"Miguel?"

"You are wrong again. You have a poor memory, mam'selle. It is Manuel. But I am pleased that you were close. Come with me, please, Monsier Phenwick is waiting for you."

"Here? For lunch?" she questioned incredulously. "I was to meet him in the Strand."

"That was merely to distract you," Manuel said. "No one was to know that you were to come here."

Alexandria stepped from the car, avoiding Manuel's assistance. "What are you doing in England, Manuel?"

"I have business. I am not always a waiter, mam'selle."

Reluctantly Alexandria went toward the hideous old building and hesitated before mounting the front steps.

"You don't wish to keep Monsieur Phenwick waiting, do you?" Manuel questioned as he attempted to prod her.

"How do I know Monsieur Phenwick is in there?"

"You will not know unless you enter, mam'selle."

"Believe me, if he is here, I'll tell him how you've treated me, Manuel."

Manuel shrugged. "It is beginning to rain, mam'selle. You will get your pretty dress all wet if you do not get into the house." He opened the door and held it for her to enter. As she entered with trepidation, Manuel closed the door firmly behind him, turned the key in the lock and removed it.

"What is that all about?" Alexandria asked.

"A precaution, in case we were followed here."

"We were not. I periodically looked back and there were no cars on the road whatsoever."

"Still, one cannot be too careful, mam'selle." Manuel struck a match and lit five candles in a candelabra.

"Where is Monsieur Phenwick?"

"Upstairs, mam'selle. I will lead the way."

The stairs were basically sturdy, but they were noisy. The candlelight created eerie shadows along the wall. Alexandria was shown into a room on the second floor that was fairly well furnished and relatively neat appearing.

"You will wait in here, mam'selle," Manuel instructed.

Alexandria scanned the furnishings, the four portraits of eighteenth-century ancestors. She watched as Manuel methodically lit several candles in the room and went back toward the door.

"Make yourself comfortable, mam'selle. I will return shortly." Manuel gave a condescending smile, stepped from the room and locked the door behind him.

Fear catapulted through Alexandria as she heard the key in the lock. Anxiously she ran to the door and tried to open it. "Manuel! What is the meaning of this?" she called but there was no reply.

After banging at the door several times, Alexandria turned back into the room. Apprehension, mixed with stark terror, clouded her mind. She tried not to panic, but she sensed hysteria rising within her.

Why? What was happening? Why had she been brought to that place? She had to think rationally, sort through her memory.

"Think, Alexandria, think!" she said aloud. She paced the room and examined the shuttered window where rainwater was running between the boards and the windowpane. She tried a second door to the room, but knew before she touched it that it would be securely locked. Why? What could anyone possibly want of her in that place?

After staring at a flickering candle-flame for several minutes and trying her best to soothe her alarmed emotions, Alexandria sat in the chair that appeared to be the most comfortable. As she searched her memory, she recalled that Guy Croisant was to come to her hotel that afternoon to help her move. Guy Croisant? She had met him in La Petite Fleur Café—and Manuel had been a waiter in the same place. Was there a connection? What had she told Guy? That she had planned to marry in two weeks and that she would stay at Somerset until two days prior to the ceremony which was being arranged by the Phenwicks.

Guy had told her that he had come to London to raise support for French defense. How could he possibly? And he did mention that he had met someone familiar on the boat during the Channel crossing. Had it been Manuel? Quite possibly. She had explained that she could not move her things until mid to late afternoon because of her luncheon engagement with Letitia Phenwick and her cousin Hayden. And she had related that she was to be picked up by a chauffeur at her hotel. Of course. That much was comprehensible. Guy may have kept his contact with Manuel while in London, but had not realized that he was being used to conspire against her. But what was the conspiracy?

* * *

Hayden had gotten into the back seat beside Guy Croisant for ease of conversation. Popkin kept his eyes on the road and listened to overhear as much of their conversation as he possibly could.

"Have you heard of Philippe de Marco?" Hayden asked as he sat back and observed the young man's reactions.

"I have heard of Count Philippe de Marco, if that is who you are speaking of," Guy replied. "He is a scoundrel and, I suspect, a traitor to France."

"Why do you say that?"

"He is aristocracy, but he pretends to be sympathetic to the people of the street," Guy said. "He even consorts with them. He has a notorious reputation. Why do you ask about him? Are you his friend?"

"I know of him. But I am curious to hear your opinion."

"I hate nobility!"

"You are a radical?"

"But of course!"

Hayden realized only too well the sort of person he was dealing with. "What do you do for a living?"

"I live off the streets. I am a student."

"At the university?"

"No, in the school of life! I read constantly and observe and gather others into conversation," Guy boasted.

"But how do you exist?"

"I do whatever I can. Unfortunately, one has to eat."

"I see. Do you know women of the streets? Courtesans?"

"I know many."

"A woman by the name of Monique Dupree?"

Guy stared with a wild-eyed expression. "I've heard of Monique Dupree. She isn't of the streets any more. Oh, no, she's a grand lady now—but there was a time . . ."

234

"Tell me about her."

"I know nothing. Why do you ask me such things?"

"Do you know that she is presently married to Count de Marco?"

"I had heard that."

"Did you also know that Alexandria Muzakova is her daughter?"

"She is?" Guy's look of absolute astonishment told Hayden that the youth was basically unaware of what was happening as far as Alexandria was concerned. He had obviously been unwittingly used to gather information, perhaps without knowing that he was doing so.

"We may encounter trouble up ahead," Hayden explained a short while later. "Can you defend yourself?"

"I can and do constantly. Will you tell me what this is all about?"

"I cannot, because I do not know. I had hoped to glean certain information from you."

"And have you?" Guy questioned.

"Some, yes." Hayden glanced out the window. "We are nearing Dover."

"I want my money."

"I'll give you half of it to show my sincerity," Hayden said, "but you will not get the rest until the task is complete." He now knew exactly the kind of person with whom he was dealing.

Alexandria judged that she had been waiting in that room for nearly half an hour. Straining to hear, she listened for the tiniest sound. Only once did she detect the sound of footsteps. She perceived that there was no one in the house at the present time but Manuel, and that he was waiting for someone to arrive. Having completely searched the room, she had begun to devise a plan. But the plan would not work if Manuel didn't return alone. Her mother had taught her a man's most vulnerable spot,

235

where pain could be induced with a single blow. The thought of doing such a thing was repulsive to her; still, she reasoned she must do whatever she could do for her own protection.

Again she paced about the room, stopping briefly to observe the cracked oil portraits. She wondered who they were likenesses of, and why they were hanging in that particular room. She had already made a search for any object that could be used as a weapon. There was none.

Sitting with the chair facing the door, Alexandria brooded over the situation. Finally, in an attempt to keep her irrational thoughts from leading her to the point of absolute panic, she decided she must force herself to remember something pleasant. Memory immediately went to Oliver and the time they had spent together in Berlin. That man's love and her love for him might have been strong enough to cause her to abandon her aspirations as a ballerina. How could love be such a powerful force?

After contemplating those moments with Oliver, Alexandria turned her thoughts to Charles Phenwick. He was a man who she could admire and respect, and perhaps love in a limited way; yet he was one who would permit her the freedom she required to continue with her career. From the time they had first met, she had found him agreeable and had quickly developed a liking for him. He was comfortable to be with, polite and protective, and he represented the epitome of security. She recalled her mother's words when she had discussed her decision to marry Philippe de Marco. Alexandria had to conclude that she had made a wise choice in accepting Charles Phenwick as a prospective husband.

Still, in that time of cogitation, Alexandria could not help but wonder the sort of husband Oliver would make. She, of course, thought of him as the future Baron von Klootz, not a revered son of the prominent Phenwick family. She concluded that he would be a devoted spouse, in his way, loving and considerate, but he might want to be dominating and adventurous. She wondered why that had occurred to her. Perhaps it was because she compared him with Charles Phenwick, who was basically docile and not particularly aggressive. One can be impractical in chosing a lover, but must be extremely pragmatic when selecting a husband.

A single pair of footsteps approached the room. Alexandria rose from the chair and positioned herself beside the door. Her pulse was racing in anticipation, and she trembled for fear she might make a blunder. There would be only one opportunity, and she had to take full advantage of it.

The key made a scratching sound before it was placed into the lock. Alexandria put her index finger between her teeth and bit on it to keep from making any noise. The key turned in the lock. She remembered Manuel's height. The door was pushed open. She saw candlelight before Manuel stepped into the room.

Alexandria's legs and feet were strong and agile from years of dancing. Her balance was excellent, since she could stand flawlessly steady on point on one foot. On seeing the man, her movement was swift and fiercely dynamic. Her foot was like a rock when it struck its mark. Manuel yelled as if he had been struck with a bullet, the force of which caused the candelabra to fall from his grasp as he doubled over from excruciating pain.

As Manuel writhed on the floor, Alexandria attempted to remove the key from his hand. He held tightly to it until she put her foot over his wrist and applied as much pressure as she could. When he rolled over onto his side, she kicked him again in the same place. They key was released as he contorted with stinging spasms.

Key in hand, Alexandria leaped from the room,

pulled the door closed and locked it. Leaning against the door, she could hear him cursing her as he moaned in agony. Second thoughts revealed that she should have rendered him unconscious, if possible, and gone through his pockets for the front door key. It was too late for that.

Alexandria had not foreseen the abject darkness in the hallway. Her eyes had become accustomed to candlelight, but not to stark blackness. Inching away from the door, she tried to remember the physical attributes of the corridor when she had initially passed through it. She could only remember the direction of the stairway. Shins were knocked and her hands scraped over unfamiliar objects. Reaching the stairs sooner than she had anticipated, she missed the first step and went plunging down them, only catching herself against the railing after she had descended partway.

TWENTY-FIVE

Somewhat **shaken by the fall** down the stairs, more winded than anything else, Alexandria managed to get to her feet and navigate the remaining steps without futher mishap. Faint late-afternoon light entered through the narrow stained-glass windows beside the front door. Recalling that Manuel had taken a match from a box on the foyer table, she searched for the box. Two matches were left. With one she lit a solitary candle, and put the other match in her bodice to have handy in case of emergency.

Alexandria carried the candle protectively into the adjoining room to her right, where she found a candelabra with partly burnt candles. In the next few moments, she lit several other candles. With lumination, she went to examine the windows. They were securely closed and would not move as she applied her full strength to them. She suspected that the shutters on the outside had been nailed tight, so it would do no good to risk breaking a window glass.

While catching her breath and bracing herself to venture from that room, which was obviously the parlor, Alexandria browsed about. The furniture was old but it did not appear to be badly worn, leading her to the conclusion that it had not been extensively used. A box grand piano was at one end of the room, over which was the portrait of a young man who somewhat resembled Worth Bassett; and she concluded that it may have been a picture of Bassett when he was a young man. Several photographs were in frames on a library table near the piano. The one she most clearly recognized was that of Jeremiah James.

Alexandria was about to leave the room, candelabra in hand, when her attention was drawn to a dossier folder with the name of Frederick von Klootz upon it. In it was statistical information about Freddie, including the account of his alleged assassination. A photograph of Freddie, age sixteen, was among the papers. Part of the documents were written in English and the rest were in German. A quick check proved that one was a translation of the other. Under the papers was a second photograph, which looked to have been taken of Freddie a year after the first picture. It looked more like the young man with whom she had fallen in love. She was about to put the second photograph back in place when she saw the photographer's signature at the bottom of it and the words "Denver, Colorado."

Excitement throbbing with her pulse, Alexandria hurriedly compared the two photographs. The resemblance was uncanny, but upon extremely close scrutiny, she could detect a definite difference in the two. The shape of the eyelids was not the same. She used papers to cover the other features in each, to isolate the eyes. One set of eyes had an expression that was unfamiliar to her, while the eyes in the photograph with the Denver, Colorado marking were well known to her. And, as she ruminated, she knew that the eyes in the first photograph were eyes she had seen on another man than the person she knew as Frederick von Klootz.

Due to the location of the dossier on Frederick von Klootz, Alexandria suspected that it had been set out to be removed, probably by Manuel when he returned to the continent. She took the folder from where it had been positioned and, after deliberation, slid it beneath the carpet near the box grand piano.

Carrying the candelabra, Alexandria moved through the rooms on the first floor of the old house. With the exception of the parlor and the room in which she had been on the second floor, the decor of the rest of the rooms was unconventional, with bizarre artifacts and peculiar devices which were unfamiliar to her. She guessed they were marks of the owner's eccentricity, the purposes of which were only known to him. There were three exits other than the front door, and all were stoutly locked.

After checking the kitchen cupboards in search of keys, Alexandria examined the pantry, which was poorly stocked, indicating that the house had not been recently occupied for any period of time.

A teapot was on the kitchen table. It was warm. Apparently Manuel had made tea prior to going upstairs. There was still another cup of tea in it. She poured it into a cup. Tepid but refreshing. She sat at the table to enjoy it while she considered her next move.

It occurred to her that the old house would have a basement. Since the kitchen had the aroma of burnt coal, she suspected that the fuel was stored in the basement. Even if the regular lower exit had been locked, there was a chance that the opening to the coal chute had been overlooked.

Periodic banging noises came from the second

floor, causing Alexandria to suspect that Manuel might be attempting to break his way out. Leaving the remaining tea, she went to find the stairs leading to the basement.

A door opening off the pantry revealed the stairway. Halfway down, Alexandria stopped dead in her tracks as she heard the sound of muffled voices coming from below. Inching farther down, she perceived that one voice was speaking German, but she could not make out the words.

The door to a basement room was ajar and a dim glimmer of light came from it. The sound was coming from there.

"The girl will have to remain in the house tonight," Alexandria translated. "The Channel is too rough to bring a boat ashore."

Alexandria got as close to the room as she dared. She could see no movement within the room.

"Manuel, are you there?" said one of the voices.

"A wireless transmitter," Alexandria whispered to herself and stepped closer to the open door.

"He has probably not got the girl yet," one voice said in German over the receiver.

"He has had plenty of time. He should have been back five minutes ago."

"Do you think there was trouble?"

"I don't know."

"Maybe we had better go and investigate."

A sputtering sound crackled over the set, followed by silence.

Alexandria peered into the small room. A single oil lantern was burning near to where the wireless transmitter was located. Finding nothing more of significance, she went in search of the coal bin. As she passed the stairs, a crashing noise came from above. Had Manuel managed to break down the door? Fear caused her to rush in the opposite direction of the wireless room. Two of the five candles went out. She didn't take time to relight them.

The coal bin was in need of replenishing. The chute above was too high for Alexandria to reach. Even if she could get to it, climbing up would be almost an impossibility. She decided that what she must do was to find a place to hide. Still, since there wouldn't be any evidence that she had broken her way out of the house, he would know that she was there somewhere and come searching for her. That was a chance she had to take.

There was another small room near the coal bin, wherein were stored several large trunks. Most of them were locked, but upon closer examination, Alexandria discovered that two of them were open and one was empty. If need be, she would be able to fold herself into it to avoid detection. Leaving the door slightly ajar, she extinguished the candles and waited in the darkness.

"The limousine is parked on the side of the house," Vladimir Popkin related as he joined Hayden and Guy Croisant after they had broken in the front door.

"Looks as if we interrupted a little party," Hayden commented as he observed all the candles lit in the parlor. "Vladimir, you take the rear of the house; Croisant, check the rooms to the right; and I'll go to the left. We'll meet back here in five minutes. If you find anything unusual, try to give a warning. Remember, there may be more than one—and they may be armed."

After making the search, the men reported back to the parlor. Popkin was the first to arrive.

"I found an empty teapot and two cups and saucers in the kitchen," Popkin explained. "One cup still had tea in it. I suspect both cups of tea were not drunk at the same time. The empty cup only had a small residue of tea leaves, while the other had several good-size leaves in the bottom. A man may have drunk from the first cup, but I believe a

243

woman drank from the second. Men have a tendency to empty cups, but women don't."

"Most observant, Vladimir," Hayden commented.

Guy Croisant had nothing unusual to report.

"We'll go to the second floor together," Hayden said as he gave each of the others a candle. "You'd think Bassett would have this place wired for electricity."

"He would have had," Popkin replied, "if the LeVeque company had decided to use it. I understand this place was left to him, and he doesn't come here often."

After investigating other rooms, Popkin found the one in which Alexandria had been held. Putting his ear against the door, when finding it locked, he detected a faint moaning sound coming from within. Together the three men used a small but solid table to batter the door open. They found Manuel moaning but unconscious.

"His pulse is very weak," Popkin said after checking it.

Hayden knelt beside Manuel and pulled back his eyelids. "I suspect he's dying from poison."

"From poison?" Popkin exclaimed.

"It may have been in that tea you found in the kitchen," Hayden suggested.

"Then if Alexandria drank it, too—?" Popkin's eyes widened. "We must find her as quickly as possible."

"If your supposition is correct, Vladimir, she may not have drunk too much of it. But we have no time to waste."

"Where do you suggest we look?"

Hayden instructed Guy to see if he could find an attic.

"We'll try to locate the basement," Hayden told Vladimir.

When they reached the kitchen, Popkin stopped

Hayden. "Did you notice Croisant's look when I said Manuel had been poisoned?"

"Can't say that I did," Hayden returned. "Why?"

"I must have worn an expression of surprise and you looked shocked," Popkin explained, "but Croisant displayed no reaction whatsover."

"Which means?"

"He may have expected the announcement."

"Possibly," Hayden said as he examined the tea-cups. "The one that is empty had been sugared; the other one had not. I'm not familiar with poisons, but we can only hope the toxin was in the sugar."

Hayden discovered the door leading to the base-ment.

Alexandria had become drowsy, which she could only attribute to the fact that she had suddenly become quiet after moving about so rapidly; besides, the small room she was in lacked fresh air. The sound of footsteps on the stairs suddenly made her become alert. A heaviness had filled her body, and she had difficulty getting to her feet. Her intention was to hide in the empty trunk, but she lacked the energy to do it.

Popkin went to the small room where the wire-less was kept. "Hayden—over here!"

"Hayden?" Alexandria questioned aloud. She pushed against the empty trunk and knocked it over; at the same time she lost her balance and fell.

"What was that?" Hayden questioned.

Popkin pointed in the direction of the fallen trunk. He found a piece of pipe, which he gripped tightly and went toward the sound. Hayden merely observed the wireless before he followed Vladimir.

Alexandria had pulled herself into a sitting posi-tion on a small trunk. Her eyes appeared glazed, as the candlelight reflected in them.

"Alexandria?" Hayden questioned.

"I suddenly feel very sleepy," Alexandria mum-bled as her head slumped forward.

Hayden quickly had his arm about her and gripped her shoulders. "Sorry to have to do this, old girl, but it's unavoidable." With one hand he forced her head back, and as her jaw sagged he rammed his long fingers into her mouth and reached down her throat to cause her to regurgitate whatever was in her stomach.

Nearly ten minutes later Hayden carried Alexandria's limp body up to the main floor. "We've got to get her to a physician in Dover as fast as possible."

"What about Guy Croisant?" Popkin asked as he followed Hayden to the front door.

"Call him. If he doesn't come immediately, we'll have to come back for him," Hayden replied.

Popkin went back to the foot of the staircase and held onto the balustrade while he called Guy Croisant. There was no response. He called a second time.

Hayden was in the backseat of the automobile, cradling Alexandria, who appeared to only be semiconscious, when Popkin arrived.

"He didn't answer."

"We'll have to come back. Drive to Dover and hurry," Hayden ordered.

"One minute," Popkin said as a thought struck him. Slopping through puddles of water left from the rain, he went to the side of the house and immediately returned to the car. He climbed into the driver's seat. "I thought I had heard a motor."

"What did you mean by that?" Hayden asked after the car began to move toward the gates.

"The limousine is gone," Popkin called back to him.

"What do you suppose happened to it?" Hayden asked.

Popkin shook his head and shrugged. Then, with all the skill at driving he possessed, he navigated the automobile down the incline and along the wet road to Dover.

Alexandria was taken to the infirmary, where Hayden gave instructions that she was to have the best treatment possible. When he was satisfied that the best physician available was tending to her, Hayden left word with the attendant that he and Popkin would be back within an hour to check on her progress.

Back at the Bassett house, Hayden and Vladimir made a complete search of the building. Not only was Guy Croisant nowhere to be found, but Manuel was missing, too, which led them to speculate that Croisant might have taken Manuel and the limousine, or that a third party or parties had removed them from the premises.

Alexandria's condition had greatly improved by the time the men returned to the infirmary. Although weak, she insisted upon going back to London, assuring Hayden that she was able to ride.

After conferring with the physician who treated her, Hayden consented to her wish. He was told that the chemical she had ingested was not fatal unless taken in extremely large doses and that it was usually used as a sedative and to induce sleep. He promised Alexandria would be as good as new the next day.

TWENTY-SIX

The following day, as the physician had promised, Alexandria was in good health and her usual energetic self. Many questions, however, plagued her mind, answers to which might never be found.

During the next two weeks, although the police had been called in to investigate, neither Guy Croisant nor Manuel Catalon was located. Hayden suspected that Croisant had simply taken the money he had been given and seized the opportunity to get back to France. On the other hand, it was speculated that Croisant and Catalon had been conspiring together over a period of time and Guy had escaped with Manuel while Alexandria was being rescued.

In time it would be learned that Worth Bassett had rented the old house to Manuel Catalon through an agency in Paris, and that the owner was completely unaware of Manuel's purpose for using the house. When the police investigated, there was no sign of a wireless transmitter and receiver in the basement. The room where it had been seen appeared dusty and unused for a long period of time. That aspect of the story remained a mystery for the present. Furthermore, it could only be presumed that Count Philippe de Marco was behind the kidnapping attempt on Alexandria; the solution of that, too, would take time to unfold.

Word had been sent to Monique Dupree de Marco that her daughter was to be wed to Charles Ross Phenwick in London. Monique sent a message explaining that she could not attend, but that she wished the best for the newlyweds.

"You're distressed because your mother won't be at your wedding, aren't you, Alexandria?" Letty questioned the day before the ceremony was to take place.

"I have never depended on Mama for support in personal matters like this," Alexandria replied. "Financial support was really what I could ever expect from her. I am not distressed, not actually—but I do have a feeling of having been let down by her *again*."

"It was sweet of Cousin Hayden to offer to stand with you."

"Hayden Phenwick is a remarkable man, Letitia, most remarkable," Alexandria said. "With Charles busy the entire afternoon, I am taking tea with Hayden. He will personally pick me up this time."

"And you're finally becoming a Phenwick woman," Letty sighed. "It seemed from the first day I met you, I just had the feeling that it would happen someday." She kissed her friend.

"It's not too late to make it a double wedding," Alexandria suggested. "Plans will have to be altered, of course, but it could be done."

"No, Alexandria," Letty replied. "I'm not ready for marriage yet. I do love Tim in my way, but now, with the war and all, I want more time to really make up my mind."

"My feelings for Charles are probably not near as

249

great as yours are for Tim, Letitia, but all things considered, I believe I am doing the right thing."

"You know, in my romantic fantasies," Letty added, "I always thought something magic would happen and you would meet my cousin Oliver and fall in love with him. Silly, isn't it? It's just that you used to mention his name so often."

Alexandria laughed. "Dearest Letitia, fantasies and realities are really two different things. Oliver was one of those ships that pass in the night. I'm being practical by marrying Charles. And you would be just as practical and sensible to wed Tim."

"Someday, perhaps, Alexandria, someday—perhaps."

Hayden wore white, with a gray morning coat and top hat. Always stylishly handsome, his appearance was more outstanding than ever. He carried gloves and a gold knobbed walking stick, a white carnation at his lapel. "I hope you don't think a gray morning coat is out of place at teatime. I've had appointments all day, and simply have not had time to change."

Sitting opposite Hayden in the open-air restaurant, Alexandria appraised his appearance again. "I doubt that you would ever look improper at any time, Hayden." Biscuits and tea had been served. "Do you suppose we should have a taster for the tea?" She laughed.

"I doubt if it will be necessary," Hayden replied. "Is everything in order for tomorrow?"

"Quite in order."

"Are you looking forward to it?"

"That seems an odd question, Hayden."

"Perhaps not." He stared into her face with an understanding smile. Gently he placed his hand atop hers. "You're extremely brave, Alexandria. Courageous is perhaps a better word."

Alexandria thought for a moment. "Maybe *am-*

bivalent is the best word to describe me, Hayden."
She looked away, folded and unfolded her napkin
before she spoke again. "There is something I must
tell you, Hayden." She was looking down.

"Do you feel you really should?"

She glanced up into his eyes and held her attention there for several seconds. "Yes." Another pause.
"While I was at the house in Dover I stumbled
across a dossier on Frederick von Klootz. It was
quite detailed and informative. A photograph of
him at the age of sixteen was included."

"Had he changed much since he was sixteen?"

Alexandria bit her lip. "There was also a photograph of Oliver Phenwick among the documents."

"Of Oliver?"

Alexandria watched for his reactions. Hayden's
expression was almost bland. "I can see where Freddie and Oliver resembled one another—except for
their eyes. I isolated their eyes in the pictures and I
could see that there was a vast difference. Oliver's
were the eyes that I knew. Never fear, Hayden;
you're the only person I ever intend to tell that to."

"Why do you wish to tell me?" Hayden asked.

"Do you recall me talking of the time Freddie
mentioned a favorite uncle of his? He made a mistake
at first and tried to cover it over by saying his
uncle's name was Hyman."

"I don't believe you ever told me that, Alexandria." Hayden refilled their cups.

"Didn't I?" Alexandria asked, a whimsical smile
at her lips. "Oh, no, I forgot. It was that Major
Rittenburg I met en route to Paris from Berlin
whom I told."

"Major Rittenburg?"

"I was concerned about Major Rittenburg the next
morning when I awakened and learned that he had
disappeared shortly after we crossed the border into
France." Alexandria etched the rim of her teacup
with her index finger. "Major Rittenburg's eyes fas-

cinated me because they reminded me of Freddie von Klootz's eyes."

"Eyes are difficult to disguise."

"It seems to me Major Rittenburg said practically the same thing, only in German, of course."

"Of course." Hayden raised his cup to her. "I like you, Alexandria. "We're much alike."

"Perhaps that is because we both love the same person."

"Perhaps." Hayden fell into contemplative silence. "You know this—I mean about Frederick von Klootz —and you love him as much as you say you do; still you're going to marry Charles tomorrow. You amaze me."

Alexandria studied his face for a moment and smiled before she stared into her teacup. "I found myself with two conflicting wishes, wishes which I believe are incompatible with each other. Maybe I should say, with two conflicting loves: my desire to be a truly great artist, and Freddie. One ultimately would have to take preference over the other because I couldn't give my complete self to each. I have admiration and respect for Charles and I appreciate him for the man that he is, but I do not have that obsessive, all-compelling love for him that I have for—" her gaze went into the distance "—that I have for my artistry as a dancer."

"Dear Alexandria—I do believe you. I can understand because we are similar in many ways," Hayden commented. "Does Charles understand this about you?"

"I doubt it. But I believe I understand Charles and I know that his needs are simple," Alexandria replied. "He has neither strong emotional drives nor ambitions. In time he will probably become patronizing and stodgy, but he will be proud of me and my accomplishments. His thrills in life come vicariously."

"And Charles will enable you to become a most

unique and extraordinary Phenwick woman." Hayden sat back as he appraised Alexandria. "Oh, how I wish my wife Olga were as independent as you are. Had she been, she might not have the problems she has today." He cleared his throat and again reached to pat her hand. "Have you considered what may occur once this war nonsense is over and this man you know as Freddie survives and comes to renew his love?"

"One starts off on a journey one step at a time," Alexandria said. "The road up ahead has its own complications but those situations do not have to be confronted until they are reached. I cannot project my imagination toward a nebulous tomorrow that may never be. I have only today and the reality of it. The most valued assets I have, besides my talent, are your friendship, Hayden, and that of Letitia. Perhaps the love of friendship is the greatest expression of love that there actually is."

Hayden stood as he embraced her. "I shall always cherish your friendship, Alexandria."

Louise Phenwick had taken charge of the wedding arrangements. The marriage of her eldest son was meant to be socially prestigious. Daniel Charles permitted his wife to handle the details.

"Are you excited about the ceremony, Charles?" Louise asked her eldest son. "That's foolish of me to ask, isn't it? I've never known you to be truly excited about anything." She patted her handsome son affectionately and understandingly, and went back to her preoccupation with plans.

Charles chuckled in agreement. "I say, Augustus has arranged a bit of a bloody bash for the bachelor party tonight. It's going to be quite a cause for celebration—a dual-purpose celebration, Mums. Rather."

"How's that Charles? What are you going on about?" Louise asked as she glanced up from the paper on which she had been writing. "Dual-purpose celebration."

"This may come as a bit of a blow, old girl," Charlie said as he wore a broad grin. "I will be going into the army in two weeks."

"You'll be doing *what?*" Louise leaned forward. "Into the army? That's impossible! You're a Phenwick!"

"It's quite possible, Mums, Phenwick or not. I say, Augustus will be in right behind me," Charlie continued. "I do believe, if Father can pull the proper strings, Augustus and I will be together."

"Does your father know about this?" Louise asked.

"He's arranging it for me—us."

"Well, we'll see about that!" Louise rose, fuming.

Charlie went behind her and put his arms about her shoulders. "Mums, don't interfere. Please don't do that. There's a war to be fought, don't you know—a bloody war. Let me be a real person just once in my life."

"What nonsense! You've always been a real person, Charles! What an outrageous notion!" Louise turned toward him. "You're being married tomorrow. Are you simply going to abandon your wife to go to war after such a brief period of married life?"

"In my quiet way, Mums, I love Alexandria," Charlie said as he went to the window. "I will probably always love her. But I believe you know as well as I do that I'm not destined to be the most satisfactory husband in the world. Rather the contrary, I should imagine. One can't do battle with facts. Yet I swear that I will do everything in my power to make Alexandria happy."

"And do you think going off to war is going to make her happy?"

Charlie tried not to look embarrassed, but his attitude was difficult to disguise. "It may well do just that, Mums. Excuse me."

"Charles!" Louise called as her son left the room.

254

"Charles! I hadn't dismissed you! Charles!" She fumed a moment, then passed over the matter for more important details concerning the reception.

Letitia sat at the dressing table, studying her reflection, her eyes periodically going to the bouquet of white roses she was to carry as maid of honor. Then her attention went to Alexandria, who was being helped into the white satin bridal gown.

"Such a fuss," Alexandria exclaimed. "It's only just another performance."

"Your wedding?" Letitia asked.

"Yes. Well, isn't it? We're putting on a show for London society," Alexandria returned. "There will be no applause, no curtain falling, no lights, only—"

Letitia went to her. "Alexandria? Are you all right?"

"I'm perfectly fine. Just a bit of preperformance jitters, I suppose. It will pass." Alexandria sent the maid out on an errand. "They'll all be there, and Charles and I will be center stage. And in less than an hour I will be a Phenwick woman."

"You don't want to go through with this, do you, Alexandria?"

"But I do. It's just that my heart isn't fully in it." Alexandria sighed.

"Where *is* your heart?" Letitia curiously asked. "Back in Berlin?"

Alexandria had never disclosed to Letty the events that had happened in Berlin, nor had she discussed Frederick von Klootz or anything about the situation. "Berlin? Berlin was just another holiday, a retreat from dancing. Why would my heart be back in Berlin?"

Letty stepped away. "You know what form of fantasies my dreams take, Alexandria. While you were on holiday, I tried to imagine—"

Alexandria touched her friend to interrupt. "You are far, far more of a romantic than I am, Letitia."

255

They embraced. "Someday you may understand. Now it is time for me to become a Phenwick woman."

Letty smiled, but tears had come to her eyes.

As Alexandria took Hayden's arm and they proceeded down the aisle, she glanced to her left, where she saw a familiar face. He held a red rose toward her as if presenting a toast. The scent of roses surrounded her and she knew, beyond a doubt, that she was doing exactly what she had to do.

Author's note: The special trilogy begun in Book #35 will continue in Book #37 as the stories of Letitia, Alexandria and Romula, and the effect of World War I upon their lives and loves, are ultimately resolved.